the
Summer
of
Permanent
Wants

Also by Jamieson Findlay:

THE BLUE ROAN CHILD

the *Summer* *of* Permanent Wants

JAMIESON FINDLAY

Doubleday Canada

Doubleday Canada and colophon are registered trademarks

Library and Archives Canada Cataloguing in Publication

Findlay, Jamieson
The summer of permanent wants / Jamieson Findlay.

Issued also in electronic format.
ISBN 978-0-385-66928-3

I. Title.

PS8561.I5386S85 2011   jc813'.6   C2011-902494-2

The author gratefully acknowledges the financial support of the city of Ottawa.

The author is donating a portion of the royalties from
this book to WWF-Canada's tiger campaign.

Text and cover design by Kelly Hill

Cover images: (cat) Yorrico, (boat) patrimonio designs limited ,
(books) John Pagliuca, (cattails) Lfoxy, all Shutterstock.com;
(girl) Grynold/Dreamstime.com

Ancient forest-friendly
Printed and bound in the USA

Published in Canada by Doubleday Canada,
a division of Random House of Canada Limited

Visit Random House of Canada Limited's website: www.randomhouse.ca

10 9 8 7 6 5 4 3 2 1

To my nieces—Anneke, Aiden, Saraya,
Maeve, Brigh and Eibhlin

Contents

Author's Note

Adventures happen to people who travel old waterways, especially if the people go slowly, watching for muskrats and yard sales, trying lots of crazy foods at the local garlic festival, staying up late to catch a meteor shower, listening to the chip-wagon lady talk about the movie that Hollywood made down the road (her grandson was in it, along with Nicolas Cage), and generally just drifting along in the Finnish style (Huck Finnish, that is). The Rideau Canal Waterway is a good place to do all these things. Stretching for about two hundred kilometres between the cities of Kingston and Ottawa, it flows through farmland, forest, meadow, and village. Sometimes it is a channel no more than a stone's throw wide. Sometimes it is a slow, sweet-tempered river. Many times it opens up to become a series of blue lakes dotted with islands. These different sections are linked by forty-five lockstations, many of which work exactly as they did when the waterway was first built, between 1826 and 1832. It is North America's oldest operating canal system. Recently it was named a World Heritage Site by the United Nations.

All this is just to say that the setting of this book is real. I did make up a few places along the waterway when I wanted an unusual backdrop for an adventure, but I like to think that even these made-up destinations have a Rideau flavour. They are as rooted in the land as genuine places like Merrickville and Chaffeys Locks and Poonamalie; they just belong to what Robert Louis Stevenson called "some different parish of the infinite."

No sailor would have called *Permanent Wants* graceful or sea-kindly, but the crickets liked it well enough. They didn't seem to notice it was a boat. To them, it was just a floating patch of backyard, free of toads and mantises and other enemies, and moated with stars on a fine night. There were two crickets, Cass and Nova. Emmeline had got the idea of bringing them on board after hearing about the legendary Joshua Slocum, author of *Sailing Alone Around the World*, who had once brought two crickets and a tree crab on board *his* boat. Several people had warned Emmeline that the chirping of crickets might get very tiresome after a while, but everybody agreed that crickets were a better idea than crabs. So on the night before the sailing of *Permanent Wants,* she went out into the long grass behind her house and caught two crickets. Into a jar they went, a very large jar—really a transparent world. It had grass and earth in the bottom, air holes in the lid, and sections of egg carton in the corner. The crickets must have felt right at home, for on the first night aboard, they started up their singing at around nine o'clock. Lafcadio, the shipboard cat, pricked up his ears in disbelief

3

when he heard them. He probably wondered what kind of strange, cross-grained, weather-beaten, gone-to-seed, lumpish misfit of a broken-down hobo boat he was sailing on. It would not be the last time he would wonder that.

This old but ardent vessel belonged to Emmeline's grandmother, Mrs. Teolani McHovec. Mrs. McHovec ("Gran" to eleven-year-old Emmeline; "Teo" to her friends) was sixty-four years old. She had short silver hair and eyes the colour of seawater flowing over an ice-berg. She loved wind. Had she been born during the Middle Ages, she might have been one of those witches who caught wind, tied it up in knots of rope, and then sold the knotted rope to sailors. But she was born much later, and so she just did a lot of sports that used wind. She had flown glider planes in her youth, and now she sailed keelboats and flew kites. Her friend Picardy Bob, who loved danger as much as the crickets loved night music, had tried to get her to go hang-gliding once, but she said no. "That is a wild and irresponsible suggestion," she told him, "even for a former forger."

I should describe Picardy Bob at once, before he is arrested. He is a small, friendly-fierce man, gifted at adventure and bicycle repair. Though he doesn't look it, he is actually a few years older than Gran. He wears his long grey hair in a ponytail and once won a prize at a local fair for the magnificence of his moustache. At the time of this story, he was a book scout—that is, somebody who hunts down valuable old books for dealers and private buyers. He was very good at picking out genuine rare volumes from fakes, which wasn't sur-prising, given his background. Years before, when he was living in England, he had actually forged a rare book himself. He did it out of curiosity and then decided that the experiment wouldn't be com-plete unless he actually tried to sell the book, and . . . well, this is how criminal careers are made. He had served time for his crimes, and afterwards, back in Canada, he had decided to get into the book business. He always had piles of old books in the shed behind his little trailer, where he lived with a parrot named Django and a pug dog named Holden Caulfield.

The adventure of *Permanent Wants* really began with Picardy Bob, and it happened this way.

One day Bob was in his shed, sorting through boxes of books, when Emmeline and her grandmother visited him with some exciting news: Gran had inherited a boat from a distant cousin! And what a homely old boat it was. Gran had taken one look at it and decided that it should really go into some kind of home. It was broad and battered and peeling, with a low cabin and a rounded bow like a tug's. The engine was an ancient diesel inboard that hadn't worked in years. As a joke (apparently), somebody had plunked down a mast right in front of the cabin. "A barge with a sail" was Gran's description of it. What could you possibly do with a boat like that? She put this question to Picardy Bob while he was sifting through his books, and—perhaps because he wasn't getting much work done that day—he replied shortly: "I'll tell you what you can do, Teo dear. Take some of my paperbacks here, put 'em on your big, ugly boat, and take a trip down the Rideau Canal Waterway. You'll be the first floating bookstore in Cottage Country. They'll love you."

There was a silence. Even Django was silent. Emmeline gave her grandmother a long, eager blue-water look.

"Don't be a romantic fool, Bob," said Gran. "There's no space on a boat for books."

Picardy Bob plucked impatiently at his moustache. "I used to know a bookseller in London who hauled around his stock on a *bicycle*. He had a little trailer full of paperbacks and miniature books, and he did a brisk business at lunch hour. Sure, you could make a boat into a secondhand bookstore. And you're the one to do it, Teo. Who here is always talking about the Strange Untried, the Unshored?"

"That would be you, Bob."

This was true. Picardy Bob often spoke about the Strange Untried, the Unshored, whenever he wanted Gran to go hang-gliding or something like that. (The phrase came from one of his favourite books, *Moby Dick*.) But deep down, Gran understood his love of adventure. Her late husband, Silas, had believed that everyone should have a half-decent adventure every two years—more often if you lived in Ottawa. And she herself was long overdue. Her last adventure was twelve years before, when she and Silas had sailed halfway around the world in their sloop, the *Cygnus*.

That winter, without telling anyone, she began work on the boat. She scraped and painted the hull. She polished the metal fixtures, taking special care with the quaint stern lamp. She found a mechanic to fix up the engine. (As a lover of wind, she disliked engines, but she knew she couldn't do without one.) And gradually she discovered the attractions of this strange, ugly flat-bottomed vessel. Its ancestors were clearly the old canal boats and sailing barges of England and Holland. It had no keel, but rather two leeboards—large, broad wooden paddles attached to the sides of the boat. They looked something like the blunt, powerful flippers of a right whale. The leeboards could be lowered into the water to keep the vessel steady while under sail. Gran also discovered that the mast itself could be raised and lowered using an anchor winch. This meant that you could easily get the boat under a low bridge if you had to. All these features, along with its flat bottom, made it the perfect waterway boat.

When Gran found herself thumbing through the IKEA catalogue, looking for stackable bookshelves, she realized that the project had captured her completely. She wondered what kind of permit she would need to moor at public docks and sell books.

But her last task was the most difficult—to convince her daughter, Emmeline's mother, to let the girl go along.

Emmeline's mother had serious doubts about the voyage. She thought that *Permanent Wants* was far too big a boat to be handled by a grandmother and an eleven-year-old girl. "And this idea of selling *books*," she said one evening, when Emmeline was upstairs practising her violin. "That means a till on board, which means cash, which means an open invitation to every lowlife from here to Joyceville."

"Dear, you are forgetting that I sailed the South China Sea," said Gran. "The pirates there were thicker than flying fish."

"But Dad was with you!" objected her daughter.

"Well, this time Lafcadio the cat is with me."

Her daughter said something like *puh* and frowned. She had no time for the Strange Untried.

"Anyway," added Gran pacifically, "we can always pack a slingshot."

Emmeline's father now entered the discussion.

"If the goal of this voyage," he said, "is to bring culture to the heathen cottagers and civilization to the land of the satellite dish, then I think a slingshot would be incompatible with your intentions. I suggest bear spray."

"Don't talk as if this were a good idea," said his wife. "It is not a good idea. It is a *crazy* idea."

"It may be crazy," declared Gran, "but I can't do it by *myself*."

She was about to add that life on a boat was life intensified, and that a water voyage had the power to transform and heal—something her beloved Silas had always believed. But all she said was, "I think it would be good for Emmeline."

Upstairs in her room, Emmeline gave an excited smile. It wouldn't be good for her; it would be *fantastic* for her. She wanted more than anything to go on this trip, just Gran and her—and Lafcadio and the crickets, of course. And maybe Picardy Bob once in a while. And all right, her parents sometimes, since they would miss her. But mainly just Gran and her. She heard silence below, so she took a step into her room and, putting her violin to her shoulder, played a quick phrase. She didn't want them to know she was listening.

Emmeline was the sort of person who could *almost* disappear in a crowd. Her face was narrow and quiet and undramatic. Her hair—a thin, flat brown—lay thinly and flatly on her head. She had no elvish ears or Cleopatra nose. The only thing striking about her was her eyes, which were as clear as winter twilight in an alpine valley. They were restless, curious eyes: they dreamed a lot, observed people and stars, and studied old houses for signs of being haunted. Once, under the influence of a book called *How to Be a Detective*, she had cut eyeholes in *The Globe and Mail* newspaper and sat at a local bus stop, pretending to read while secretly watching passers-by. She was discovered when a woman noticed a pair of intense blue eyes watching her from the middle of an article entitled "Important People Who Have Gone Blond." But apart from this (her eyes, I mean), she was no different from the thousands of other eleven-year-olds who are good at undercover work—except that if you had looked closely at her left wrist, you would have noticed a medical ID bracelet.

Downstairs, Picardy Bob was speaking.

"And it just so happens that I myself aim to take a few trips along the Rideau this summer, for the auctions. I'd be happy to look in on the two sailors and serve as deckhand from time to time. I can't say I'm much of an old salt, but I did once take an extensive correspondence course in celestial navigation."

Bob didn't add that he had done this course while in jail. He didn't need to. Emmeline's mother and father knew him quite well.

"I appreciate the offer, Bob," said Emmeline's mother, who never gave in easily. "But with that big old boat, I think we need something more in the way of qualifications."

"Well, he's read *Moby Dick*," said Gran. "The unabridged version, I would guess, just from listening to him."

"Also *Swallows and Amazons*," put in Picardy Bob.

"That seems . . . satisfactory," said Emmeline's father, with a glance at his wife.

Which brings me to the books they had on board.

They had lighthearted books that were not necessarily lightweight and a few heavy, serious books just for ballast, but mainly they had a lot of old-fashioned books that always get read, generation after generation, even by people who say they've grown out of them. There was *The Haunted Bookshop* by Christopher Morley. There was *King Solomon's Mines* by Rider Haggard ("the most amazing book ever written," according to the cover). There were detective stories by Josephine Tey and G.K. Chesterton. There were anthologies: *A Century of Creepy Stories* and *Victorian Ghosts and Ghouls*. There were books about the ocean (*Two Years Before the Mast, Typhoon, Twenty Thousand Leagues Under the Sea*) and books about rivers (*The Wind in the Willows, Huckleberry Finn, Slowly Down the Ganges*). There were titles that made you smile (*Why God Loves the Irish* by Humphrey Desmond), and titles that gave you a bit of a chill (*The Rivet in Grandfather's Neck* by James Branch Cabell). There was *Speakable and Unspeakable in Quantum Mechanics* by Dr. J.S. Bell and *Green Eggs and Ham* by Doctor Seuss. There was an illustrated encyclopedia of "paranormal and occult worlds." There was an old manual of stage magic, an old book of Ontario folk songs, and a *very* old atlas. There were books that people remembered from some distant, sun-flooded place in their lives, or maybe even from another life; books that seemed to come with the smell of cedar and the lap of waves under the dock; books that people seemed to have read in dreams. In other words, the books were all perfect cottage books.

Gran printed up a list of the stock, put it inside clear plastic, and tucked it into the drawer that held the navigation charts. Most of the books were paperbacks, of course, to save on weight. The stock wasn't large—it would barely have filled a wall in Picardy Bob's shed—but Gran believed she had just the right titles. After looking over her list again, she decided to add a few more books by P.G. Wodehouse.

When Emmeline's mother saw all these preparations, she just looked grim and started making curtains for the cabin windows.

Eventually, the great day arrived. Emmeline and Gran had spent the previous night on *Permanent Wants*, after catching the crickets, and soon everything was ready for sailing. Emmeline had stowed her most important belongings: her dream catcher had been hung over her bunk, her violin and sketchbook were in the cupboard, and her yellow karate belt was rolled up beside them. She had suggested *strongly* that her Johnny Depp poster be taped up in the galley. Gran hadn't known who Johnny Depp was until Emmeline's mother explained, but she had agreed to have the poster there. She knew that she would have to get used to Emmeline's whims, just as Emmeline would have to get used to *hers*. After all, they now had to share a very small living space.

It *was* a small living space, but cozy. Once inside the cabin, you came first to the galley, or kitchen. It had a two-burner stove, a tiny fridge, and a little table attached to the wall. The two bunk beds were next to the galley, in the little alcove that made up their living space. Right at the end of the alcove was the head, or bathroom. The sign on the door said "Strategy Room," and inside was a small sink and composting toilet. The books themselves were stored in light plastic cases that could be stacked on top of one another.

Some cases were stowed inside the cabin, but most were kept in the bow storage compartments. Picardy Bob had showed them how to line the cases with pressure-treated plastic so there would be no mould or water damage. It was also Picardy Bob who had painted the name *Permanent Wants* on the bow and stern, along with the words "The Floating Bookstore." He had a very careful hand, being a forger.

A few well-wishers had gathered on the dock. There were Picardy Bob and Emmeline's parents; there was Gran's friend Sheila, who lived on the Rideau River and would give them harbourage the next night; and there was a tall white-haired man who had the sparse elegance of an old willow tree. This was none other than Captain Lillwyn, explorer in residence at the Royal Bytown Yacht and Lawn Bowling Club. He had been asked to say a few words to mark the occasion, which he agreed to do, being a secret admirer of Gran's. He talked about all experience being an arch, "where-through gleams that untravelled world" (the way he said it, you knew it was from a poem), and he urged Gran and Emmeline "to strive, to seek, to find, and not to yield."

"If I hear one more quote today," said Emmeline's mother through her teeth, "I am going to commit a *crime.*"

She gazed at her only child with a fierce, tender look. Was she doing the right thing, letting Emmeline go off like this? The old boat didn't look particularly seaworthy, despite its fresh coat of blue and white paint. And what a sinkhole for money it had turned out to be! (*Permanent Debts*, she called it.)

As for Emmeline, she was happy for the first time in a long while; you could see it in her face. But she didn't call out to her parents, or chatter to Gran, or make jokes. Emmeline hadn't spoken a word in almost a year. Ever since their fateful vacation in Kenya, Africa, when she had fallen sick and lain in a coma for a month, her language had

been broken. Often she couldn't remember words. Sometimes—
and this was even worse—she could only half-remember them. Her
mind was filled with word bits and shadow words and word lumps.
And when she tried to put them together . . . you can't imagine the
effort. After chasing around a few words in her head, and getting her
lips and tongue to shape them, she would heave out a three-word
sentence like somebody heaving a bag of cement to her shoulders—
and the words would be *in the wrong order*. She had struggled and
raged and cried, and one day she had just given up.

We don't really know what it's like to be someone else, to be
looking out at the world from inside her head, to hear her speaking to herself in that inner voice we all have. But if we know the
person well, we can get a good idea. On that day of the sailing,
with Emmeline waving goodbye to her mum and dad and Picardy
Bob and Holden Caulfield (the latter barking away as usual), her
thoughts probably went something like this:

wavingevery

one

sunwaving and

bye Dad!

picardy bog . . . no picardy bob and holdenbarking and

Mum bye!   *woof! woof!*

I've taken on the task of telling Emmeline's stories for her because I've learned so much from them. I've learned that an island
can be an animal power, that there is an old and a new darkness,
that spirits can move in and out of music, and a bunch of other

things that even the Friends of the Rideau don't know. But mainly I've learned that the Strange Untried, the Unshored, is there for everybody, even those without language. Sometimes, in fact, it can be warm sunlight for a wintered-off mind. And that's my big interest in these stories, since I work every day with the icebound ones.

First Tale

The Discovery of Zeya Shan

The road to Zeya Shan led from an old atlas into the night sky, and Emmeline followed it as far as she could before it disappeared among the stars. Along the way, she discovered a beautiful city right out of that ancient Middle Eastern classic, *The Thousand and One Nights*. Two people travelled with her—Gran and Captain Lillwyn, the explorer. But Emmeline was the one who first stumbled on the trail. She liked to think that one day, perhaps when she was very old, she would look out the window and know that her time had come, and then she would pack her bags and leave for Zeya Shan.

The adventure began on a fine, cool, star-petalled night, their first one out. They had come through the three lockstations of the city, starting with the Ottawa one in the morning and ending with Hogsback in the afternoon. By then, they were both tired and head-achy from the glare of the sun off the water. Luckily Gran's friend Sheila was there to look after them. They all went for a long, re-freshing swim at Mooney's Bay, and then Sheila treated them to a big dinner. Now they were back on board *Permanent Wants*, snug in their bunks, with the dark-sutured moon shining through the cabin window and the waves lapping gently against the hull. Emmeline had just finished making an entry in the scrapbook that served as the ship's log—not in writing but in pictures, for writing and reading were almost as hard for her as speaking. Pictures, colours, shapes, and sounds were everything to her now.

First she'd pasted in her log a cut-out map from a Parks Canada brochure, with the Ottawa lockstations circled in red marker. She'd also drawn a human figure with a red-pencil face—the man who'd called out to them, "Lord love a duck! What kind of boat is *that*?" (She couldn't call up the words in her mind, but she could remember perfectly his heavy, flushed, unshaven face and his dark hair, curiously thick and smooth, like a pelt.) Finally, she'd pasted in the bright blue label from her new . . . She tried to find the word in her head. Those dark things that you put on your eyes to keep the sun out. *Glosses*, that was it. Her new Mountain Equipment sunglosses.

Putting away the scrapbook, she got out her nighttime book—which happened to be the old atlas from their stock, the *Innes-Adaire Atlas and Gazetteer of the World*, published in 1908. (In the bunk underneath, Gran was deep into *The Collected Essays of Robert Louis Stevenson*.) Emmeline had always loved maps, especially antique maps that had faded colours and smelled like old corn husks—maps with plenty of blank spaces on them. In a few minutes, she was no longer in her nook on *Permanent Wants* but was travelling through the world of Teddy Roosevelt and King Edward VII and the last czars. Every page held storied names. Abyssinia was there, and Persia and Siam. The deep interior of Antarctica was blank, for Scott and Amundsen had yet to reach the South Pole. The Ottoman Empire was there, though coming apart fast, and the Balkans were in one of their endless temporary alignments, the result of secret negotiations among men in old-fashioned stiff collars and pince-nez. Large cruel colonies were still in place, the sea was home to both full-rigged ships and steamers, and every continent held a mountain range that had yet to be explored.

Emmeline didn't read the words, just the maps. She climbed the mountains by following the hair-fine whiplash lines, rode the black stitchings of railroads, and drifted with the tiny red arrows of the trade winds. She sailed the blues of the oceans and trudged the bone-coloured deserts. She conjured up the dusty heat of terra-cotta countries and the cool breezes of lettuce-green coasts. And thus it was that, turning the pages slowly, noting every detail, she discovered a tiny, beautiful country.

She noticed it only because of its colour—a soft orange-apricot, like a fleck of dawn on the page. It was a small wedge of a country in south-central Asia, tucked between two beige-coloured lands (Persia and Trans-Caucasia, for those who could read easily). It had mountains to the south and a curving river to the north. She could see no railroads or roads within its boundaries. Though small, it showed up clearly between the drab countries that surrounded it. To Emmeline it looked as if it had drifted in, like a winged seed from a maple tree, and got caught in that crevice between the mountains and the river. She imagined it floating over the world of the atlas, a tiny bit of life fluttering furiously, like a haiku poem struggling to get written. She studied the name; it was in two words. Z. E. (She knew "E"; it was in her name.) Y. A. She sighed. Maybe she would just read that far for tonight. But when she stopped trying to read the words and just looked at them as a design, they were mysterious—like an unknown constellation or the sign of an old inn.

"Goodnight, Emmeline," called Gran from the lower bunk as she switched off her light. "Don't read too long."

Emmeline stuck her hand over edge of the bunk and waved goodnight to Gran. Then she lay still, feeling the gentle rock of the boat around her. Above her, the dream catcher was a spidery shape in the gloom. They were still inside the city limits—she could hear the cars on Hogsback Road—but for her, this was the real beginning of the adventure. She closed the atlas, put it in the net holder beside her bunk, and switched off the light. She still saw the country vividly in her mind, coloured like the rising sun. And no roads or railroads . . . She smiled. She liked countries like that.

"Zeya Shan," read Gran out of the gazetteer section of the atlas. "'Small monarchic state between Persia and the Trans-Caucasus. Approximately 220 square miles in size. Zeya Shan has existed as a sovereign kingdom for at least a thousand years. Its topography has been a major factor in its preservation, for it is bounded on the south by the Talish Mountains and in the north by the River Hinzer, which curves around the country in the form of a protective C. The language of the Zeyans has evolved independently of Turkish and Persian, though it has similarities to both. The only city is the capital, Arjish, whose citizens pursue the most cherished avocations in the country: astronomy, chess, and falconry.'"

They were all sitting at Sheila's kitchen table, the breakfast dishes around them, the early morning sun pouring through the window.

"Sounds like a wonderful place," Sheila remarked. "I've never heard of it."

"*Nobody* seems to have heard of it," said Gran. She and Emmeline had already gone to Sheila's computer and typed in "Zeya Shan"; the Internet had nothing to say about the place. There was no state, region, or principality in south-central Asia that even resembled Zeya Shan. Puzzled, Gran had gone to Google and found a very precise map of the region. (Persia, she explained, was now called

Iran, and Trans-Caucasia was known as Azerbaijan—although the names evaporated in Emmeline's mind as soon as she heard them.) The area north of the Talish Mountains was empty of any kingdoms or city-states; there was nothing of significance until the Azerbaijani port city of Baku.

"Well," added Gran, draining her coffee cup, "the history of the world is full of tiny countries that were swallowed up by bigger ones." Emmeline was frowning.

"She disagrees," observed Sheila, who knew all about Emmeline's difficulties with language. "You tell her the way of the world, and she disagrees. Good for you, Em."

"Well, let's send Picardy Bob an email," suggested Gran. "Maybe he can find the place. I know he's got plenty of old atlases in his shed." She had other things to think about right then; she wanted to make a last trip to the hardware store before they started upriver.

Picardy Bob was usually online on Saturday mornings; it was his busiest day. When Gran and Emmeline returned from shopping a few hours later, his note was waiting.

"Hello, you two!" he wrote. "I've got two old atlases, one published in 1903 and the other in 1916. I also have a Baedeker's *Guide to the Middle East* from 1924. No Zeya Shan in any of them, sorry to say. But I've forwarded your email to that explorer chap from the yacht club, Captain Lillwyn. I know he's got a good library of old maps and travel books. Maybe he can find your country."

Emmeline's brow was furrowed. As usual, her thoughts were in a swirl of words and word stumps, but she knew what she wanted to say. She closed her eyes.

thousandyears and
　　　　　　　　not there?
　　thousand not nowhere?

"Maybe it was a very *short-lived* country," remarked Sheila.

"But the gazetteer says it's been around for a thousand years," said Gran.

Emmeline's eyes lit up: that was exactly what *she* was thinking. Her grandmother had an amazing ability to speak her thoughts without all that smudging. Now how had she said it? *thousandyears around thousand* . . .

"I suppose it could just be a mistake," observed Sheila. "It wouldn't be the first time that an American atlas got things wrong about the Middle East. Anyway, maybe this Captain Lillwyn can help you out. If anybody can find a lost country, it's an explorer."

Privately, Gran wished that Picardy Bob had not brought in Captain Lillwyn to help. He was a nice enough old guy, but he was so *accomplished*. Gran always felt overshadowed in his presence. (If you know Gran, you will understand what an achievement this is.)

It was funny how Zeya Shan flitted through Emmeline's mind that day. The kingdom came back to her at odd moments—when she saw the sway and scatter of freckled light in the trees, or the rippling sunbloom on the river bottom, or the fish idling green-glazed just below the surface. In the afternoon, the river widened enough for them to try a bit of sailing. Emmeline took the wheel at this point, while Gran lowered the leeboards and raised the sail. For a minute or two they drifted with the sail flapping, but eventually the sail filled and they shut off the engine. The breeze was light and their progress slow—laughably slow, to people who passed in motorboats.

"Oh, well," said Gran. "We're not in a hurry."

Emmeline was too busy steering to look up. Gazing at her, Gran remembered the *old* Emmeline—the Emmeline who talked nonstop, who loved Scrabble, who sometimes even made up her own definitions of words ("phony," she told her mother once, should really mean that you talked on the phone too much). The old

Emmeline had been lost to that strange African sickness. She had to crawl after words now. Gran remembered a time last fall when the girl had caught Lafcadio the cat lapping milk from her cereal bowl and had stormed towards him, trying to find the words to scold him. Lafcadio had coolly jumped down from the kitchen table and darted away when Emmeline finally managed "Bad . . . dog!" Then, as Gran watched, the girl closed her eyes and stood still, her brow wrinkled. No, that wasn't right. She *knew* it wasn't right. Not *dog*, but something like it. A little word . . . She stood there for half a minute, racking her brain, and then her face cleared.

"Bad . . . *god!*" she yelled after Lafcadio.

And then, looking at Gran's face, Emmeline must have guessed that *god* wasn't right either. She had rushed from the room, and from that day on, she would not say a word.

Now Gran remembered a line from Robert Louis Stevenson, who said of some unlucky people that "they are tied for life inside a bag that no one can undo." Was that Emmeline's fate? Gran suddenly looked angry and determined. No! This voyage would bring out the old Emmeline. The words she longed for were right there, in the books they carried. Gran would help her find them; together they would untie the bag and throw it over the side of *Permanent Wants*.

And then she turned away. She didn't want Emmeline to see her face.

That evening they made it as far as Manotick, and after dinner they inflated their Sea King rubber dinghy. When darkness came, they rowed out to the middle of the river and had a swim, surrounded by the steadfastness and sanity of the stars. Emmeline remembered what Captain Lillwyn had said at the sailing: all experience was an arch, through which you could see the untravelled world. She saw the arch in her mind, and the world unrolling beyond it, a vast tapestry of greens and browns. Like the African plains . . . And then she was travelling back in her mind to their vacation of two years before, to Kenya and its great cloud-like trees, its termite mounds like crumbly standing stones, and its creatures. On their safari, they had come across a huge scorpion that made her shiver now in the dinghy. It wasn't black but a glistening dark blue, as if it were made of plastic. And then one morning she'd woken up feeling strange—groggy and achy. All day long she had stayed in the tent with a damp cloth on her forehead and cool drinks by her side. But by evening she was seeing things, and that big scorpion kept appearing on her bed . . .

She didn't remember much after that, except waking up in a hospital to see people around her—people who were crying with happiness, now that she was out of her coma. But she didn't recognize her mum and dad and gran. In fact, she had nothing in her head: no names, no words, no memories. And so began the long journey of remembering. Flying over to Nairobi, Gran had brought some of her things—her PlayStation, her two stuffed bears, her photos of the family skating on the Rideau Canal—and the adults took turns holding her and telling her about herself. All this continued when they flew back to Canada. Many things came back to her, but her language stayed lost, damaged . . .

"Everything okay, Em?" said Gran as the dinghy turned lazily in the darkness.

Emmeline nodded, leaving Africa behind, and turned her attention back to the stars. The people of Zeya Shan loved stars, too, she remembered. It suddenly seemed to her that although they were sailing down the good old Rideau River, they were somehow moving closer and closer to Zeya Shan.

The next day, for the first time, they opened for business. (The Manotick town council had granted them a special permit to set up shop at the waterfront, as long as they gave some of their profits to a local literacy organization.) They raised their two yellow patio umbrellas on the forward and stern decks. Under these they set up their stackable bookcases, along with some flower boxes. Luckily *Permanent Wants* had a large foredeck, so most of the stock went there. Single bookcases were placed on top of the low cabin. Since there was a comfortably wide walkway on either side of the cabin, people would be able to stroll right around the vessel, browsing. Travel books were shelved just inside the cabin; all Gran had to do there was prop open the door. On the marina dock in front of the boat, they placed a box of "bargain books." Finally, next to the bargain books, they set up their sandwich board advertising the bookstore.

Gran saw at once that the arrangement left a lot to be desired. At most, they could handle about ten people on the boat at a time. Fortunately, they had just a trickle of customers that day, and at least everybody seemed to enjoy themselves. An old man with a Scottish accent said that a floating bookstore was "a wonderfully quaint and impractical idea."

"That's what *I* thought," replied Gran.

But she enjoyed telling the customers about *Permanent Wants* and all the work she had put into it. Many people were impressed that she and Emmeline were handling this big boat by themselves. But really, as Gran explained, canal boats were *made* to be handled by a small crew. She had discovered that in the old days, even large canal boats were often handled by just a father and son. The only time she really had to be careful was when docking. The waterway could get crowded, and she often didn't have a lot of space to man-oeuvre. But Emmeline would stand at the bow, directing with her hands, and Gran would gingerly bring the boat in—slipping the throttle into neutral, then into forward, then into neutral again. It was really no more difficult than docking a houseboat. In fact, it was probably easier: a houseboat, being tall, could sometimes catch winds that would nudge the vessel out of line.

For Emmeline, the best part of that day was the evening, just as they were closing up the bookstore. A station wagon pulled into the marina lot, and she recognized the tall, stooped figure that emerged.

"Your friend Picardy Bob said I could find you here," said Captain Lillwyn, smiling his worn smile. "Has the trip been a success so far?"

"We made sixty-seven dollars today," said Gran. "But what about this Zeya Shan?"

"I have a very curious story about your country. *Your* country, Emmeline. Can I come aboard?"

Emmeline beamed at him, and Gran smiled bravely.

They moved the last of the bookshelves inside, set up the deck chairs behind the cabin, and lit a mosquito coil; and while the kettle was boiling, they watched a great blue heron wing its way through the dusk. Emmeline got out the atlas and showed it to the captain, who chuckled quietly.

"I was interested in Zeya Shan from the start," he said. "I looked through dozens of travel books and histories of this region, and found no mention of the place. I was ready to give up when I came across this book."

From his briefcase he withdrew an old volume that seemed to be the same soft blue of the dusk around them.

"*Journey to Kaspi*," said the captain. "Written by somebody named St. John Sheraton. Privately printed in 1884. It describes Sheraton's journey from Istanbul to the Caspian Sea; Kaspi is his name for that famous body of water." He opened the book. "According to his account, the weather had been extremely dry, and at one place the River Hinzer was low enough for him to ford on his horse. He took this route southeast across the Hinzer because he had heard stories of"—here the captain cleared his throat, settled himself in his deck chair, and began reading—"'a small kingdom near the Talish Mountains, blessed by an almost complete lack of access, where the people apparently live as they have for centuries . . . '"

The dusk deepened, the crickets sang from the darkness inside the cabin, and the captain read on in his stately, old-school voice. Slowly, the kingdom of Zeya Shan began to take shape in Emmeline's mind. She saw the dark-skinned Zeyans—the men in turbans, the women in brightly coloured head scarves—harvesting pistachios and melons in the fields near the capital city of Arjish. She saw them fashioning tools in small forges, or tending goats and cattle in the foothills, or playing chess under spreading fig trees. And strangely enough, she heard them *speaking*. With the images came words—faint at first, but then louder—words like sparks, words like darting minnows, words dipping and rising like goldfinches in flight, words sustained in an arc like cast fishing flies. The veer and tumble of an ancient, lively language.

"'Like the Persians, the Zeyans are grave and courteous,'" read the captain, speaking in the voice of St. John Sheraton. "'They are also completely ignorant of the outside world and have never heard of Paris or London. I consider them the most civilized people I have ever known, and Arjish to be a rival of any European capital.'"

Arjish. Emmeline was there in her mind, walking through the central bazaar, where the street merchants sold damask, licorice, and star calendars, and where brown children skittered like blown leaves through the alleys. Then it was night; she was standing on the crest of a large breakwater that looked out on the River Hinzer, which seemed to reflect the entire Milky Way in its swirling surface. The words of the captain, speaking from the corner of the deck, drifted into her mind: "'The Zeyans have an almost mystical regard for astronomy—not just astrology, but *real* astronomy.'" She stood on a rooftop beside the traveller Sheraton and his host, a merchant named Lazar, with the heavens spread out above them. And there she saw what Sheraton saw . . .

"'The sky was brilliantly clear,'" read Captain Lillwyn, "'and from where we stood, we could see the crescent moon just above the mountains. And immediately adjacent to it, looking in on its bay, was a bright body that I took to be Venus. But this was only part of the spectacle. There were two faint imminences near Venus—undoubtedly other planets, though I am not, alas, enough of an astronomer to tell their names. I gazed at them through Lazar's telescope; the three heavenly bodies formed a small and perfect triangle near the crescent moon. Lazar told me that this planetary grouping had a special significance for the Zeyan people. The first and greatest sultan of the kingdom, Hara the Great, had been born under this conjunction. Indeed, the ruler had designed his realm to reflect the arrangement: the curving Hinzer was taken to represent the crescent moon, and the triangle of planets was taken to be Zeya Shan itself, which has a triangular shape. Whenever this conjunction appeared, Lazar added, Zeyans celebrated for as long as the planets remained in this position. Unfortunately, I was unable to find out how often this conjunction occurred. Lazar could only say that a Zeyan counted himself fortunate if it happened twice in his lifetime. When I indicated to him how gratified I was to be able to witness this spectacle, he smiled and replied that the stars had their own hospitality.'"

At the end of the chapter, when St. John Sheraton had regretfully taken leave of the Zeyans and made it through a pass in the Talish Mountains, the captain closed the book.

"So Zeya Shan *is* a real place!" exclaimed Gran.

The captain smiled sadly. "It's convincing, isn't it? Unfortunately, I suspect that Zeya Shan is completely invented."

"*What?*"

Gran glanced at Emmeline, who had never taken her eyes off Captain Lillwyn.

"I would stake my reputation on it," declared the explorer. "Problem is, you will not find it in any other history of the region. *Factual* history, that is. But if you turn to the imaginative literature of the Middle East, you get another story. Zeya (or Zeyna) Shan is mentioned in a number of Persian and Turkish epics dating from about AD 700 to the nineteenth century. There was even a famous Turkish poet, a friend of Lord Byron's, who claimed to have visited it in 1847. Apparently, he told Byron that a person could enter the kingdom only with"—here the captain wiggled his fingers to signify quotation marks—"'the assent of the minor gods.'"

"The assent of the minor gods?" repeated Gran.

The captain nodded. "It's often the way with these mythical kingdoms: the minor gods are the gatekeepers."

"But who *are* the minor gods?"

The explorer shrugged his narrow shoulders. "No idea. I can only say that Zeya Shan is like Shangri-La, or Oz, or the Blessed Isles of Prester John—the only map you will find it on is the map of our imagination. I suspect this St. John Sheraton meant it as a scholarly joke. He guessed that some of his more knowledgable readers, knowing the legends about Zeya Shan, would enjoy the joke. Its name, incidentally, means 'star kingdom' in Old Azerbaijani." He chuckled. "My Old Azerbaijani is a bit rusty, but I can still make out simple phrases."

"But Zeya Shan is in that atlas of ours," objected Gran, "and atlases don't contain mythical countries."

The captain gave another melancholy smile. "Of course—you trust the authorities. You trust the experts to be what they claim. But sometimes . . ." His voice trailed off as he looked across the water.

"I'm not sure what the explanation is," he continued. "It used to be that atlas publishers would deliberately include small mistakes in their more insignificant maps so that if the maps were copied without permission, the theft could be detected. Perhaps that's what happened here."

"But is there *anything* factual in this account of Sheraton's?" persisted Gran.

"Oh, yes," said the captain. "The River Hinzer is real. That was the first thing I checked. Apparently in the early eighties, the Soviets tried to change its course as part of a grand engineering project. The land proved to be very hostile, and they had to abandon the project; the river didn't seem to want to shift. Needless to say, there were no reports of a kingdom, even a ruined kingdom, in that area. Nothing there but rocks and dirt." He looked at Emmeline. "Never mind, Emmeline. You might want to hold on to that book. I bet there are very few atlases with imaginary countries in them."

But Gran wasn't sure who looked more unhappy, Emmeline or Captain Lillwyn.

Emmeline had to use everything she could to get her thoughts across, and one of the things that helped her was American Sign Language—the language of many deaf people in North America.

Now, Sign (as it's called) is a real language, like French or English. It's not just pointing at what you want or shaking your head at what you don't want. It uses gestures and hand shapes to "talk" in space. And generally, when somebody suffers damage to the language centre in her brain, she can't use *any* language, whether it's English or French or Sign. But Emmeline surprised her doctors. She was able to learn some signs—not a lot, but some—and she seemed to use these as pictures of ideas. She had always been good at seeing shapes in space, which was why she so liked drawing and sculpting and geometry.

Still, she never got very good at Sign. The signs she knew were mainly those that looked like the thing they represented—like the sign for *baby*, where the signer makes a rocking gesture with her arms. But the great thing about Sign, for Emmeline, was that she could *move*, and sometimes moving helped unblock her. By using her hands to communicate, she found that words would sometimes float to the surface of her mind like loose tea leaves. And when Gran saw how Emmeline persisted at Sign, she decided to learn it, too. As a result, Emmeline often told Gran things that she wouldn't tell her mum and dad.

Heard speaking, Emmeline signed to Gran, the morning after the captain's visit.

Gran didn't quite catch the gestures at first. She made the sign for *again*—opening her left hand, palm up, and then darting her curved right hand over to touch it.

Emmeline signed again, making sure she had the gestures right. Her right index finger touched her chest—*I*—and then moved to cup her ear—*hear.* Then she made the sign for *speaking,* which you might be able to guess even if you don't know Sign: the index finger, pointing left, makes a small circle in front of the mouth. Finally, she held up her right hand, her thumb at her chin, and then moved it back towards her ear; this put the whole sentence back a day in time. Gran was concentrating mightily.

"You hear . . . no, *heard* somebody speaking yesterday," she translated. "Um, who, sweetie?"

Emmeline hesitated, wondering how she could explain this part. She made the sign for *star,* and then—unsure about how to express the idea of kingdom—just swept a hand around her to indicate a place. Gran got this only because she herself had been thinking about "star kingdom."

"Zeya Shan," she said. "You mean you heard the people of Zeya Shan?"

Emmeline gave a flash of a smile. She meant the sun-darkened farmers, and the tiny brown children scampering through the alleys, and the mothers in bright head scarves and flowing dark robes, and the old men whose silver beards glistened with frankincense. But she had no signs for all this, just pictures in her head. She so envied the deaf storytellers she had seen on YouTube, who could create a kind of ballet with their hands—weaving faces and figures into the air just as some gymnasts weave long, flowing ribbons, making them shimmer and dance before the spectators.

"You mean, when the captain was reading that book?" pursued Gran. "You heard these people?"

Again Emmeline nodded. Very slowly, she signed, *Star kingdom.* Then she moved her index finger straight out from her lips, a gesture that means *real, certain, actual, sure, genuine, true, indeed.* At the same time, she moved even closer to Gran and fixed her gaze on her. Gran blinked at her granddaughter: Sign could be *so* intense.

"You may be right, sweetie," she said. "I think we should find out more about Zeya Shan."

Emmeline was looking away absent-mindedly, her hands still fluttering. She was thinking hard—not in words, but in pictures. In her mind now was the strange astronomical sight that St. John Sheraton had reported—three bright planets in a triangle, right beside the crescent moon. Her hands moved again, trying to stir up words.

moon

moonandplanets

so real and so moonmade

> *he is*
>   *nightspeaking*
> *making up? all it?*

Then Emmeline looked straight at her grandmother and signed, *No way, Gran!* (Gran knew this one, she got it so often.)

What Emmeline meant—it came out later in bits and pieces—was this: if the account was a hoax, then St. John Sheraton was a very thorough hoaxer. He was so careful in describing this sight and Lazar's explanation of its importance. Sheraton *couldn't* be making it all up.

"Well," said Gran, a bit at a loss, "I say we talk to Picardy Bob about it."

Picardy Bob, naturally, could not resist the riddle of Zeya Shan.

"Your atlas will be even more valuable to collectors if it's got a mythical country in it," he told them. "Maybe you should do some research on this publisher, Innes-Adaire. There may be a good story about how Zeya Shan got into the atlas."

And so, after their grocery shopping the next day, Gran and Emmeline went online at an Internet cafe and found a publishers directory. There were several paragraphs about Innes-Adaire, which Gran summarized for Emmeline. The firm seemed to have specialized in atlases and books about map-making, and though it was quite successful, winning a number of prizes, it went out of business in 1934. They checked to see which of its books were still in print; none was. The only one still around was a 1920 book called *Taming the Haggard*, by a man named Alan Racette. Apparently it was not about maps but about falconry; the subtitle was *Notes from a Falconer's Life*. (A haggard, Gran learned, was a wild mature hawk that had been caught for training.) Though out of print, the book was considered a minor classic and could still be found in many libraries across North America—including, they were surprised to see, the public library in Manotick.

That had been in the afternoon, and now Gran and Emmeline were on the deck of *Permanent Wants*, eating a late dinner of veggie burgers. They were in no hurry to leave Manotick; each day, they were selling a few more books. Emmeline was making a small sketch of a hawk in her scrapbook, to remind her of the book *Taming the Haggard*. Just then, they heard footsteps at the end of the dock. An RCMP officer was approaching, a tall man in a shiny peaked cap and thick policeman's shoes.

"Excuse me, ma'am," he said to Gran. "Are you Mrs. Teolani McHovec?"

"In person," replied Gran warmly.

"Corporal Barrington is my name. The secretary of the Bytown Yacht Club said I might find you here." He was immaculately dressed: grey shirt, blue tie, and blue pants with a gold stripe down the side. His face was round and boyish, but his eyes were a cool, clement grey. Emmeline was reminded of somebody from a book she knew. Now what was the name?

"I am looking for somebody I believe you know—a Mr. Dillwyn Lillwyn," continued the RCMP man. "He sometimes calls himself Captain Lillwyn."

"What's wrong?" said Gran. "Has something happened?"

"Nothing has happened," said the officer calmly. "We are just very interested in talking to this individual. When did you last see him?"

"Well, just last week, as a matter of fact. He dropped by the boat for a visit."

"And where did he go after that?"

"I assume he drove back to Ottawa. Can I ask why you want to talk to him?"

The officer touched the peak of his cap. "I am afraid I am not at liberty to say, ma'am."

"What do you mean, you are not at liberty to say?"

The RCMP man continued to look over *Permanent Wants*. His eyes moved from Lafcadio (who was lounging on the cabin roof) to the deck and then back to Gran. The crickets kept up their chirping in the background. Tin Tin, remembered Emmeline. He reminded her of Tin Tin. Same boyish, eager face. And why was he looking for the captain? She suddenly felt that there might be more to Captain Lillwyn than they guessed.

"Are you good friends with Mr. Dillwyn Lillwyn?" he asked easily.

"More like acquaintances," replied Gran. (She was thinking, Is that his first name, *Dillwyn*? No wonder he wants people to call him Captain.)

The officer ducked his head ever so slightly, and Gran wondered if he was trying to see into the cabin. "And you are the only occupants of this vessel?" he said. "You and this young person?"

"No," said Gran shortly. "There's the crickets, God love them." She threw a glance over her shoulder. "Cass and Nova, shut up!" She ran the two names together, as she usually did, and so it came out, "Casanova, shut up!"

The RCMP man raised an eyebrow.

"Anyway," continued Gran, "we are not hiding Captain Lillwyn on this boat, if that's what you're thinking. Listen, young man, I might be able to help you if I knew why you were looking for him."

In reply, the policeman took a card from his wallet. "If this Dillwyn Lillwyn should happen to get in touch with you, I would greatly appreciate a call. Here is my card."

Gran gave the card a stony glance; her question had remained unanswered.

The RCMP officer turned to go, but then he hesitated. "By the way," he said, "this man Lillwyn is not a captain."

"I beg your pardon?"

"I understand he refers to himself as a retired captain in the Royal Navy. The British navy has never heard of him." He drew himself up and saluted. "Ladies."

Turning, he walked along the dock to his RCMP cruiser, his large policeman's shoes making a faint *squeak-squeak*.

"So *he* says," remarked Gran.

But Emmeline was thinking of how worn and worried the explorer always looked—as if he was tired of being hunted.

Next evening, Em told Gran that she wanted to go to the library by herself, to get the book *Taming the Haggard*. Gran was frankly nervous. Em sometimes got confused on her own; she had great difficulty reading street signs, and even had a hard time with telephone numbers. In the end she gave in, writing down the book title for the girl, but insisted that Em take the emergency whistle with her.

Em was tempted to give a good blast of the whistle right in the library—the old librarian moved *so* slowly—but when she finally got the book, she studied it as carefully as she had the atlas. It was an old hardcover, with ivory pages and little gold ridges on the leather-bound spine. It was full of illustrations—woodcuts, some of them very detailed, of falcons and falconers. Yes, this was the book. Two minutes later she was outside in the twilight, walking towards the marina, book in hand.

Since Emmeline read pictures rather than print, she had developed the somewhat dangerous habit of skimming a book while she walked. She was about a block from the library, her eyes gliding over the first chapter, when she stopped. Before her was a woodcut of a night scene—falconers flying their hawks by moonlight, their horses tied nearby. The artist had cleverly created the effect of darkness through a white dappling of moonlight on the horses. The setting was clearly the Middle East, for the falconers wore the traditional long robes and headdresses of the region. But what had caught her attention was the moon, a bright crescent. Around it, the artist had drawn three little white circles with lines radiating from them.

Stars or planets . . . and they formed a perfect triangle.

Emmeline stood still for a second, staring at the book, and then broke into a run. Ten minutes later, completely out of breath, she reached the waterfront. As she pounded down the dock towards *Permanent Wants*, Gran opened the door of the cabin and, after looking around furtively, beckoned to her.

Emmeline jumped on board, bursting with her news, but Gran just said urgently, "Come inside *quickly*, Em," and disappeared again. Puzzled, the girl followed her grandmother inside. At the end of the cabin, just emerging from under the bunk, was Captain Lillwyn. He smiled shakily.

"Emmeline," he said, "did you see any *plainclothes men* out there?"

Emmeline thought for a moment. While running through the parking lot near the wharf, she *had* noticed two serious-looking men sitting in a car. She nodded vigorously.

"It looks like the game is up, Captain," said Gran.

"It's not a game anymore," replied the captain unhappily. Standing up with an effort, he peered through the curtained window of the cabin. "It's a good thing I got here when I did; I just managed to beat them. But they'll be there all night, watching the road. Getting out of here is going to be impossible."

"You are not getting out of here until you tell us why the RCMP is after you," said Gran, rather severely. "And if you really *are* a captain."

The captain sighed and turned to face them. He looked much the worse for wear since they had last seen him: there was dirt in the creases of his tweed jacket, and his pants had bits of bracken clinging to them. He looked as though he had slept several nights in the open.

"No, I am not a captain," he said morosely. "And I'm not an explorer. And I'm not an honorary lifetime member of the Royal Geographical Society. I am a *fraud*."

He sat down heavily on the bed, but he forgot to duck his head, and so banged it on the upper bunk. Gran and Emmeline winced.

"A *criminal* fraud," he added, rubbing his head. "If I were just playing at being an explorer, then I wouldn't have the RCMP after me. But I have made a living off my deception—a very good living, in fact." He drew a small flask from his jacket pocket, unscrewed it, and poured a bit into the cap. "Brandy?" he offered.

Emmeline reached for the cup, but Gran said: "Don't be ridiculous, Emmeline. Go on, Captain. I'll call you that because I'm in the habit."

The captain downed the brandy in a single gulp. "It all started years ago. I always wanted to be an explorer, but I wasn't cut out for it. Too timid, too bookish, too fond of the good life." He held up the flask of brandy. "This is Courvoisier, you know. The yacht club always has plenty on hand. You wouldn't be able to get *this* in the heart of Amazonia, would you?" He poured himself another capful. "Anyway, I would have been quite happy just dreaming about being an explorer, if it hadn't been for a fateful letter. From a cruise ship company—don't they always traffic in false dreams? They had addressed it to 'Mr. Lillwyn Dillwyn,' but I thought they had just got my name reversed. The letter turned out to be an invitation to be a shipboard lecturer on one of their luxury cruises. As the author of many books, they wrote, I was sure to have much material for lectures, and they invited me to choose my own topics. Clearly the letter had been intended not for my humble self, Dillwyn Lillwyn, but for somebody named Lillwyn Dillwyn! Some wretched *author*. Well, I'm afraid my secret ambitions got the better of me. I wrote back to the company saying I would be glad to accept their invitation and suggesting as a lecture topic 'A Year Among the Head-Hunters of Borneo.' They were delighted."

The captain paused to down another capful of brandy, then continued in a low voice: "That was the beginning of my career. The cruise was a great success, and one of the passengers, a magazine publisher, asked me to write some articles about my explorations. One thing led to another, and soon the world knew me as an explorer. And all I did was spend even more time in my library, reading about the places I was supposed to have explored. It wasn't long before a publisher asked me to write an autobiography. I did—and it was pure fiction from beginning to end. It was the most fulfilling thing I've ever done. Then an Australian television company optioned the book, and they made a movie out of it, for which I got a handsome fee. That's when I went from being a fraud to being a con man of international proportions."

Gran couldn't believe what she was hearing.

"But what about that talk you gave at the yacht club?" she said. "You had those shrunken heads on display and—"

"Oh, anybody can whip up a shrunken head," replied the captain. "You make a clay form, wrap it in goatskin, and then add some hair—I generally use paintbrush bristles for the eyebrows. Boiling the goatskin will give it that wrinkly feel. But don't boil the head with the hair on; it'll all fall out."

Emmeline was suddenly determined to make some shrunken heads for *Permanent Wants*. She knew the perfect place for one—on the inside door of the boat's tiny bathroom. You wouldn't see it until you sat down! She wondered if she'd have time to do it before her mum and dad came for a visit.

"But you know," said the captain reflectively, "I had one thing in common with real explorers: the saddening knowledge that very little of the world remains to be explored. It became harder and harder to find exotic places that I could pretend to have visited. And that's why I was so excited when you told me about Zeya Shan. Here was a spark of hope, just a spark, that—"

At this, Emmeline remembered the book in her hand and held it up.

"What's this?" asked the captain and Gran together.

The girl had already opened the book to the drawing she had seen, and she signed to Gran, *Star kingdom.*

"More of that ruddy Zeya Shan!" exclaimed Gran. Emmeline looked gleeful.

"What!" said the captain. He rose at once, mindful of his head this time, to peer at the illustration over Gran's shoulder.

"Listen to this," said Gran, glancing at the passage opposite the woodcut. "'In Britain the peregrine falcon has long been a favourite hunting bird, but in the Middle East the preference is for the saker falcon. A few Middle Eastern countries have bred their own birds, which combine the qualities of both. In 1905 I spent some time in Zeya Shan, a small kingdom not far from the Caspian Sea, where I hunted with a falcon that had the plumage of a peregrine but the lines of a saker. The Zeyans had actually trained falcons to hunt under the stars, and I remember watching several of them sweep over a field under a brilliant crescent moon. My attention was divided between the birds and the sky, for several bright bodies—planets, I'm sure—had gathered around the moon in a perfect triangle, and I recall thinking that this sight was surely as rare as that of falcons hunting in darkness.'" She looked up from the page. "Isn't that odd! A crescent moon and three planets around it. Sheraton described exactly the same thing, Captain."

The captain turned the volume over in Gran's hand. "What is this book? *Taming the Haggard*?"

"It's from the same publisher that did the atlas," explained Gran. She flipped to the very back, where there was a note about the author.

"Listen, friends," said the captain, "I would like to believe in this country as much as you. But it takes a fraud to know a fraud, and I can tell you that Zeya Shan is nothing more than—"

"Wait a minute," said Gran. "It says here that this guy Racette was a map-maker by training."

"Yes? So?"

"A *map-maker*. And get this—he spent five years teaching map-making in Baghdad. At the Royal College of Engineers and Surveyors. So he probably knew that part of the world very well."

Emmeline understood at once; Gran could see it in her eyes.

"Racette must have drawn the map in the atlas!" Gran continued. "He would have been the perfect choice. He wasn't just a map-maker; he had actually lived in the Middle East. Maybe he had some arrangement with them—he would do their maps, and they would publish his book on falconry." She glanced at the captain in triumph. "*That's* why Zeya Shan is in the atlas, Captain. Racette had actually been to the place."

"But he *couldn't* have been to the place," countered the captain heatedly. "It doesn't exist. There are lots of explorers who travelled through that region and found no trace of it. And what about the Soviet engineers in the eighties? They mucked around in that area for months, and there was nothing there."

"It's not there *now*," said Gran. "But could it have been there once?"

"What on earth do you mean?"

"I'm not sure, but . . . could Zeya Shan have been destroyed and buried by an earthquake?"

"An entire *kingdom*?" The captain plucked the book out of Gran's hands and began flipping through it in agitation.

"Well, it's just a suggestion. Is there anything else about Zeya Shan?"

"I don't see anything," said the captain, still flipping the pages. "But it's a good, thick book, and there's no index. I wonder . . ." He stood there irresolutely, book in hand. "Could it be true? Could there be a buried kingdom out there?" He glanced from Emmeline to Gran. "Or is the secret even more stupendous than that?"

Just then, in the silence, they heard the sound of a car's wheels on gravel. Headlights flickered over the boat.

"There are *two* cars out there now," said the captain, peering through the porthole. "This doesn't look good." He continued to watch for a moment, his face tense, then turned to Gran. "Teo—may I call you Teo?—I noticed you have a dinghy tied to the stern."

"You want to escape in our dinghy?" said Gran sharply. "Then *we'll* get hauled in for helping you."

"They won't be able to prove I was here," said the captain. "And they won't see me go. And if I turn myself in, how can I pursue the riddle of Zeya Shan?" He moved close to Gran. "Dear lady, all my life I have longed to be an explorer. Maybe this is my last chance. Zeya Shan may be a fable, a chimera, a fabrication, but I *have* to find out."

Emmeline wordlessly pleaded with Gran to let the captain take the dinghy, but Gran was not easily moved.

"Listen," she told the girl, "this man cheated innocent people."

"No, not *innocent* people," corrected the captain. "Just television producers and publishers."

"Well, you cheated *me*," shot back Gran. "All this time I thought you were the real thing. What about that speech you gave at the sailing of *Permanent Wants*? All those grand words about striving and seeking and not yielding. And this from a man who cooks up his shrunken heads like hot dogs!"

"The words were true, Teo," said the captain humbly. "Spoken by a fraud, but true nonetheless." He lowered his voice to an urgent whisper. "Please, we don't have much time. I promise I will tie the dinghy on the opposite shore, hidden in the big willows. You can retrieve it when it's safe." He held up *Taming the Haggard*. "And may I take this with me, Emmeline?"

"It's a *library* book," said Gran sternly.

Captain Lillwyn may have been a con man, but he would never have jeopardized the library privileges of a fellow human being.

"I promise I will mail it back to you as soon as I can," he said to Emmeline. "Er, you may need to renew it once or twice."

Gran saw to her irritation that he had made an ally out of Emmeline. "Even if we do give you the dinghy," she said, "how far do you think you're going to get? You have no car, you have no money, and you're a wanted man."

"Teo dear," said the captain, "for years I have lived a comfortably false life. Now I ask for something else: danger, risk, impossible odds. Give me all the hardships that *real* explorers face. I will be content."

Gran gave an exasperated sigh. She knew that if Picardy Bob had been there, he would have been defending the captain—and probably pelting her with lots of quotes from *Moby Dick*.

"All right, all right," she agreed crossly. "Go, Emmeline—get the dinghy tie rope and bring it alongside. Keep low so they don't see you."

Emmeline darted out the door, untied the painter of the dinghy, and brought it alongside the boat. The captain slipped out, keeping low as well. He had a bit of difficulty getting over the gunwale without a ladder, but he managed eventually. From the darkness of the dinghy, he looked up at them.

"Goodbye, friends," he said. "You will hear from me again one day." He sat down to take the oars, then glanced up again. "Teo, they'll wonder at the yacht club what happened to me. Please tell them that the call of adventure became too strong. Please tell them I got tired of being an explorer in *residence;* I wanted to be an explorer in *action.*"

"The real story is going to come out soon," warned Gran.

"The real story," echoed the captain. "What *is* the real story? Maybe the real story of my life is out there in the darkness, and maybe I'm on my way to find it." He paused, his hands on the oars, and when he spoke again, they could hear the emotion in his voice. "Remember that, Emmeline. You are not your circumstances, you are not your weaknesses, you are not your mistakes. Your real story is there for the making—no, the *taking.* Remember that."

And settling himself into the dinghy, he began quietly working the plastic oars. Cass and Nova provided the goodbye music.

The RCMP gave up on the search eventually, concluding that "Captain" Dillwyn Lillwyn was no longer in the country. As for the man himself, he was as good as his word. A month later, in the middle of the adventures that make up this book, a parcel arrived for Emmeline and Gran. They were astonished to see that it had come all the way from Tehran, Iran. It was the library copy of *Taming the Haggard,* and there was a note with it.

"Dear Emmeline and Teo," wrote the captain. "I am returning the book you so kindly lent me. Of it, I can say that the old cliché is true: this book changed my life. I don't expect to see you two, or any of my old friends, again. But please don't worry about me. I am about to set off on an adventure beyond imagining. I just have to wait for 'the assent of the minor gods.' And I believe that will happen in the next few years, if my astronomical research is sound. P.S. For more about the minor gods, take another look at that wonderful illustration you showed me."

Gran turned to the woodcut in *Taming the Haggard*, which showed the Zeyan falconers flying their birds at night.

"What's he talking about?" said Gran. "I can't see—"

But Emmeline pointed excitedly to the three little circles that were arranged in a triangle around the moon.

"You mean, the minor gods are the *planets*?" said Gran. "Get out!"

Emmeline reached a hand up to Gran's chin, fixed her gaze on her, and nodded forcefully several times. Gran, glaring back stubbornly, reached out her hand to cup Emmeline's chin. They remained that way for a moment, and then Emmeline stretched her *other* hand towards Gran's face. She thought she might use both hands to make Gran's head nod, but she couldn't quite reach. They stood there for a moment at arm's length.

"I still say that man's a fraud," mumbled Gran. The word actually came out *fwaud* because of the pressure from Emmeline's hand.

It was Picardy Bob, naturally, who had the last word.

He came for a visit one evening when they were having halibut-and-zucchini kebabs for dinner. Gran and Emmeline always worked as a team on this dish: while the girl sliced the zucchini into thick half moons, Gran prepared the marinade—vegetable oil, salt, pepper, and cumin. ("Don't forget the cumin!" Bob said.) Then they threaded the zucchini and halibut onto wooden skewers and grilled them on the boat's hibachi. Sometimes they made rice to go with the meal, but this time they just had lots of kebabs and potato chips.

After hearing the whole story of Zeya Shan, Bob put down his kebab and pondered for a moment. "I've never been much on astrology," he said finally, "but I can't help thinking that there might be something to the idea that heavenly bodies *do* have some effect on our world. Maybe certain conjunctions of planets will open up pathways, secret avenues here on earth. And maybe those avenues can lead to some very strange places—but only for as long as the conjunction lasts."

"Oh, *Bob*," said Gran. She often felt that she had to be the anti-mystical one, with all the mystics in her life.

"As for the captain's story about the River Hinzer," continued Picardy Bob, ignoring the interruption, "here's *my* explanation: The Soviet engineers couldn't shift the river from its bed, right? Well, maybe they couldn't because Zeya Shan was *still there*, in some sense. Maybe it will always be there. We can't see it, we can't sense it, but the land will always carry some memory of it, a permanent image. That's your kingdom, Emmeline—eternal but cyclical, like the stars themselves. And protected forever by the planets." He picked up his kebab. "Just the right amount of cumin, girls."

Emmeline was absent-mindedly tugging at her medical ID bracelet, wishing she could tell her friend Madison about this adventure. Madison didn't seem to mind that Emmeline couldn't speak. Sometimes the two friends would call each other and have what Gran called a "communing": Emmeline would listen while Madison talked away about her week at riding camp, or the three goals she had scored in a soccer game, or her new iPod Nano ("It's, like, as big as a matchbox!"). Eventually, Madison would talk herself out, and Emmeline would tap the receiver to say goodbye, and that would be it. Madison thoroughly enjoyed it, and Emmeline . . . well, she put up with it. She had lost a lot of friends because of her language problem, and at least Madison was still her friend.

As for Gran, looking at the girl, she was thinking of Captain Lillwyn's parting words to Emmeline. *Your real story is out there*, he had told her. It reminded Gran of something an African friend of hers, a wise and well-travelled man named Tibeli, had said about Emmeline. He had listened soberly as Gran explained how the girl's language had been stolen from her, but he didn't say that it was awful, or how sorry he was, or anything Gran was used to hearing. He just said that the girl had stumbled into a *mauvaise histoire*, a wrong story. Once she found herself in her *true* story, the names of things would return to her, and words would come again like rain after a dry season . . .

All Gran said aloud, however, was this: "Well, I think the captain, that old fraud, could have sent us some money. That library book was two weeks overdue."

The Language of Eden

O ne of the pleasures of travelling the Rideau Waterway is "locking through." The waterway winds through land that gently slopes up and then down, and locks were built to move boats from one water level to another. A lock is really nothing more than an elevator of water. It consists of a long stone chamber and a set of gates at each end. In the old-style locks, the gates are opened and closed by means of a large hand-operated winch, called a "crab." Once the gates are closed, water can be let into the chamber or out of it, thereby raising or lowering the boats. It sounds like a slow process, and it is—pleasantly so.

The only time the process isn't so pleasant is on busy weekends, when there are many boats and space is tight. Then the "lockies" (the Parks Canada people who work the locks) have less time to chat, and pilots have to be careful in steering around other vessels. Gran and Emmeline found themselves in just such a situation one Saturday morning while locking through the pretty lockstation of Poonamalie. There was a whole flotilla of boats, big and small, waiting to get into Lower Rideau Lake. As one of the larger vessels,

Permanent Wants was first into the lock chamber, then all the other boats were packed around it. There were so many of them that little open water was left, and some boats were moored two and three abreast.

Emmeline, looking around at the boats, felt sure that everyone on them was living a normal life. Some people were sunburned, some were pale; some wore straw hats with paisley bands, some baseball caps; some wore too-tight bathing suits, some drooping bathing suits. But all were talking and laughing easily. They probably didn't even realize how normal they were. She used to have a normal life, too—*blazingly* normal. She could play Scrabble with Gran and write emails to her friends. She could go tobogganing on her Crazy Carpet with her cousins Shelby and Todd and scream her head off (sometimes even in French). She could watch movies—*Get Smart, Toy Story, Back to the Future*—and repeat all the funny lines for her mum and dad. She never had to visit doctors and speech therapists; she never took five minutes to print her own name; she never had to put up little labels—"wall," "light switch," "desk"—around her room so she could remember the names of things. Now, looking out at the boats, she suddenly decided that this summer was going to be normal. She and Gran would do all the ordinary things that people did on their vacations. And if she didn't speak . . . well, that wasn't so abnormal, was it? Her dad didn't say much and he was pretty normal, for a dad.

Nudging against the gunwales of *Permanent Wants* was a cedar-strip canoe. The canoeists were a man and a woman in expensive khaki travel clothes, the kind with lots of snap pockets. The man looked to be a bit younger than Gran, the woman younger still. They seemed completely untouched by the wild world. Both were short and pudgy, with pinkish indoor faces and old-young smiles. The man's belt neatly bisected his paunch, as the equator does the globe.

He wore an old-fashioned pith helmet, the kind that Victorian explorers used to wear, and the woman wore an Australian bush hat. Her pants must have been well pressed for the journey, for they still held their pleat.

But the most curious thing about them was their shipmate—a large, ragged crow. It seemed as tame as a pirate's parrot, and moved back and forth on the middle seat of the canoe, its head bobbing like a pigeon's. It was clearly fascinated by all the commotion around it.

Eventually, all the boats were inside the lock chamber. Bumpers were secured, and tie ropes were looped around the black cables that ran down the lock wall. Engines were turned off, although some big boats kept their engine fans going (to get rid of gasoline fumes). Then the gates were cranked shut, and the lockies moved to the upstream end of the lock to open the sluice valves. Water flooded into the lock chamber. Looking over the side, Emmeline watched the swirls and eddies on the surface. She and Gran settled back to wait, the tie ropes held loosely in their hands. When the water level had risen to that of the lake at the upper end of the lock, the gates would be cranked open and all the boats would be on their way.

Naturally, Gran said hello to the couple in the cedar canoe, and they said hello back. Then the crow jumped in.

"Ahoy, mateys!" it said. "Ahoy, mateys!"

Gran and Emmeline stared, as did people in the neighbouring boats. Even a passing lockie stopped to have a look—and lockies are not easily impressed.

"Don't mind Crow," said the man in the canoe, chuckling. "He usually takes over the conversation."

"I don't think I've ever seen a talking crow before," said Gran.

"Oh, crows are pretty good mimics," returned the man. "This one knows dozens of words."

"Most of them rude," added his wife.

"He didn't learn those from *me*, dear," said the man, unclipping his sunglasses from his spectacles. He had watery blue eyes and a face like an underbaked bun.

"I'm Professor Henry Van Troon," he said to Gran, "and this is my better half, Prue."

"I'm Teo and this is Emmeline," said Gran. "Are you from around here?"

The professor nodded. "Just outside Smiths Falls. We've been canoeing for a week in the area. We're on an expedition, you might say."

"Might say," croaked the crow. Prue, the professor's wife, rolled her eyes.

"What kind of expedition?" asked Gran curiously.

The professor put his sunglasses back on and sat up straighter in the stern seat. "I am looking for something," he said, slowly and impressively, "as important as the lost continent of Atlantis, or the Holy Grail, or the Ark of the Covenant."

"Ark!" said the crow. The professor chuckled.

"Yes, Crow knows," he said. "He knows better than anybody." He paused again, head held high, like an actor on stage. "I am looking for a vanished language."

Emmeline, who was at the bow of *Permanent Wants*, stood up and moved closer, holding her tie rope at arm's length.

"A Native language, you mean?" asked Gran.

The professor shook his head. "Even more spectacular than that. I am looking for the first language ever spoken by humans—the ancestor language, the dawn language, the seed from which all other languages grew. I am looking for the mother tongue of the world."

Prue had obviously heard it all before: she was gazing through the porthole of *Permanent Wants*, smiling faintly at Lafcadio, who had been banished to the cabin during the locking-through.

"It's *here*?" said Gran in astonishment.

"Oh, yes," said the professor. "Crow knows. Don't you, Crow?"

"Boop!" said Crow. "Boop-boop-a-doop! Rama lama ding dong! Mee mee na na noo noo!"

"That's not it," said the professor hastily. "Crow's vocabulary is like his nest—bits and pieces from everywhere. Come on, Crow. Say a few words of the mother tongue." But Crow had seen Lafcadio, too, and just flapped his wings at the cat. Lafcadio, for his part, looked out at the canoe's occupants with relaxed contempt.

"He's so contrary," sighed the professor. "He'll never say anything you want him to. But yes, he knows a few words of the ancestor language—just picked them up. And I'm quite sure it happened in this area."

"Really?" said Gran, giving her tie rope a gentle jerk upwards. (You often have to do this while locking through, sliding your tie rope up the cable as your boat rises.)

"It all started in the spring," began the professor. "*Everything* starts in the spring for Crow, because he gets so restless then. He often goes flyabout—just takes off to explore on his own. Generally he comes back after a few days, but this time he was away for a week in April, and we got worried. So we stocked up on roasted sunflower seeds, which he loves, and headed out onto Highway 43. Crow is not hard to track, since he's such a social butterfly. We found a gas station owner who had heard him imitating a cell ringtone, and not far away, there was an outdoor yoga camp where he would sit in a tree and chant *Ommm*. Well, we found him without much problem. He was hanging around the Tay Dairy Queen and Mini-Putt, near Port Elmsley, mooching ice cream. You ate *so* much junk on that flyabout, Crow. Anyway, we plunked him into a cage and that was that.

"Well, it was two mornings later—I was sitting on the veranda reading the paper, and Crow was on his perch yakking away—when

I heard him say an extraordinary phrase. It was as small and bright as a jewel. I am a student of languages, you see, and I knew immediately it was no modern language he was speaking. I got out my tape recorder, and sure enough, after a while he said the same phrase, along with several others that had the same quality. The next day I drove into Kingston to see a colleague of mine, an expert in primitive languages. He was even more excited than I was. Apparently, the phrases reminded him of the dialects spoken by two Stone Age tribes that had been discovered many years ago—one in the Amazon, and one in the Philippines."

Crow said "Ahoy!" to Lafcadio and flapped his wings provokingly, but the cat paid no attention. He was used to birds with attitude.

"There was something very interesting about these two tribes," continued the professor. "They were true children of nature, living in grass huts, hunting with blowguns, and speaking a simple and beautiful language. But amazingly, some of the same words could be found in the two dialects—and yet the tribes lived on different continents! That's when people began to think that maybe these tribes were speaking remnants of one very old language, maybe the *original* language. Some scholars had always believed in a mother tongue spoken by all of humanity in the morning of the world. They also thought it was as extinct as the sabre-toothed tiger. But these two tribes, hidden away in the jungle, must have kept the original speech—some of it, anyway."

The professor paused, looking fondly at Crow in the centre of the canoe. "I got all this from my colleague in Kingston, who had tapes of these two tribal dialects. And guess what? After a few days of listening, we heard words and phrases that sounded very close to Crow's utterances. I came away convinced that they were indeed the same phrases, but that Crow was speaking them with a local accent. And he must have picked them up on his flyabout."

"But where would he have heard them?" asked Gran. "I mean, a Stone Age dialect?"

"I suggested the gas station," remarked the professor's wife, "judging by the staff."

The professor gave his wife a brief tolerant smile, then continued as earnestly as before: "I knew the answer lay in the countryside where Crow had gone, so I spent all of May and June driving and walking the area west of Smiths Falls. And that's when I made a second stupendous discovery."

Emmeline thought he was going to stand up in the canoe, so excited was he. He shifted and wriggled like a small boy who had just caught his first fish. His wife put both hands on the canoe gunwales to steady the vessel.

"Just a charcoal drawing on rock," he said. "A very simple drawing, done in the hollow of an outcrop. Yet it reminded me strongly of the Stone Age cave paintings at Lascaux and Chauvet in France. I thought at first it was very old and had been done by the Native people of this area. But then I had a bit of the charcoal analyzed, and the lab told me it had been freshly applied."

"Probably just a weekend artist," observed Gran.

"Possibly," said the professor. "But the lab also told me that it was *natural* charcoal—from burned wood of the area, not from an artists' supply store. Do weekend artists make their own charcoal?" Before Gran could reply, he continued: "And what's more, the drawing was done on a rock face miles from anywhere. Why would a weekend artist choose such a spot?"

Gran was silent. The professor nodded solemnly.

"First Crow picks up some words of a Stone Age dialect," he said slowly. "Then I discover a drawing done in a Stone Age style—using the materials of a Stone Age artist. I can draw only one conclusion." He looked from Gran to Emmeline. "Somewhere between Smiths Falls and Port Elmsley lives an undiscovered Stone Age tribe."

Very soon, Emmeline and Gran had been recruited to join the expedition. Gran did so with good humour, thinking that it would make a good story and nothing else. But Emmeline was completely captured by the idea of an ancestor language—a language that had emerged in the long-lost world of mammoths and sabre-toothed tigers and cave bears. And who on earth would be speaking it around Smiths Falls?

When Gran explained (with Emmeline's consent) that the girl was trying to recover her own lost language, the professor and his wife were completely captured by *her*.

"Remarkable!" said Henry. "I think you're the very person for our expedition, Emmeline. But my word, it must be hard for you."

Em wished she could tell him that she did have *some* language. She could usually remember simple words like *friend, salt, sad, children, Gran,* and even a few less common words like *apricot, shrimp,* and *wild*. But she had so few words altogether that she had to make them stretch. That was why, when she named things in her mind, every small animal was a shrimp and every piece of fruit an apricot.

"Well, Em," said Prue, "we are delighted to have you along. And you know some Sign language—that's wonderful. Can you tell me your name in Sign?"

Em was caught off guard. She knew her name in Sign, of course, but just then, it wasn't within reach inside her mind. She closed her eyes: this happened so often.

Gran watched her for a moment and then said gently, "You remember, Em. It starts like this." She held up her right hand, fingers curled towards the palm, to finger-spell *E*. "And *M* is . . . What was it, now?"

Emmeline remembered then, and made a fist with three fingers over the thumb.

"That's it," said Gran.

Em sighed. Yes, she was just the person for this expedition.

Before the professor and his wife went their own way, Henry gave Gran directions. "You can moor at Joe Michaud's dock, just down from the lockstation," he said, pointing to his map. "He can rent you a canoe as well. Then you want to go down this little tributary as far as Hadley Cove, right here. It's not quite an hour's paddle. We'll meet there at, say, noon?"

Joe Michaud's place turned out to be a repair shop for almost everything. He had a neat little frame house behind the shop, white with blue trim and flowerpots on the front porch. Apart from that, the place was mainly junk. There were washing machines and ovens and tractor parts and piles of aluminum siding and a rack of bikes (even some old "banana bikes," with the long seats and Y-shaped handlebars). On the wall of the repair shop was a gun rack that held nothing but hockey sticks. Maybe to hide some of the junk, Joe's wife, Sally, grew flowers and plants wherever she could. A field was being cleared behind the shop—for a big vegetable garden, Sally explained—and smoke could be seen rising from a small brush fire. Joe wasn't at home, but Sally said *Permanent Wants* could moor there for the weekend. While they were chatting, Gran asked her about the countryside they were about to explore.

"Well, there's not much there," she said. "A few old houses and *lots* of old appliances. Joe'll be out there doing his rounds this afternoon." She looked up from the dock at a crowd of children in the yard. "Y'all! Time for chores!"

"That's quite a family," remarked Gran with a smile.

"Oh, they're not all mine, thank goodness," said Sally. "We take in foster kids sometimes—we got three right now. No, four."

Emmeline, looking up at the yard, saw one little girl who was standing apart from the others. She seemed as skinny as a leaf stalk, and her pale blonde hair stood out even at that distance. Emmeline noticed that she had hadn't looked up at Sally's voice; only when the other children moved away did she follow.

"The city kids really like it here," continued Sally. "If Joe's going to any of the farms, he generally takes a few with him." She pocketed the money Gran had given her. "Don't you worry, I'll look after your cat. So you're going to do a bit of paddling today?"

"We're off to Hadley Cove," said Gran.

"Oh, that's nice. There's a ruined orphanage not far from the cove—very picturesque. Have a look if you get a chance."

When Gran and Emmeline set out ten minutes later in their rented canoe, the pale-haired girl watched them from the lawn. She wore odd-coloured socks, Emmeline noticed—one with blue trim, the other with red. Her thick glasses seemed too big for her face. She seemed as frail as a seedling in a junkyard. Emmeline waved, but the other girl didn't move. Still, Emmeline felt that they might have things to say to each other, if they met.

Soon the tributary narrowed and the banks grew thick with trees. Emmeline could easily see the bottom, layered in old leaves. The water became even shallower as they passed through a small flooded forest, and they often sank their paddles into the leaf bed. Two mallard ducks paddled through the green light; Emmeline could see their pale orange feet working under the surface. She watched as the birds came to a thick floating branch, casually waddled over it, and then resumed their paddling. A kingfisher swooped through the soft light, making its strange rattling cry. They were only a few kilometres from Joe's shop, but Emmeline felt as if she were leaving civilization.

The river dipped into a little inlet—Hadley Cove—and on the shore they spied the professor and his wife, sitting on folding camp chairs, a map spread between them.

"So this is the place," said Gran as the bow of her canoe nudged the grassy bank.

The professor got to his feet. "Nice, don't you think? The cave drawing is just up here. It hasn't been touched, as far as I can tell."

They followed him along a forest trail. Bits of fluff from cottonwood trees floated like snowflakes through the green light. A few big trees had been blown down near the trail and lay twisted and splintered at their trunks, their great white bones revealed. They seemed like great sculptures, peaceful and not tragic despite their yellowing leaves. By falling, they had created a place for the sun to get through, and they lay in a bright marinade of dandelion light. They seemed to have passed on to a higher life, and continued to sip water and carbon in another world.

"It feels like the primeval forest, doesn't it?" said the professor. "Just the place where you'd find the primeval language. The language of Eden—that's what people used to call it. For centuries, it was thought that Adam and Eve spoke the oldest and most perfect language of all. But humanity had cut itself off from God, scholars believed, and so had lost that language. Only birds kept it alive—birds and elementals."

"Elementals?" said Gran.

"Yes, otherworldly beings—spirits, angels, ghosts."

"I'm starting to think," said Prue dryly, "that our primitive tribe belongs in just that category."

Her eyes, Emmeline noticed, were not as summer-mild as her husband's. They were tired, careful, disbelieving eyes—not blue or grey but some washed-out colour, a shade away from being no colour at all.

"Speaking of otherworldly beings," remarked Gran, "where's Crow?"

"Oh, he'll show up when he's hungry," said the professor. "Here, this is what I wanted to show you."

They had come to an outcrop of whitish rock fronted by small trees. The professor led them through the trees to a hollow—not so much a cave as a scooped-out section of the rock, about two metres high and half a metre deep. There, all of them stood still, gazing in wonder at the charcoal drawing on the rock face.

Most of the shapes were animals—a horse with a thick mane, a smallish bear, a few rabbits. Above the animals were birds: one of these, a small, slender arrowhead with a long beak, was clearly a hummingbird. All the shapes were drawn roughly, with streaks of charcoal that wavered over the bumpy, cracked face of the rock, and yet they showed touches of close detail. One of the rabbits had a floppy ear, and the horse had a forelock of mane between its ears. Besides the animals, there were two small human figures with long, wavy lines coming from their heads. They seemed to be floating in the air above the animals. Oddly, the two figures were drawn over each other; one pair of legs intersected the second pair. Emmeline wondered if the figures were supposed to be transparent.

The only material used in the drawing was charcoal, but the artist had cleverly used the colours and shapes of the rock to give the animals depth. The figure of the bear, for example, had been drawn around a rusty patch of rock that bulged out a bit, as if the bear were forcing its way out of the rock.

The only other marking on the rock was a line drawing of a human hand, palm facing out, the thumb tucked in.

"How strange," remarked Gran.

The professor nodded. "Strange and yet familiar—to someone who knows Stone Age art. Horses and bears are common motifs in the cave paintings of Europe. So are hand drawings like this. But usually they are simple stencils—a hand held up against the rock and paint blown around it. This one has much more detail. Most remarkable."

Emmeline, fascinated, went close to the drawn hand. She felt that it was different from the other shapes, that it was a symbol or code of some kind. She held up her own hand as a comparison, and at once the professor exclaimed: "Don't touch it!"

Emmeline snatched her hand back and glared at the professor: she knew better than *that*. She didn't move from where she was standing, to make a point to the professor.

Prue said wearily, "Oh, keep your hair on, Henry."

"Sorry," said the professor, looking abashed. "I *am* jumpy around this drawing. But you've noticed something important, Emmeline: that hand *is* small. These Stone Age people are probably diminutive. They may even be of pygmy origin. Look at how small the floating figures are, compared to the animals."

"It's almost as if they can pass *through* one another," remarked Gran, pointing to their intersecting legs.

The professor nodded. "My guess is that these figures are shamans, travelling through the spirit realm. The flowing lines coming from their heads may be headdresses worn for the magical journey."

"Or maybe just hair," observed Gran.

"Maybe," said the professor, but he clearly preferred his magic-headdress theory. "Anyway, you see why I want to protect this drawing. Now, let's get you a map, and I'll show you our search terrain."

Along with the map, the professor gave them some little orange flags and told them to be on the watch for anything out of the ordinary—shaped stones and sharpened sticks, for example, that might be tools. If they found anything, they were *not* to pick it up. Rather, they should flag it and mark it on the map.

"Sally at the shop mentioned something about a ruined or-phanage," remarked Gran. "Is that near here?"

The professor pointed to the map. "Right there, on the edge of your search area. You can take a look if you want."

"It's a sad place," remarked Prue.

Her husband glanced at her uneasily. Emmeline sensed in that glance a whole unspoken dialogue between the professor and his wife. Gran must have sensed it as well, for she said briskly: "Well, we'll take a look at it if we get a chance. Shall we meet back here for a late lunch at two?"

For an hour, Gran and Emmeline wandered through their area, stopping often to listen, their eyes moving from the ground to the trees. Once Emmeline saw a small, bright fleck beside the trail, but it turned out to be nothing more than an old shotgun shell. She found it pleasant walking in the ancient ruined light of the forest, and she walked with all her senses alert. She was good at this, much better than Gran. It was as if, having lost much of her own language, she found it in other things—in landscapes, birdsong, the sound of wind, the drift of sunlight, the echoing silences. Now she stopped trying to find the words for things and just let the mood of the forest wash over her. She sensed something like a melancholy, a forgot-tenness that she hadn't felt in the woods earlier.

After a while, she got a bit bored with looking for signs of the tribe, and her mind turned to other things. She hadn't practised her karate for a few weeks, and soon she was stopping briefly to—hi-ya!—try a block or a kick. Karate was the other thing she loved, besides the violin. She'd been doing it for eight months now and knew five kicks, seven punches, and three blocks (for both low and high blows). She liked kicks better than punches, because they were more like dancing. And what she *really* liked was making the karate sounds. You were allowed to say things like *tsah!* and *hi-ya!* when you did karate moves, since that helped to get the adrenalin going. They weren't words, just sounds, and she didn't have too much difficulty saying them. In fact, sometimes she shouted them. Once she'd said *hi-ya!* so loudly that they'd heard her all the way down in the kitchen of the community centre, where there was an adult night class going on in "Survival Skills for the Kitchen." The instructor was so startled, she dropped a bowl of palak paneer.

"Okay," said Gran, "I'm a hooligan after your Johnny Depp poster," and she came at her granddaughter with arms held out menacingly. She launched a roundhouse blow that moved in a languid arc, as if she were doing tai chi. Emmeline blocked the blow and, with equal grace, pivoted and swung a foot sideways, landing a kick on Gran's kidney with all the force of a falling snowflake.

"That three-week layoff hasn't hurt *you*," declared Gran.

Around noon, they came out of the woods to see a stone house across a meadow, a house with bright white sheets billowing on the clothesline.

"I could use a drink of water," said Gran. "How about stopping there? They might know something about the drawing on the rock face."

The house turned out to be small but well kept, with large blue shutters and orderly rapids of ivy flowing down the facade. Gran knocked using the old-fashioned brass knocker, and the door was opened by a pleasant-looking woman in a white apron and a nurse's spongy-soled shoes. When she heard Gran's request, she said cheerfully: "How about some iced tea? I just made some."

"That would be lovely," said Gran.

They followed her into the living room, where an old woman sat in a rocking chair. She wore a loose grey sweater despite the warm day, flesh-coloured stockings that bunched at her ankles, and embroidered slippers. Her hair was very white and reminded Emmeline of the enriched bread that you can usually buy on sale—three loaves for two dollars.

"Just some hikers, Auntie," said the woman in the apron. "I'm going to get them some iced tea. I'll get you some, shall I?"

The old woman was looking off into the distance, her chin raised, her hands on the arms of the rocking chair. The bones of her hand stood out against the skin like the frame of a paper lantern.

"Poor dear," said the woman in the apron as they passed into the kitchen. "She had a stroke in the spring and isn't doing too well. Sometimes I think she can see things I can't see—ghosts from the past." She withdrew a jug of iced tea from the fridge. "She's had a hard life. Grew up at the old orphanage, the Paulker place. Have you seen it?"

"Not yet," said Gran.

The woman poured out the iced tea with a clink of ice cubes. "I call her Aunt Tilley, but she isn't really my aunt. She's got no one left, so I come here to help out a couple of times a week."

"That's nice of you."

The woman shrugged. "Well, I feel sorry for her. Lived in that orphanage all her childhood—she and her two sisters. Both her sisters died in an influenza outbreak in the thirties. *Both* sisters. Isn't that sad?" She handed them each a glass of iced tea. "She was frail to begin with, and now she's lost her speech. Can't say a word."

Gran and Emmeline exchanged glances, and the girl gave the barest nod.

"Emmeline here has a similar problem," said Gran quietly.

"Really?" The woman looked hard at Emmeline. "I've never heard of that with kids."

"Yes, well, it happens. Shall we go back into the living room?"

They took their iced tea and went to join Aunt Tilley. The old woman smiled weakly at Emmeline and then turned to gaze out the window again.

"Are you birdwatchers?" said the woman in the apron, noting Gran's binoculars.

Gran shook her head. "We're actually doing . . . anthropological research."

"How interesting. What's that?"

While they drank their iced tea, Gran explained to the woman (whose name turned out to be Miriam) that they were helping a professor research ancient cultures.

"He's especially interested in old languages," added Gran. "In fact, he seems to think that there's one still spoken around here."

"Hmm," said Miriam. "Well, I don't know of any ancient languages in these parts. Although sometimes our handyman lets fly with some fine old Anglo-Saxon words."

"That wouldn't be Joe Michaud, would it?" said Gran. Joe seemed to be the local jack of all trades.

Miriam nodded, chuckling. "Joe's actually been a real help. He's coming out today to look at our washing machine. So you know the Michauds and their horde?"

They chatted for a while more, but Miriam could shed no light on the mystery of the rock drawing; she guessed it had been done by kids. All the time, Aunt Tilley sat apart from them, looking out the window. Emmeline didn't know whether she was even listening to their conversation.

"Well, we should be on our way," said Gran eventually. "The professor will want a report. Thank you so much for the iced tea."

They had gone barely a few metres from the house when, looking up, Emmeline saw Crow sitting in a tree, watching them with bright eyes.

When Emmeline and Gran got back to the site of the rock art, they found the professor looking tired and hot. He greeted them listlessly.

"Where's Prue?" asked Gran.

The professor waved his hand vaguely. "Oh, she's looking for the graveyard."

"The graveyard?"

"Yes, there's supposed to be an old graveyard associated with the orphanage."

He no longer seemed charged with the excitement of the expedition. His pith hat in his lap, his shirt drenched with sweat, he sat wiping his face with a handkerchief. This was the first time they'd seen him without his hat, and his hair looked like half a toupée put on crookedly.

Gran sat down on a log and got out their sandwiches. Emmeline, however, had pulled her sketchbook from her knapsack, and moving through the underbrush, she now stood in front of the charcoal drawing. She was thinking about Aunt Tilley. Surely anybody who had lived in this area all her life would know if there was a primitive tribe in this forest. And since Aunt Tilley couldn't come to see the drawing, Emmeline was determined to take it to her.

Once they were alone, the professor moved close to Gran. "Teo, I wonder if you could have a talk with Prue. She's . . . not quite her old self today. She won't really open up to me, and I thought . . ."

"I'd be glad to talk to her," said Gran. "Is she coming back for lunch?"

The professor shrugged. "I don't know. Maybe we can just go ahead."

"Em?" called Gran. "Want some lunch?"

But Emmeline was intent on capturing the design on the rock face. She drew everything as accurately as she could, right down to the crooked ear of the rabbit. As always, copying a drawing helped her to see it better. Sketching out the floating figures, she thought the lines coming from their heads might indeed be hair, just as Gran had suggested. She took special care with the hand design; once again, she thought it might be the most important element of the whole picture. Now, in drawing it, she had the odd feeling that she should really know what it meant.

Five minutes later, when Gran and the professor were still munching away, she emerged from the undergrowth and signed to Gran that she was going back to the house.

"Now, sweetie?" said Gran. "We just got back."

Emmeline nodded vigorously and stooped to grab a sandwich.

"Okay," said Gran, "but take the emergency whistle. Are you sure you don't want to wait until—"

But Emmeline was off through the trees.

Reaching the house fifteen minutes later, she stopped to get her breath. She felt nervous, as she always did when she had to be on her own around people, but after quieting her breathing, she went up to the door. Miriam answered the knock.

"Well, hello again," she said. "Did you forget something?"

Emmeline shook her head and showed Miriam the drawing.

"How nice," said the woman, a bit puzzled. "You want to show it to Tilley, do you?" Emmeline kept looking around her, trying to see into the living room. "Come right in. More iced tea?"

Emmeline was shown into the living room, and Aunt Tilley smiled her faded smile. The light in the old woman's eyes seemed to be that of the forest—shadow and leaflight commingled, the light of forgotten ages. She was at least seventy years older than Emmeline, and yet for both of them, language was no more than a faint memory in their minds. But it wasn't *completely* gone. Emmeline suddenly felt that if they could put their minds together, they might be able to speak. They were like two islands far apart in the ocean, joined beneath the waves by an undersea continent; it was a matter of going deep to meet up.

She laid her sketchbook before Aunt Tilley. She felt helpless. How could she explain the story behind it? The old woman put a trembling hand on the drawing. Her eyes no longer held old forest light; they were bright and curious. She leaned closer to the drawing, her gaze moving from the animals to the strange floating beings. The flowing shapes, so primitive but so alive, seemed even more mysterious in the stillness of the old house. Aunt Tilley touched the hummingbird, and her brow wrinkled. Was she trying to find the word? Emmeline herself looked far inside her own mind, sifting through the shapes and colours, looking for *words*.

Some people say that we can't really think unless we have language—that we need words to make thoughts. I don't think that's true. Thought is a kind of underwater wave, and when it rises to the surface of the mind, it breaks in the form of words. Words are the *foam* of thought, not the substance. For Emmeline, the wave of thought was as strong as it was for other people; it just didn't carry words. And though she found this very hard, she knew there were others who were just as badly off as she was.

Or even *worse* off. I myself have known others—both adults and children—who had to struggle even more than Emmeline.

Miriam, coming down the hall with two glasses of iced tea, was surprised to see Aunt Tilley and Emmeline moving towards her. The old woman was holding on to the girl's elbow.

"Er . . . do you want to go to the bathroom, Auntie?" Miriam asked.

Aunt Tilley shook her head firmly and kept walking. Emmeline darted a quick glance at Miriam—not exactly impolite, but not inviting either. Miriam stood aside to let them through. The old woman stopped at an open door; inside, Emmeline could see a four-poster bed, a small sofa, and a dresser. Both the dresser and the bed had white coverings, very clean, with lace trim. Aunt Tilley beckoned her inside, closing the door decisively on the surprised Miriam. Then, moving over to a bedside table, she picked up a framed picture and handed it to Emmeline.

It was an old black-and-white photo that showed three girls, each seven or eight years old, standing before a Victorian-style house with decorated gables and a porch swing. The girls were all wearing white dresses and looked exactly alike, with their long braided hair and shy smiles. Emmeline had long forgotten the word *triplets*, but the picture captured the idea even better than the word. She remembered what Miriam had said—that Tilley had grown up with her sisters at the orphanage. So this was a picture of Tilley and her two sisters. And the house in the background must be the old orphanage. Why was Aunt Tilley showing her this?

Just then, her thoughts were interrupted by the sound of a vehicle outside the house. A car door slammed.

"Hey, all!" said a man's cheerful voice.

"Oh, there you are, Joe," said Miriam from the front of the house.

"Sorry I'm late," said the man. "So your washing machine is acting up again. I'm not surprised—it's older than I am."

Emmeline darted to the door of Aunt Tilley's room and peeked out. She saw a heavy-set balding man with a cheerful, ruddy face—Joe Michaud, she guessed. Behind him was a boy with red hair and freckles; she remembered him as one of the children at the Michaud place. And beyond the boy, hovering timidly at the door, was the pale blonde girl with the thick glasses.

At the edge of the yard, the two girls glanced up to see Crow in his usual place, looking down at them with a bright, disreputable eye. In the old days, Emmeline remembered, people believed that birds could talk to ghosts and other "elementals." Elementals. Emmeline didn't recall the word, just the idea—the image of beings like wind-blown wisps of snow. It was, in fact, very close to the image of the small floating beings she had seen on the cave wall.

She looked at the pale-haired girl. Did her new friend know Crow? Just then, the bird gave a loud *caw*. Emmeline's eyes flickered up to the bird, then back; her companion's gaze had not moved. She suddenly knew for certain what she had sensed before—the girl was deaf.

She signed to the girl: *Know Sign?*

The girl nodded and then beckoned eagerly: *Come on!*

She seemed to have the run of the property; neither Joe nor the boy had paid any attention when she darted out the door. And she had obviously been here before. Moving ahead of Emmeline, she veered without hesitation down the path that led to the rock drawing. Emmeline caught up to her and touched her arm.

You . . . know . . . this . . . Emmeline paused, searching for the sign for *forest*, but the girl understood anyway. Pointing to herself, she touched her two middle fingers together and then traced a circle with her hands: *My place.* She added something else, something too quick for Emmeline to catch. But she obviously didn't want to waste time gabbing. They ran, and then walked, and then half-ran through the sun-flecked greenery.

As they approached the rock drawing, Emmeline heard Gran and the professor talking. The other girl, not hearing the voices, was completely caught off guard when, bursting into the glade just ahead of Emmeline, she saw the adults sitting around drinking tea. She stopped short, dismayed. The professor's wife had joined the other two but sat apart.

"Well, hello," said Gran. "Who's this, Emmeline?"

Friend, Emmeline signed. Then, to the pale girl, she signed, *My gran*, indicating her grandmother with a nod of her head.

"Oh, she knows Sign?" said Gran.

Emmeline touched her ear, and Gran understood at once. Getting to her feet, she signed *welcome*, raising her open hand and then sweeping it down in an arc so that it finished palm up.

Prue was watching them keenly. "I know this girl," she said. "She's one of the Michaud kids."

The girl seemed overwhelmed by all the adults. She turned to flee, but Emmeline put a hand on her arm.

The girl shook her head, frowning. *My place*, she signed, quickly and urgently.

Your place? Emmeline repeated.

The girl nodded vigorously. *They must go*, she added.

Why?

They must.

"Emmeline, please ask her to stay," said Prue. She had noticed that the girl's eyes kept darting to the undergrowth beyond them, the site of the rock drawing. "Maybe she can help us."

Emmeline hesitated, searching for the sign for *help*. It was two hands, one helping the other. Yes, she remembered. She placed one fist in the other palm and then raised them together.

But the pale-haired girl clearly didn't want to help. She shook her head again, signing, *My friends will not come.*

Your friends?

"They're having quite a conversation," remarked the professor, clearly feeling a bit left out.

"This seems to be a special place for her," said Gran. She hadn't quite understood the last exchange, but she could sense the girl's dismay at finding people here.

"In that case," declared Prue, "we should leave."

"What?" said her husband, startled.

Prue was already gathering up the lunch things. "Let's go, everybody."

"I am not comfortable with leaving this girl here alone," said the professor. "It's a valuable archeological site."

"Oh, pish," said his wife. "She has as much right to be here as you do. In fact, probably more."

"What on earth are you talking about?" demanded her husband.

Prue sighed. "Oh, Henry, you *are* blind. It was this girl who did the rock drawing."

Emmeline closed her eyes. Of course. She should have seen it before.

The professor stared. With his mouth open and his chin thrust forward, he looked as if someone had just given him a clip on the back of the head.

"Don't be ridiculous," he sputtered.

"You're the one who's being ridiculous," said Prue. "Look at her hand: that's your 'diminutive tribesman.'"

The girl was watching Prue intently, and Emmeline wondered if she could lip-read.

"What am I doing talking about her as if she's not even here?" continued Prue, straightening. "What's her name, Emmeline?"

Emmeline was quite sure even before asking that the girl's name started with B. Sure enough, the girl held up her right hand, fingers extended and thumb tucked into her palm—the same hand shape that was sketched on the cave wall. (It is part of the manual alphabet of Sign, and one of the first signs Emmeline had learned.) Then, very quickly, the girl circled her face with her open hand. Emmeline was trying to put these signs together when Gran said: "It's a name that begins with B and means *beautiful*. Maybe Belle. Or Bella."

But the professor was too distracted to pay much attention. "We will *not* leave," he fumed.

Emmeline was getting impatient: she wanted to find out more about these mysterious friends of the girl's. But the girl herself had clearly had enough. She turned suddenly and was off through the trees, Emmeline at her heels.

"Well done, Henry," said Prue.

In her husband's drawn and bewildered face, one emotion stood out—the loss of a dream. Gran decided to step in.

"Professor," she said, "I'm not sure it really matters who did the drawing. It doesn't solve the big mystery—where Crow learned to speak that tribal language."

"If it *is* a tribal language," said Prue.

This was too much for the professor. "It *is*," he insisted, his mouth twitching. "Didn't you hear Crow while we were canoeing up here? He was back in the country he knew, and he was *telling* us about it."

"I just heard a lot of cawing," said Prue.

"He wasn't saying *caw*," protested her husband. "He was saying *a-kau*." He turned desperately to Gran. "It's one of the oldest of all ancestor words. It means *water* or *stream*, and you'll find descendants of it everywhere. In Latin it became *aqua*; in Japanese, *aka*; in the African Bushman dialect—"

"Whatever you say, Henry," said Prue.

Her husband stared at his wife, no longer an authority, no longer sure about anything.

"What's got into you, Prue?" he said hopelessly. "You've been like this all weekend."

His wife shrugged heavily. "I guess I'm just tired, Henry. Tired of all this."

"What? All this what?"

"All *this*. Running around helping you make a name for yourself. That's been my life for twenty years." She stooped to pick up a bag. "Whatever happened to *my* life?"

Henry could only blink and breathe hard. Once more, Gran decided to speak up.

"I think I'll find out where those girls have got to," she said. "Why don't we all go up to the house? I still say there's a mystery here, Professor. And I bet Crow knows something about it."

It was later in the afternoon—after Joe had left with his son and the pale-haired girl, when everybody was sitting around the garden table, drinking iced tea and watching the hummingbirds at the feeder—that Crow said something memorable.

A single, brilliant word.

When she tried to recall the word later, Gran could only remember that it was there and gone in her mind like a shooting star. None of them had ever heard anything like it before. For Emmeline, it didn't even seem to be a word; it was something alive. She could guess what it meant: *hummingbird*. It resembled a hummingbird—small and swift, with colours that shifted and glimmered like a rainbow. They all stared at Crow open-mouthed, except Aunt Tilley, who smiled delightedly.

"I told you, Prue," breathed the professor. "I *told* you."

Prue said nothing. She was as astonished as anybody else.

"The language of Eden," continued the professor, his voice shaking. "I *knew* it."

"The language of *what*?" said Miriam.

The professor's attention was on Crow. "You old shyster," he said. "You were just playing with us. You could speak it all along."

"But where on earth did he learn it?" asked Gran in wonder.

Prue had noticed Aunt Tilley's reaction when Crow spoke. She leaned closer to the old woman.

"Do *you* know that language, Aunt Tilley?" she asked clearly.

They all looked at the old woman, who nodded, still smiling. The professor gripped the arms of his deck chair.

"Madam," he said, "where on earth did you learn it?"

Aunt Tilley's smile faded, and again her eyes filled with the soft forest light. Emmeline knew then that the mystery there was even stranger than the one they had originally come to solve. The pale-haired girl knew something about it, but she had revealed very little to Emmeline—the secrets surrounding "her place" were clearly precious to her.

Emmeline turned to Gran so the other could see the puzzlement in her face.

"You and me both, Em," said Gran. She turned to Miriam. "You're going to have to be Aunt Tilley's voice, Miriam. Her voice and her memory."

"Me!" said Miriam, looking flustered. "I'm just the housekeeper. I don't know where to start."

But Emmeline knew—with the photo of Aunt Tilley's sisters. She slipped off her chair and moved close to Aunt Tilley, who seemed to understand what the girl wanted. Shakily, the old woman rose to her feet, helped by the professor.

"Mee mee na na noo noo," said Crow in a pleased voice.

They found the graveyard at twilight, less than thirty metres from the rock drawing. It was completely covered by young spruce trees and low ferns; Emmeline and the others had walked right by it several times. For a minute or so, they stood looking down at the tiny white crosses.

"We've forgotten just how severe influenza could be back then," said Gran.

The woods were filled with a stillness, an everlastingness that comes to an old forest at twilight. Emmeline could easily understand why the pale-haired girl had been drawn to this place. The venerable trees, the hidden graveyard, the light like bottle glass, the ancient rock face . . . The city had no places like this, where ghosts might breathe the same piney air as the animals. Once here, the girl had sketched what was strange and exciting for her—and being from the city, she found horses just as strange as bears. And her charcoal? From the brush fire at Joe's yard; that was Emmeline's guess. But there were still things that Emmeline didn't understand—like the floating beings in the drawing. Were they the mysterious friends the girl had spoken of?

Emmeline wished she knew Sign as well as her friend; maybe then the pale-haired girl would have shared the secrets of this place. She looked down at the cracked and peeling crosses, some of which stood crookedly because of the shifting ground. Sometimes she felt that her disability put her in the loneliest place imaginable. She wasn't part of the deaf world, and she wasn't part of the speaking world. And she didn't have any *jokes*. Even in Sign, she couldn't make a joke. If only she had just one joke—she would use it all the time. If she could manage to laugh herself, then others would laugh, too, wouldn't they?

"I wonder why the orphanage had its own graveyard," remarked Gran.

"They didn't have any money," said the professor. He was quiet but not downcast—not after the excitement of the afternoon. "Gravestones and plots cost money. So they buried the victims here . . . in paupers' graves."

"Let's go," said Prue. "This place is too lonely."

They moved out of the shadowed silence into the light of early evening. Emmeline went reluctantly, wondering which of the little crosses marked the graves of Tilley's sisters. Everybody seemed to be wrapped up in his or her own thoughts. Emmeline turned to give the now-hidden graveyard one last look. She wished she could describe the whole adventure to her friend Madison by making a charcoal drawing on a rock. Telling a story with words was (for her) like trying to run with cats clinging to your ankles. Even now, thinking of the day's events, she had a swirl of only two words in her head:

crow-caw

    caw-crow

        crow-caw

And she could just imagine what Madison would say to *that*.

"Professor," said Gran, "I've heard that twins sometimes develop their own language—a secret language that they use only with each other."

"That can happen, yes," said the professor.

"And I suppose the same thing could happen with *triplets*?"

The professor gave her a sharp glance. "You may be on to something there, Teo. Yes, the orphanage would probably have been a strange and threatening place to those three girls, and they may well have retreated into their own world—and their own language." He was silent for moment. "And what a language it must have been! Look at the word for *hummingbird*—I've forgotten it now, but I can still see it flashing in my mind. Where on earth could they have gotten that? I almost think . . ."

"Yes?" said Gran.

"Well, maybe they tapped into some ancestral memory of language. I might almost say a memory of Eden." His eyes shone with the light of unwritten academic papers.

"But we're still left with a mystery," said Gran. "If Tilley can't speak, how could she have taught the language to Crow?"

"Maybe she *can* speak," said the professor. "She just can't speak *English*."

Gran gave him a doubtful look. "Is that possible?"

The professor nodded vigorously. "It's rare, but it happens. People who suffer a stroke can sometimes lose a language they learned recently but *not* one they learned long before." He tilted his pith helmet up on his head. "And imagine how precious this first language must have been to Aunt Tilley. She needed to hear it again, to *live* it—and so she taught a few words to Crow. I do believe we've solved the puzzle, Teo." The professor glanced at his wife. "What do you think, dear?"

But Prue didn't seem to hear; she was looking back through the trees at the rock drawing. On her face was a look of wonder and perplexity.

"That girl is an artist," she said. "She sees things we don't see."

Henry tentatively put an arm around Prue. "We can stop at the Michauds', dear. I'd like to see more of the girl's art."

"Yes," said Prue. "I'd like that."

They stepped out of the brush and began making their way down the path. The wind had died, and the birds chirped their evening song. Prue, looking up, seemed to come out of a trance.

"But you know," she remarked, "we *haven't* solved the puzzle."

Both Gran and the professor stopped walking.

"What do you mean, dear?" said Henry cautiously.

"I spoke to Miriam while we were washing the tea things," said Prue. "She said that Aunt Tilley had her stroke in March and then spent three months in hospital. That means she wasn't even here in April, when Crow got loose." She looked from Gran to her husband. "That bird didn't learn the language from Aunt Tilley."

"But—" Gran stared at her—"where *did* he learn it?"

They were startled by a sudden *caw*. Crow dropped from nowhere into the column of mauve air above them. For a moment he circled, looking every bit the scruffy forest gypsy; then he disappeared in the direction of the cave, flying to a place beyond their vision.

At War with the Caliph of Darkness

Though a loner in some ways, Picardy Bob had friends all around the world. He knew a pickpocket in Calcutta, a retired rodeo cowboy in Arizona, a bomb-disposal expert in Toronto, a husband-and-wife team of cosmologists in Hawaii, a man who faked Bigfoot photos in Oregon, and some real old-fashioned hoboes who were riding the freight trains in Saskatchewan. Not surprisingly, he also happened to know someone who lived along the Rideau Waterway, a "fine old pirate," and suggested that Gran and Emmeline look him up.

"And what does this pirate do?" asked Gran, who was always a bit wary of Picardy Bob's friends.

"Well, he's retired now," said Bob, "but he used to be a real pirate—at least, a real *movie* pirate. It was his second career, actually. He was captain of an old freight boat, working the route between Halifax and Boston, when a casting director saw him and said, 'There's our Captain Blood!' So he signed on to play Captain Blood. And they liked him so much he went on to play Jean Lafitte, and his career was launched."

"Well, we'll see if we have time," said Gran. "Where does he live, anyway?"

"You'll be coming to the place soon—Slackwater Bay." Picardy Bob shook his head. "Not exactly the most picturesque place to retire. There's a fertilizer plant there and not much else. But I suppose the property was dirt cheap."

That was how Gran and Emmeline found themselves motoring into Slackwater Bay one cool, rainy evening, looking for the house of Kingman Drake, retired movie pirate. They found the place easily enough—it was the only house on the bay. Gazing at the tiny bungalow through the drizzle, Gran had misgivings. She had asked Picardy Bob to call the pirate beforehand, but unbelievably, the man had no phone. Kingman Drake kept pretty much to himself.

"But don't worry about that," Picardy Bob had said. "Just tell him you're friends of mine. And bring a bottle of rum."

"I don't know, Emmeline," said Gran now, slowing the engine down. "I'm not sure about dropping in on someone who likes to keep to himself."

Emmeline wondered if he actually *liked* to keep to himself. Maybe it was just that nobody visited him.

"Anyway," said Gran, peering through the drizzle, "he certainly has a nice long dock, big enough even for us."

She steered the boat towards the dock, keeping an eye on the depth sounder. Emmeline went forward to get the bumpers out. The rain was very fine, almost a mist, and the whole bay was sunk in the gloom. The lights from the bungalow were yellow smudges on the shore. Across the bay, Emmeline could just make out a cluster of larger lights—the fertilizer plant, she guessed. Clumps of seaweed dotted the water and swirled lazily in the wake of *Permanent Wants*. She could see the patterns of light and dark on the water, like unpainted patches on an old barn, created by the mix of rain and currents.

Gran shut off the engine as they nudged close to the dock. Emmeline, boathook in hand, brought the vessel safely in and then jumped lightly onto the dock. After securing the stern, Gran surveyed the bay. Weeds and algae were everywhere.

"Picardy Bob was right," said Gran. "It's not exactly a picturesque place."

Just then, they heard a door bang. A large man in a fisherman's oilskin jacket and a sou'wester hat was lumbering towards them, holding something that glittered. As he came closer, they gasped. The glittering thing was a cutlass.

"Here!" said the man as he stepped onto the dock. He was wheezing heavily. "What do you think you're doing?"

"Mr. Kingman Drake?" said Gran, keeping calm.

"Who wants to know?"

"My name is Teo McHovec. I'm a friend of Picardy Bob's."

"Picardy Bob!" exclaimed the man. He stood with the point of the cutlass resting on the dock, the rain dripping off his sou'wester. He was still wheezing. "You mean the Picardy Bob who did time for forgery?" he said, less gruffly.

"That's the one. He . . . ah, hopes you are well."

"That flea-sized little flimflammer!" exclaimed Kingman Drake with enthusiasm. "No, I *ain't* well. Tell him that. How can I be well in this tame, stiff-necked, fancy-pants age?" His eyes moved over *Permanent Wants*. "Where'd you get this ship, woman?"

"I inherited it," said Gran shortly, resisting the temptation to add "man," or even "bub."

Kingman Drake shuffled down the length of the dock, looking the boat over with interest. "I sailed something like this in Holland," he remarked. "She was faster than she looked, with a good, thick hull. So you're friends of Picardy Bob's, eh?"

"Yes. This is my granddaughter—"

"Why didn't you bring Bob along with you? Don't tell me he's in jail again."

"No, no, he's travelling to see customers. He's in the antiquarian book business now."

Kingman chuckled. "Good old Bob. I knew he'd never go straight. Well, you two look a bit clean and churchy to be comfortable in *my* house, but any friends of—"

He suddenly stopped and stood gazing out at the bay, where the patterns of light and dark water drifted lazily under the leaden sky. For a second he seemed to breathe in the air. Then he moved to the end of the dock, flipped his sou'wester off so it hung by its cord, and peered down into the water. "It's here," Emmeline heard him mutter. Then he turned back to face them again. "Any friends of Picardy Bob's are welcome in my house," he said in his raspy voice. "Come in, come in!"

Gran scooped up the paper bag that held the bottle of rum, and she and Emmeline followed Kingman up the path towards the tiny house. It didn't look like much from the path, but it turned out to be quite cozy inside. There was a fire crackling in the little fireplace, and on the floor was a thick cream-coloured rug with a black skull and crossbones embroidered on it. The tabletops held lots of framed photographs, almost all of them stills from Kingman's movies. And of course, there were ships in bottles. One in particular caught Emmeline's eye: a small, high-prowed vessel like the kind that Columbus had sailed, inside a large round bottle. It had painted gun ports along the side and a pirate flag the size of her little fingernail. The masts were made of two matchsticks bound together with black thread, and the sails seemed to have been snipped out of a handkerchief. It was sailing on realistic-looking waves of blue putty. Emmeline was entranced.

Gran presented their host with the bottle of rum, saying she wasn't *that* churchy, and Kingman gave a flicker of a smile. With his sou'wester off, they could see that he *did* look like a pirate—thick silver-black hair, brambly eyebrows, a complexion like that of the planet Mars, and eyes fired dark and bleared. He wore faded blue suspenders that traced a parallel track down his huge chest and then diverged slightly, following his even more expansive belly. His worn corduroy pants were big enough for a circus bear. Emmeline wondered how he got around his tiny house without constantly knocking things over.

"You know what that is, girl?" he said to Emmeline, who was looking at an unusual knick-knack—something greyish white and slug-like, about the size of a small squash, floating in a large jar. "Bit of a giant squid. The old worm tried to wrap itself around my sloop once. I cut off a chunk of his arm with my fish knife. Thought about making a steak out of it, but I was told those big fellows taste like ammonia, so I just put him on my mantelpiece."

Emmeline, fascinated, gestured Gran over. The object in the jar looked more like a big chunk of old cheese than an arm tip, although it had one suction cup as large as a drink holder. Emmeline wondered how big the squid itself must have been. Quickly she made the sign for *enormous* to Gran—her two hands, index fingers curved and thumbs up, moving away from each other until her arms were extended. Kingman caught it.

"That girl deaf?" he said bluntly.

Emmeline and Gran looked a bit taken aback. This man clearly said whatever came into his mind.

"No," said Gran. "She has a . . . condition, a problem with language."

"She can't speak, is that it?"

"That's right. She got sick when she was in Africa, and . . . It's a long story."

"Let her tell it."

Gran eyed him coldly. "I just told you, she can't—"

"Let her tell it her own way."

Gran and Emmeline looked at each other. Emmeline shrugged, then began telling the story in the language she used with Gran. She made the sign for Africa: her right hand went up, fingers curled and thumb raised, to sign *A*, and then she traced the shape of the continent in the air. Next she described the sickness, how it had come in the night and left her in a coma. (She didn't know the sign for *coma*, and the gesture for *sleep* didn't seem strong enough, so she just closed her eyes tightly for a few seconds.) She made the sign for *gone*, or *empty*, to describe how she felt when she woke up from her coma. Then she made the sign for *trying*—her palms facing out, pushing through something—to describe what her life had been like since then. But of course, she couldn't tell Kingman what it had really been like. She couldn't talk about how she constantly mixed words up, calling a thimble a pimple, the carpet a car kit, and Santa a panda. She couldn't talk about the time she had burst into tears because her soccer coach had asked her name and she couldn't remember it. She couldn't tell him how she had decided, one despairing day, not to speak at all. Above all, she couldn't talk about how scared she was sometimes—scared that she would be thought weird, *retarded*, for the rest of her life. All she could do, at the end of the story, was sign: *It's not finished.*

"Well," said Gran to the pirate, "did you understand?"

"No," said Kingman. "But I liked it anyway. What was that last part?"

"She said it's not finished," explained Gran.

"You got that right, kid," said Kingman, speaking more to himself than to her, and he smiled his flickering smile. "Now, tea?"

They had tea in front of the fire, Kingman mixing the rum into his. On the end tables were framed movie stills showing the pirate in various poses and costumes. Gran noticed that Emmeline, after telling her story, had no self-consciousness about signing, as she often did with strangers. At one point, she turned to the pirate and made a few signs that Gran knew well.

"I think she wants to know if you like Johnny Depp," interpreted Gran.

"Who?" said Kingman.

Emmeline stared at him, astonished.

Gran said smoothly: "Just another movie pirate—though not with your range, Mr. Drake. I must say you were very convincing as"—she leaned close to read one of the photo captions—"the Sea Raven of Gibraltar."

"Sure I was good," said Kingman moodily. "It ain't hard playing yourself." He raised his bloodshot eyes to Gran. "But I'll tell you something nobody knows: I was a *real* pirate once. I sailed a blue sea under a pirate flag, and fought with a cutlass and blunderbuss, and drank rum out of a skin bottle. In another time, another world."

"Another world?" repeated Gran, not sure how to take this.

Kingman's gaze was far away. "I never even told Picardy Bob about it, and he was the one guy who might have believed me. But it don't matter. Tonight you're going to hear it *all*."

Suddenly he stood up and, yanking down the neck of his unbuttoned shirt, revealed a thick white scar that slanted away from his collarbone.

"See that?" he said. "That's a little something I got from the cutlass of Jacques Sans Merci, also known as Lamprey Jack, also known as Joachim Barbare, the Caliph of Darkness—the cruellest, meanest, most savage, most foul-smelling, most lice-infested, most morally stunted pirate who ever lived. He made Blackbeard look like Walt Disney."

He sat down again, the chair creaking with his weight. Gran wondered if he was talking about a movie director he hadn't liked.

"It was an epic battle," Kingman continued. "Just me and him. Our crews were all dead, our ships were sinking under us, but we fought on—with cutlasses and daggers and then our bare hands, jumping from one bit of wreckage to another. In the Bight of Blight, it was, with the water dark as oil around us. We were drifting close to the whirlpool at the centre of the bight, and I could barely stand, I was so weak from loss of blood, when I caught him with a cuff to the head. I remember his curses as he disappeared into the swirling waters." He moved his arm, wincing a bit. "I've done lots of things in my life I ain't proud of. I've stolen and brawled and made women weep. But when the final reckoning comes, I hope they'll remember my one great deed—I vanquished Lamprey Jack. I freed the Sea of Corsairs from his reign of darkness."

Gran and Emmeline exchanged glances, wondering what they had got themselves into.

"That was a long time ago," continued the pirate. "The wound healed. All these years, I have carried the scar with pride. But lately"—once more he moved his arm gingerly—"the pain is there again. Sometimes the scar is reddish, like it never really healed. The wound has come back, there's no doubt about it. And that can mean only one thing."

"What?" said Gran.

Kingman turned to look at her. "The task I thought was finished *ain't* finished. Lamprey Jack didn't die that day. Somehow he escaped the whirlpool; somehow he got a crew together again. And now he's sailing the Sea of Corsairs in his old ship, the *Deathsmear*, trailed by his flock of black seagulls, his pets and his spies. The pain I feel is a messenger, calling me back. I got to return to the Sea of Corsairs."

Silence reigned in the little house. The drizzle pattered on the windowpanes. Kingman took a sip from his mug and stared into the fire.

"Just where is this Sea of Corsairs?" asked Gran carefully.

Kingman smiled his flickering smile. "As the great Melville said about one of his own destinations, it ain't on any map—true places never are. I can tell you that it's linked to our world by water. But the how and why of it, I don't know. I just know I have to go there."

Gran decided to take the charitable view and assume that the poor man simply wanted to return to a place where he had played a memorable movie role.

"Well, why can't you?" she said. "I've never heard of this Sea of Corsairs, but nowadays you can get a cheap flight to almost any—"

"Up till tonight I've lacked two things," continued Kingman, as if Gran hadn't spoken. "A crew and a ship. But now . . ."

And he turned his brooding gaze on Gran and Emmeline.

"Well!" said Gran. "That's quite a story. But really, we're probably not the ones to help you, Mr. Drake. It sounds like you need a real ocean-going ship, and . . . um, a crew that shares your interest in history."

Kingman nodded slowly, still staring at the fire. "You think I'm crazy."

Gran gave Emmeline a glance to say, *Help me out here.*

"Of course not," she assured him. "But we're on a tight schedule, you know, and I'm afraid we don't have time for . . . side trips."

There was an uncomfortable silence. Gran and Emmeline could only listen to the ticking of the wall clock, which was shaped like the miniature steering wheel of a ship.

At length, Kingman said with finality: "Yeah, sure. You're on a schedule—like the rest of the world. I understand."

Emmeline looked at Gran reproachfully. Gran took a long breath.

"Let me see you off," said Kingman. He stood up.

They had no choice but to put on their still-damp raincoats, pull on their wet shoes, and troop out into the darkness. The rain had stopped, but a thick fog had fallen with the night. Gran felt very awkward. She did not look forward to manoeuvring out of the bay in these conditions, but now she couldn't very well ask Kingman if they could moor there for the night. She sighed. Picardy Bob and his friends!

As they came up to the dock, Kingman stopped at the shore. For a second he looked out at the water, breathing in heavily, as he had when they first arrived. Then he turned to Gran.

"Before you leave," he said, "maybe you could do something for me."

"What?" said Gran warily.

The pirate nodded towards the seaweed-draped shore. "Taste the water."

"I beg your pardon?"

"Taste the water. Just a small taste."

"Why?" said Gran, suspicious. "What's the matter with it?"

"Nothing. But I think you'll find it's . . . not what you'd expect."

Gran hesitated, thinking, Now what? But Emmeline stooped down and dipped a finger in the water. "Emmeline!" said Gran sharply, but the girl had already put her finger to her lips. A startled look came over her face, and she signed to Gran: *Salt!*

"What?" said Gran. She crouched down to dip a finger in, too, and her face showed her bewilderment.

"It's faint," said the pirate, "but it's definitely salt water." He took a step towards Gran. "Now, why would there be a saltwater flow in a freshwater bay? I'll tell you why: it's a ring current from the Sea of Corsairs."

"A *what*?" said Gran.

Kingman looked past her into the bay. He seemed more restless now, more alive, more eager to take on the world.

"I told you," he said. "Water is the link. There are meanders and ring currents that break away from the Sea of Corsairs and drift into this world. Sometimes they rise in saltwater bodies, sometimes in fresh. In my life, I've seen them in just two places. One was the Mediterranean—that's how I first got into the Sea of Corsairs all those years ago. The other is this ugly little bay." He snorted. "*Look* at it! Mud and weeds and that dang fertilizer plant across the way. I would never have chosen to live here—except that I discovered it's a passageway to the Sea of Corsairs." He spread his arms wide. "We don't have much time," he said urgently. "The ring current never lasts, and these days it's always weak. Are you willing to sail under me? I'd rather have *real* pirates, but you two will have to do."

"This is absolutely crazy," said Gran.

"If it's crazy," said the pirate calmly, "you have nothing to lose. Let's set sail. If the water is only the water of this world, we'll find out soon enough. But if the water is *not* of this world"—in the darkness they saw the gleam of his smile—"it will take us to where I must go."

"Somebody here is *definitely* not of this world," muttered Gran in a voice that only Emmeline heard.

The girl gestured impatiently at her grandmother, her right hand moving as if to shoo somebody away. *Give him a break!* she was saying.

"I need my cutlass and spyglass," said Kingman. "Ready the ship. I will be back."

"Now hold on just a minute," began Gran, but Kingman was already lumbering towards his house. She wondered if they should just get away now, as quickly as possible. But Emmeline seemed to guess her thought, and coming close, she took a firm hold of her hand.

"I'm sure there's a natural explanation," Gran said irritably. "For the salt, I mean." She stood there, undecided for a moment, gazing up at Kingman's house. "All right, let's get on board," she said finally. "Maybe the poor man will have come to his senses when he gets back."

They had started the engine and untied the stern line when the pirate appeared on the dock, cutlass in hand. He had moved much faster than they thought him capable.

"No engine!" he hissed. "Our lives won't be worth a match if we make noise."

He'd obviously *not* come to his senses, Gran saw. Maybe the only thing to do was to take him out for a bit. Show him it was just an ordinary bay.

"Well, if we can't use our engine, are we going to *paddle* out?" she demanded.

"It's shallow enough to pole out," said Kingman. "I hope you've got a sounding pole; you ain't much of a crew if you don't."

They didn't have a sounding pole, but they did have a boat-hook, and it was Kingman who stood in the cockpit at the stern and poled them out into the fog. The pirate had left behind his oil-skins and sou'wester, and now wore a dark jacket that did not rustle when he moved.

"No lights!" commanded Kingman as Gran bent to switch them on.

"But that's dangerous," objected Gran.

"It'll be far more dangerous *with* them, take my word. Lamprey Jack might be sitting out there with cannons ready." He leaned on the boathook, and the vessel slid into the night. "You got any weapons on board?"

Emmeline made the action of drawing a slingshot. Kingman nodded. Gran was tempted to say that she had a can of Lysol—sure to be of use against the foul-smelling Lamprey Jack—but she stayed silent.

Soon the dock behind them was swallowed up in the fog. They heard nothing except the faint lapping of water against the hull. Even the crickets were silent; maybe they didn't like the damp. Emmeline wondered if the boat was moving at all. At first she tried keeping watch from the bow, but the fog was like an eddying wall, and eventually she joined the others in the cockpit. Lafcadio sat alert in the corner, tail twitching.

They could have been anywhere, in any body of water in the world, drifting in a dead calm.

"The ring current comes only at night," said Kingman softly, "and it seems to be growing weaker. I can't figure out why. I used to be able to see bits of seafire—you know, flashes of green and blue from tiny sea creatures. Sometimes I even thought I could hear the calls of seabirds in the darkness; maybe they are carried here with the salt air that comes with the current. But I ain't seen either seafire or birds for a while."

Emmeline had the big shipboard flashlight with her but didn't turn it on, remembering Kingman's words. She was more willing than Gran to go along with the pirate, partly because the foggy night was working on *her*, too, but also because she couldn't help liking the man. He treated her as someone who could *do* things. The problem with having no voice was that people looked at you and thought: Blank. They thought that you were a blank, and that your mind was a blank. But Emmeline's mind was far from blank: it was a torrent of colours, shapes, tunes, and karate shouts. She wished she could tell Kingman that she had a yellow belt in karate. Why hadn't Gran mentioned that when he asked about weapons?

"I wish I had my old crew with me," he muttered, dipping the boathook in. "Johnny Grandshanks, the lookout man—so tall he could have looked out over this fog—and Troubadour Charlie, and little Pepé." He chuckled. "What sons of devils they were, too! Always drinking and spitting from the masts and dipping the butter knife in the jam pot, instead of using the spoon." He suddenly moved forward a step, looking over the dark water. "Johnny! Pepé!" he called softly. "Are you there, lads? It's me, Kingman! I'm back!"

His voice faded into the fog. After a moment, he sat down; they could not see his face in the darkness, but they heard his heavy, laboured breathing.

"You remind me of Pepé, kid," he said to Emmeline, his voice much weaker. "He didn't say much, but he understood a lot. He even understood the speech of animals. You can be Pepé. And *you*, woman, you can be Molly Burke, the only girl who—"

Suddenly, from the darkness ahead, there came a fluttering sound, followed by a soft *whump*. It sounded like something had fallen onto the deck of the bow. Gran and Emmeline stiffened, and Lafcadio went into a long, tense crouch. Very quietly, Kingman laid down the boathook and took up his cutlass.

For half a minute nobody moved. From far away they heard the barking of a dog. The old boat creaked beneath them. Then Kingman lowered his head and whispered: "You take the port side, and I'll take starboard. We'll come at them from both angles."

It is *not* pirates, Gran told herself, but she had the unsettling sense that *something* was keeping quiet in the darkness ahead. Emmeline crouched wide-eyed in the cockpit, feeling Lafcadio's tail flick across her legs. She wished now that she had gotten out both the slingshot *and* the bear spray.

"Take the light, woman," whispered Kingman. "Turn it on sudden when I give the word."

Telling herself again that there was a natural explanation, Gran stepped up on the gunwale catwalk, flashlight in hand. Kingman was already moving with surprising stealth along the other side, the vessel tilting slightly as he did so. Emmeline had decided to crawl forward on the roof of the cabin. The bow of the boat was pitch dark; they could see nothing.

"*Now!*" roared Kingman, and Gran switched on the light.

Before them in the bow stood a tall bird—a blue heron. It didn't seem frightened by Kingman's yell, or by the sudden light. Turning its narrow head, it eyed them imperiously.

"I *knew* it wasn't a pirate," breathed Gran.

For a second, all of them—humans and bird—regarded one another. Lafcadio had crept up beside Emmeline, who took a hold of his collar, in case he felt like going after the heron. What was the name of that bird? She went over all the animal names she knew: *dog, shrimp, god, Santa, cheep*—

"It's what we call a pacha bird on the Sea of Corsairs," said Kingman. "It was a sin to kill 'em. They were supposed to be the spirits of dead sailors." He looked past the bird into the fog. "Hide the light, Molly. It's just an invitation to others more evil."

Gran directed the flashlight beam down, but she didn't turn it off—partly because she was tired of Kingman's orders, and partly because she wanted to see the bird. Emmeline, too, was fascinated: she had never been so close to a heron before. It was just under a metre tall, half of which was legs. Its slender neck was slightly kinked (like the pipe below a sink, Emmeline thought). When it turned its head, she could see the thin plume that curled down the back of its neck; she was reminded of a pirate's pigtail. Its legs were bent at the knee, but the angle pointed backwards instead of forwards like a human's. Just then the bird opened its long, sharp beak and gave a cry, a *skrok-skrok!* The sound had something of the frog's croak in it, but also something of the metallic squeak of an old clothesline as you pull it in.

"What did it say, Pepé?" demanded Kingman, turning to Emmeline.

Emmeline shook her head helplessly. Where did he get the idea that she could understand animals? The bird fixed her with its round yellow eye—as if it shared Kingman's belief about her.

"It's just a blue heron," said Gran impatiently. "We've seen plenty of them along the river."

"Well, maybe this one *ain't* from the river," said Kingman testily. "I told you, I've heard birds out here—*ocean* birds—calling long and sad. Calling me back to the Sea of Corsairs." He took a cautious step towards the heron. "Bird, I am Kingman Drake, pirate captain and liberator of the Sea of Corsairs, and I seek Lamprey Jack, the so-called Caliph of Darkness, so I can finish the sucker. What do you know of him?"

The bird suddenly took off with a great rush of wings. Gran caught it momentarily in the flashlight beam; they could all see the creature's long legs streaming out behind it.

"It wants us to follow," said Kingman.

"Not without running lights, we're not," declared Gran.

"Hold your tongue, Molly!" growled Kingman. "Sometimes I wish I had never rescued you from that harem. Why can't you just be quiet and follow orders like Pepé?"

"Because this is *my* boat, Mr. Drake," snapped Gran, "and I am not your Molly, whoever that—"

Just then, Emmeline touched her grandmother's arm. Gran listened. In the distance, they caught the faint sound of flowing water. It came from the starboard side, where the heron had disappeared.

Kingman listened as well, then moved to the side of the boat.

"Shine your light here," he commanded, pointing down with his cutlass. Gran shone her light into the water; weeds floated on the surface.

"The sargasso," said Kingman. "The cursed sea-bloom." He looked around, his jaw set. "I know where we are: the Bight of Blight. The ring current has carried us here."

"This is *not* the Bight of Blight," said Gran in exasperation. "There are weeds everywhere in this bay."

Kingman ignored her. "Watch the sky, Pepé!" he said to Emmeline. "Jack always liked to send his seagulls as a welcoming party. Hideous things, they were—black as soot, but when they opened their beaks you could see red. They went straight for your eyes." He turned back to Gran. "If this ain't the bight, smart girl, then what's that sound of water?"

"I don't know," said Gran simply. "Let's investigate." She had given up trying to argue with him.

"We'll do that," agreed Kingman. "And you'll see—it's the sound of the whirlpool at the heart of the bight. You can turn on the engine now, woman. We'll need the power to keep us away from the vortex."

Gran took it as a good sign that he was calling her "woman" again, instead of "Molly." She switched on the inboard engine, which made a low, guttural sound in the fog. Emmeline went to the bow to keep a lookout, but the fog was thicker than ever. The surfaces of the boat were all damp, and Emmeline's sneakers squeaked faintly as she moved. With the throttle at the lowest possible setting, Gran motored in the direction of the heron. Knowing how shallow the bay was, she kept a close eye on the depth sounder, now illuminated on her dashboard.

A yellowish blur appeared through the fog ahead, and then another. Kingman nodded grimly.

"Crangs," he muttered. "The burning carcasses of dead whales. Lamprey Jack butchered sperm whales by the hundreds and set their oil alight in the darkness."

"Well, I say it's the shore," said Gran. "And if so, we need our running lights."

She flipped them on, bracing herself for hot words from Kingman. But the pirate just muttered, "So be it—no more hiding," and took a fresh grip on his cutlass. The lights really didn't improve visibility; they just showed how thick the fog was. Gran put the boat in neutral. Emmeline could hear the sound of flowing water even above the idling engine.

"This is it," said Kingman, standing in the cockpit. "This is the place where I fought Lamprey Jack." He glanced ahead at Emmeline, who had fetched both the slingshot and the bear spray and was now crouching in the bow. "Steady, Pepé. Just imagine that Johnny Grandshanks is with us. Remember how he used to watch your back in battle, you being so small? He's here in spirit. I can *feel* it."

The water beneath the boat was eddying noticeably.

It is *not* the Bight of Blight, thought Gran, but she brought the boathook close, just in case. Emmeline drew out a big marble and fitted it into the pocket of the slingshot. Kingman put one foot onto the gunwale, cutlass in hand. For a moment they drifted in silence, their nerves taut as guitar strings. Now there were four yellowish blurs ahead of them, steadily growing brighter. They all craned their necks to see in the fog, their faces beaded with moisture. Gran could see Kingman's windbreaker stretched tight across his broad back. He's got us all half-believing it, she thought.

Suddenly Emmeline sat back, the tension seeping out of her, and turned to make a sign. Gran let out a long breath.

"I think you can put your cutlass away, Mr. Drake," she said.

She peered overboard; foam could be seen on the swirling water.

"It's the fertilizer plant," she said. "And that rushing water is from an outlet pipe."

There was no doubt about it: they could all see the bank, which consisted of flat stones contained by steel netting. The yellowish haloes were clearly big industrial lights on the corners of the building.

Kingman slumped, and for a moment Gran was afraid he was going to fall overboard.

"Mr. Drake?" she said.

The pirate raised his head with an effort.

"You see the opening of the pipe there?" said Gran. "Right below the—"

"I *see* it, woman." He went down on one knee, the cutlass resting on the deck.

Emmeline took a few steps towards him along the catwalk, but he waved her away.

"I was wrong," he mumbled. "The fog misled me, the night misled me . . ."

Gran was silent. She didn't like to admit it, but once or twice during the adventure, she herself had wondered if they were still in the bay. She turned her attention back to the pipe.

"I wonder what's coming out of there," she remarked. "There seems to be a lot of foam around."

Kingman raised his head. "Foam and scum and weeds—*that's* my bay. That's my portal to the Sea of Corsairs." He gave a bark of a laugh.

"They must use the pipe only late at night," remarked Gran. "We didn't notice any outflow when we came in."

This seemed to revive Kingman, who suddenly got to his feet and moved to the bow. "That's an old outlet pipe," he said, peering through the darkness. "It ain't supposed to be used. The township already warned these guys about it."

"Maybe we should take a sample of the water," said Gran. "Em, can you get an empty jar?"

"So that's what they're doing!" muttered Kingman. "Too cheap to pay for a new wastewater system. They just use the old pipe at night—when nobody's around." He took a firm grasp of his cutlass. "I'll settle 'em. They're going to find out they have Kingman Drake living on their bay."

"Well, the best thing we can do is report it in the morning," said Gran hastily. She didn't want the pirate going after anybody with his cutlass.

Gran hooked a finger through one of Emmeline's belt loops, and the girl leaned over the side to scoop up some water. They could both hear Kingman muttering from the bow.

"All right," said Gran as Emmeline came up with the jar full. "Let's go before he starts looking for his ring current again."

"I heard you," said Kingman, scowling. "And yeah, I *will* look for it again. I'll be looking all my life." He gazed out over the water. "It comes and goes in the night, you know. Just like the birds. Sometimes I've heard 'em crying and calling right up until dawn."

But his voice had lost much of its harsh vigour. He stood in silence for a moment, then drew his sleeve across his eyes.

Gran put the engine in reverse, and after doing a wide turn, they began motoring slowly back to Kingman's dock. The pirate kept pointing to foam on the water. "Look at that," he said disgustedly, over the engine. "That run-off is carried all the way out here." For the rest of the return trip he was quiet, but he roused himself to guide them into his dock.

As for Emmeline, the discovery of the pipe didn't lessen the twitchy feeling she'd had all night. She wasn't the only one; Lafcadio was still on edge as well. From the bow she watched and listened for the heron, which she called a *skrok* in her mind. Kingman had said that in the Sea of Corsairs, they regarded *skroks* as the spirits of dead sailors. She got the odd feeling that the bird was still out there, watching over them—a sentinel, a guardian, a lookout.

And it was the *skrok*, she thought, that had led them to the outlet pipe.

But they made it to the opposite shore without seeing the bird, and the first thing Kingman did was to kneel down and dip a finger into the water.

"The ring current is gone," he said.

"Never mind, Mr. Drake," said Gran. "If we hadn't taken that late-night cruise, we wouldn't have caught them using that outlet pipe."

Kingman's wheeze had returned, along with his heaviness, the weight of the years. He didn't move as Gran and Emmeline secured the tie lines.

"Maybe," he said, getting to his feet with an effort. "But my wound ain't no better."

They stayed on the boat that night, moored at Kingman's dock. They didn't get much sleep. The least little noise would startle them wide awake, and Lafcadio prowled restlessly around the cabin all night, sometimes jumping up on Gran's bunk. They got up unusually early, just before dawn. The morning was still foggy, but the day promised to be nicer than the previous one. They could see Kingman moving about in his living room, and they prepared themselves for an awkward goodbye.

The pirate appeared red-eyed and untidy as ever, but strangely, he wasn't down in the dumps. He took the sample of water and put it on the vestibule table, saying he would run it into town that very day. Then he bustled about preparing toast and coffee.

"You know, Mr. Drake," said Gran later, as she sipped her coffee, "I *thought* there were a lot of weeds and algae in this bay. Without the run-off from the plant, conditions might improve. I bet your property values will go up."

Kingman plunked down his coffee mug and grinned. "Hang my property values!" he said. "We've solved the mystery."

"What mystery?" said Gran uneasily.

"Remember what I said about the ring current—how it's become so weak and unpredictable? Well, we found the reason: the discharge from the pipe must have muddied it." He took a big bite of toast and followed it with a gulp of coffee. "You two should be proud of yourselves. Slackwater Bay will again become a pure portal into the Sea of Corsairs."

Emmeline gave him the thumbs-up. Gran sighed.

"You two ain't pirates," said Kingman, talking with his mouth full, "but you're okay. And I still say there's a lot of Pepé in you, kid. Which reminds me . . ."

Going over to mantelpiece, he took down one of the ships in a bottle, the small one with the tiny pirate flag.

"I made this one myself," he said. "It's the ship I sailed on the Sea of Corsairs, the *Avocet*. I'd like you to have it."

Emmeline, her eyes sea-alive, took the bottle gingerly. It was just small enough to fit on the shelf beside her bunk.

"Oh, now, Mr. Drake," said Gran, "we couldn't possibly—"

Kingman glowered at her. "Yes, you could, woman. I can easily make another one. Anyway, you need it for your own ship; all you got is *books* on board."

"Yes, we do have a lot of those," returned Gran. "And we'd love to give you one, as *our* parting gift." Leaning close to Emmeline, she whispered: "What do you think—*Treasure Island*? Or maybe *Carefree Bachelor Cooking*?"

Emmeline put down the ship in the bottle and signed that she would get both.

The fog still hung in the middle of the bay, but around the shores, it had pretty well gone. After some rooting around in the boat's storage compartments, Emmeline found their large illustrated copy of *Treasure Island*. She also grabbed *Carefree Bachelor Cooking* as she came through the galley (they'd recently been trying out some of the recipes). Lafcadio had hoped he'd be able to squeeze out with her, but she pushed him inside with her foot and closed the door, ignoring his increasingly loud meows.

What? she signed in response, brushing her right index finger down her left palm. Lafcadio just kept meowing. For some reason, he was suddenly very eager to get out.

Books in hand, she stepped lightly from the transom to the dock. And then she froze.

A huge dark seagull was standing six metres away.

She had seen greyish seagulls along the river, but this one wasn't just grubby: it was the colour of volcanic ash. Its beak was long and sharp, its eyes fierce but somehow lazy. It gave a raspy *skree!* and Emmeline saw that the inside of its beak was pale red.

She backed up towards the end of the dock. The bird, opening its eagle-sized wings, gave a fluttering hop towards her.

Lafcadio scratched fiercely at the door of the cabin, meowing a screechy meow, but the latch wouldn't give. The seagull kept coming. Emmeline, desperate, planted her feet and flung the copy of *Carefree Bachelor Cooking* straight at the bird. The creature fluttered easily into the air and then settled a few metres closer to Emmeline. The book skidded, pages flapping, into the water.

Emmeline was now at the end of the dock. She clutched the large, heavy copy of *Treasure Island*; it was her only weapon. She would ward the creature off, knock it out of the air . . .

Just then, she heard a faint cry, a *skrok-skrok*. A long grey shape swung out of the fog to her left. The seagull gave an angry *caw* and rose just as the heron dived. Emmeline thought there would be a collision, but the seagull twisted in the air; and then the two strange birds, shrieking and feinting like battling spirits, disappeared into the mist of the bay.

Fourth Tale

In the Court of the Reptile King

The Bay of Small Blessings was as pretty as its name, especially in early morning, with the mist rising off the water and the birds just waking up on the shore. That was how Gran and Emmeline saw it one Saturday in late July. They had been exploring Big Rideau Lake, in the middle of the waterway, and this particular bay had just a few cottages and very little boat traffic. They decided to overnight there, not far from a small, heavily treed island. Gran thought it would be the perfect spot for an early morning swim.

Dawn arrived in soft bergs of mist. At first Emmeline was tempted to stay in bed, but looking through the open cabin door, she saw how still and otherworldly the water looked. She just *had* to swim in it. Gran was already standing at the transom ladder, pulling her bathing cap on. Emmeline soon joined her, wearing her fleece over her bathing suit. Everything on deck was damp; the metal fixtures were clouded, and Emmeline could feel the moisture on the pebbled surface of the deck. A lone bird—Gran thought it might be a cardinal—called from the shore. Sixty metres off the port side, they could just make out the vague shape of the island, a wash of shadow in the pearling cloud. The trees appeared to be treading the air. Some stood straight as soldiers; some drooped over the water; some eddied in smoking curves against the pale grey. The boat seemed to be floating on a pure membrane, a vast lens of clouded light. Looking down from the stern, Emmeline could see the ends of the transom ladder below the surface, where they were bent by the water.

Gran was already puffing in anticipation as she lowered herself down the ladder.

"Here goes, Lafcadio," she said. "*Hoo!*"

Lafcadio watched her disapprovingly. He could not understand why anybody would abandon sleep for a swim.

Emmeline followed her grandmother, catching her breath as well. The world seemed newborn, crouching in silent wonder. They swam out to a patch where the mist seemed especially thick, but once they got there, Emmeline found that she could see through it pretty well. Treading water, she signed to Gran: *So quiet*. Then she dived as silently as an otter. Turning to look up through the depths, she saw Gran's pale legs floating below the surface, making a slow pedalling motion. She rose under the legs and tweaked a toe, and very faintly, as if from several kilometres away, she heard Gran exclaim above the surface.

They swam a leisurely circle around *Permanent Wants*, and while Emmeline stayed to practise her underwater somersaults, Gran headed back to the boat. Lafcadio gave her a reproachful look as she hauled herself, dripping, up the ladder.

"You should really learn to like the water, Lafcadio," said Gran, grabbing a towel. "You're a shipboard cat now." She pulled off her bathing cap, shook her hair, and paused to take in the morning. Behind her in the stillness, she heard Emmeline surface and exhale. More of the island was visible now; the trees had acquired detail. It's going to be a beautiful day, she thought.

Just then, she heard a faint rippling sound from the port side of the boat, in the direction of the island. A muskrat? she wondered, and moved over to the railing. A dozen metres away, at about ten o'clock off the bow, a long line was gliding on the water. It was moving only a bit faster than a drifting log, gently ruffling the water surface at the front. Gran would never have heard it if the morning hadn't been so still. As it got closer, she could see that it was weaving slightly, tracing a languid S through the water. She peered, leaning over the railing, and suddenly let the towel fall, her mouth agape.

It was an enormous *snake*.

"Emmeline!" Gran cried, her face pinched in horror. The girl, treading water fifteen metres behind the boat, looked back at her grandmother.

"Saints alive," breathed Gran. The creature looked to be nearly ten metres long and as thick as Emmeline's waist. It was now abreast of the boat, swimming sternwards at an angle.

"Come here!" shouted Gran frantically. "*Quick!*"

Emmeline couldn't see the snake, but the urgency in her grandmother's voice set her churning through the water. Gran grabbed the boathook from its rack on the gunwale. The snake was still swimming at an angle, coming ever closer to the boat. She leaned over and clumsily slapped the boathook on the water.

"*Go away!*" she roared.

This had absolutely no effect on the creature. It neither sped up nor slowed down; it just kept up its easy, sinuous progress. It could have been water itself, so liquidly did it move. Gran could make out its colouring now—olive green with dark spots, like army camouflage.

And she could see that it was swimming straight into Emmeline's path.

She acted without thinking. Boathook in hand, she swung a leg over the transom railing and half-jumped, half-fell into the water. Lafcadio sprang back, startled. At the sound of the splash, Emmeline stopped swimming and looked up in alarm. She could see Gran in the water, thrashing about portside, striking out with the boathook . . .

And then she saw the snake.

Her breath went clean out of her. For a moment, all she could see were some bumps on the water. Then it raised its head, and she saw the triangular, blunted snout—larger than a Labrador dog's—and the pale tongue darting out like a bit of static electricity. The snout was greenish and covered with oblong scales that looked like closely set tiles. There was a single dark line running from each eye that almost looked like war paint. Most terrifying of all, the eyes seemed to be the same dull green colour as the skin. They were alien eyes—empty, lidless, and marble cold.

Emmeline couldn't move. Dimly she was conscious of Gran behind, yelling and slapping the water. The snake was now less than three metres from her.

Then some deep life-saving instinct kicked in. She took a huge breath and went under.

Something told her that her only hope was to vanish from the creature's field of vision. She pulled herself down, pushing furiously against the water . . . half a metre, a metre. A greenish shape glided over her. She almost opened her mouth and swallowed water at its size. It was nearly thirty centimetres thick in the middle, a great weaving dynasty of scales. The belly, like an alligator's, was much lighter in colour than its body. Even with her water-blurred vision, Emmeline could see its skin creasing a bit, like a Lycra garment, as it traced out an S-pattern in the water. Her lungs bursting, she frog-kicked upwards, away from the snake. The creature paid her no attention. Surfacing with a great gasp, she swam straight into Gran's arms. They supported each other as they made their way to the boat.

Emmeline was opening and closing her mouth in silent terror, as small birds do. At the ladder, Gran threw a glance over her shoulder; the snake had disappeared into the mist.

Once on deck, they stood huddled in each other's arms as Lafcadio padded around them, mewing out comforting remarks.

"I'm going to make some nice hot tea," said Gran at last, "and then we're going to draw anchor and get out of here. Some Bay of Small Blessings!"

She scooped up her towel and draped it over Emmeline, who was still shivering. As she did so, she gave a glance sternwards: the lake was perfectly quiet.

"And the first town we get to," she declared, "we are going to report this. That was no snake—that was a *serpent!*"

Just then, from out of the mist, they heard a *squeak-squeak*. In a few seconds they could make out a small rowboat approaching, a boy at the oars. He paused in his rowing, glancing over his shoulder, and they heard him say worriedly, "Oh, oh." Then the oars clinked in their locks, and the squeaking resumed. When he was two boat-lengths away, he let go of an oar and turned in his seat.

"Um, hi," he said nervously. "I'm looking for . . ."

He broke off, scanning their faces. He seemed to be about Emmeline's age, with a mop of reddish-blond hair.

"I guess you've already seen her," concluded the boy. "I can tell."

"Seen who?" said Gran.

The boy ducked his head slightly, looking embarrassed.

"Willa," he said. "Our anaconda."

"Your *anaconda?*" repeated Gran hoarsely. Emmeline was watching the stranger intently from the cowl of Gran's big towel.

The boy nodded and turned so he was straddling the seat. "She got loose. Sorry about that."

"That was your *pet* anaconda?" said Gran in disbelief.

Again the boy ducked his head apologetically. "Well, she's not really a pet. She's just one of our residents. Our biggest one, in fact." He added hastily, "But she's very good-natured."

"Good-natured!" exploded Gran. "That snake just tried to eat my granddaughter!"

The boy winced. "I'm sure she didn't. She *can't* be hungry. Yesterday she had half a pig and a chicken and—"

"I don't want to hear about it!" interrupted Gran furiously. "What are you doing keeping an anaconda here, anyway? They belong in ruddy South America. I'm going to report you to the *police*."

"Please don't," said the boy. "We might lose our permit."

"You *should* lose your permit," retorted Gran. "Anacondas swimming around like . . . like penguins!"

"All I can say is sorry." The boy sounded a bit defensive now. "It's not easy, you know, with just me and my uncle Digby. We've got thirty-eight snakes to look after, and forty-two geckoes, and twelve monitor lizards, and—"

"What on earth are you doing with all those reptiles?" said Gran.

"We breed them," replied the boy. "On the island there. We breed them and raise the babies, and then we give the babies to zoos. And we've won awards, lots of awards. But everything has been going wrong this summer. *Everything*. We can't get the La Gomera lizards to mate, and the motorboat broke down, and now Willa has escaped . . ." He scanned the water around his boat, and then gave Gran a pleading look. "Could you help me find her? My uncle will have a conniption if he finds out."

"No," said Gran decisively. "No more anacondas today, thank you. You need the authorities for that, and we'll be happy to get them for you."

Emmeline glanced up at her grandmother, then back at the boy. She had stopped shivering, but her face was still pale.

"Is she okay?" said the boy, nodding at her. "She's not saying anything."

"She has problems speaking," said Gran shortly.

Emmeline bit her lip; she wished Gran didn't have to constantly explain her condition.

"Oh," said the boy, looking relieved. "I thought it was Willa who did that. She has that effect on people." He half-stood in the boat, one hand on the gunwale, and scanned the water again. "Geez, it would be awful if a boat ran over her. She's got a new mate coming next month. She lost the first one—squeezed him to death by mistake. Of course she felt awful about it. *That's* the kind of summer it's been."

Emmeline signed to Gran: *Let's help him.*

Gran stared at her, suddenly feeling very old. The girl had just been terrorized by an enormous snake, and now she wanted to help *capture* it?

"Look, what can we do?" she said in exasperation. "We are *not* jumping into the water to capture him. *Her.*"

"She'll probably just swim back to the island after a while," said the boy. "She's not really a deep-water snake. We just need to follow her, make sure no boats come by."

Gran took a deep breath. When I see that uncle of his, she told herself, he's going to get an earful.

"Well," she said wearily, "I guess I can't leave a child alone to tackle an anaconda, can I?"

"No," agreed the stranger. "But actually, I'm not a child. I'm a boy."

Rowing close to *Permanent Wants*, he hefted his anchor (half a concrete block tied to a faded polypropylene rope) and tossed it overboard. Then he scampered onto the deck of the larger vessel while Gran and Emmeline drew up their own two anchors. By this time, the sun was well over the horizon, and the mist was disappearing fast. Before she started the engine, Gran peered around the starboard end of the boat; she was getting very jumpy about the snake.

It didn't take them long to find Willa. She was on the far side of the island, about ten metres from shore, swimming as lazily as before. Cautiously they followed her, Gran steering and the two children watching from the bow. The boy was clearly right about the reptile: it didn't seem interested in striking out for the middle of the lake.

"She's just getting some exercise," said the boy in relief. He straightened and glanced at Emmeline. His red-blond hair was straight except at the back, where it curled like wood shavings from a plane. He wore worn jeans, muddy running shoes, and a Hard Rock Cafe T-shirt.

"My name's Tom," he offered. "What's yours?"

This time Emmeline remembered her name in Sign. She fingerspelled *E* and *M* while Tom watched intently.

"Er, say again?"

She repeated the gesture, this time more slowly. He imitated her movements, first the *E*—hand up, fingers curled towards the palm—and then the *M*—a fist with three fingers over the thumb. She nodded, smiling at him.

"That's your name, eh?" he said. "Cool. I guess people have to *groove* when they say your name. Well"—he made the hand shapes again, this time moving his upper body like a rapper—"thanks for helping me. How do you say thanks?"

Emmeline showed him—the tips of the fingers moving away from the mouth as if blowing a kiss. He seemed a bit embarrassed by this one, but he did it anyway (quickly) and then turned his attention back to Willa.

"I wonder if your gran could go on *this* side of her," he said. "Not too close, but close enough. Maybe we can just nudge her towards shore."

Gran was able to do this, and very soon Willa, feeling crowded, headed into shore on her own. Gran put the boat in neutral as the creature slithered through the shallows. Then they were all treated to the spectacle of a full-grown anaconda drawing itself onto the pebbled beach, making a visible path in the stones as it disappeared.

"That's a *big* snake," said Tom proudly. "Twenty-seven feet, four inches. Pythons can get longer, but nothing is as heavy as—Oh, no." He was looking at a point farther down on the beach; a rather wild-looking man had appeared there.

"Tom!" called the man. "What are you doing out there?"

He wore a bulky vest with all sorts of pockets, the kind photographers wear, which made his skinny frame seem even skinner. His hair was wilder than Einstein's, a supernova of crinkly grey. He wore large green rubber boots that were caked in mud.

"Hoo boy," said Tom in a low voice. Moving closer to the deck railing, he shouted, "Willa got loose, Uncle Digby!"

His uncle's lanky frame sagged. Gran turned off the engine so man and boy could hear each other better.

"But she's back," added Tom, adjusting his voice to the sudden quiet. "She just went up on the shore there." He pointed to the spot.

"Thank goodness!" said the man. "I'll go after her. She wasn't injured, was she?"

"No, no," said Tom. "She was just in the mood for a swim." He gestured to Gran and Emmeline. "These people helped me find her."

"Thank you, thank you!" exclaimed the man, scrambling up the beach. "That was a prize green anaconda you saved."

"Listen! Hey!" called Gran—she was still keen to give the man a piece of her mind—but he had already vanished into the trees. She sighed and pressed the ignition switch. "Well, anyway, it's something for the ship's log," she said. "Let's get you back to your boat, Tom."

She'd had enough of reptiles for one day. But she couldn't help noticing that Emmeline and Tom had really hit it off. The girl was usually awkward around other children, but she had already taught him some signs, and he seemed to enjoy using them. Now that the snake was back on the island, he was much more at ease.

Permanent Wants nudged the rowboat gently, but Tom didn't move. He looked around at them, and then to the shore, and then down at his feet.

"Well, thanks," he said vaguely.

"You're welcome."

Still Tom hesitated. Gran shut off the engine.

"Hey," he said, "would you two like to come for a tour?"

Emmeline nodded vigorously, beaming at him. Gran looked defeated.

From the shore came a shout. They all turned to see the man with the wild grey hair, Tom's uncle Digby, gesturing to them with his hat.

"She's safe!" he called. "She's back in her pen. Thank you again!"

Gran waved a hand weakly. He looked so happy that she lost all desire to chew him out.

Tom called, "Hey, Uncle Digby, can they come for a tour?"

The man opened his hands wide. "That's a great idea. And perhaps you'll stay for tea on the terrace afterwards? It would be an honour."

Emmeline signed enthusiastically, working her hand in a nodding motion from her wrist.

"That means yes, Uncle Digby," Tom interpreted. "I've been learning Sign language. I already know a swear word. Look, guess what this is—"

"All right, Tom, all right," interrupted Gran curtly. "Get in your boat and show us where we can dock. Your harbour must be well hidden; we saw nothing when we passed."

"So you'll come?" said Tom. "Great!" But he made the swear word sign quickly, to himself, to make sure he still remembered it.

"For a *short* while," replied Gran, giving Emmeline a meaningful look. "Incidentally, you don't have any poisonous snakes on that island, do you?"

"No, no," said Tom emphatically. "We're not allowed."

"Thank goodness for small mercies," said Gran, reaching for the starter button. "Still, I hope it's just us *mammals* who are invited to tea."

As it turned out, Gran found it hard to resist the Squamish Island Reptile Haven. The place was home to some of the world's rarest and most endangered creatures—the kind that are glimpsed only every ten years or so, out of the corner of one's eye, in the shadow of a sand dune or at the foot of a giant jungle tree. Their very names were as strange and faraway as they were: the Angel Island chuckwalla, the Solomon Islands prehensile-tailed skink, the Mongolian frog-eyed sand gecko, and the flying snake of Singapore.

First, Gran and Emmeline were shown around "Lizard Landing." Some of the residents were housed in big wire cages; some (the smaller ones) were in plywood boxes. They saw a shingleback skink from Australia whose tail perfectly mimicked its head; they saw two flinty-eyed Bengal monitor lizards, with their powerful front limbs curved like the arms of a weightlifter; and they saw a Parson's chameleon from Madagascar carrying its baby on its back. (Emmeline laughed out loud when she saw the baby chameleon's face: it looked like a tiny Yoda.) The Mongolian frog-eyed sand geckoes turned out to be minute lizards that resembled tadpoles with legs. Finally, in a pen not much larger than a breadbox, they saw the smallest lizard in the world: the jaragua sphaero. It could just about fit onto the surface of a quarter.

"Where do you get all these animals, anyway?" said Gran.

"Most of them are on short-term loan from zoos," said Digby. "We're better at breeding reptiles than they are. *Much* better." He looked around with pleasure at the tall pines that surrounded Lizard Landing. "We're nice and isolated here—no worries about dogs and cats."

Emmeline was looking up at the trees as well. The island *was* beautiful, with the needle-strewn paths and the warm, earthy smell and the green-gold light among the trees. It had a secret, forgotten air to it. The colours in the woods were both soft and clear: the bluebells looked like delicate wreaths of violet smoke, and the old pine needles had a rich rust tint. Scattered everywhere were old, dried-out stumps and sculpted pieces of driftwood, which provided centrepieces for the cages. (Digby said that the snakes in particular loved gnarled chunks of wood to curl around.) Still, there was something about the place. It was just *too* quiet, Emmeline decided. She hadn't heard a single bird since they arrived.

From Lizard Landing, they walked along a shaded path to "Snake Town." Their first stop was the snake nursery, a small plywood hut that was kept heated even in summer. In an incubator they saw a fresh clutch of Burmese python eggs, most of them the size of large potatoes, their shells dirty white and pliant as old leather. Digby studied them carefully.

"I bet there will be dozens of baby pythons wriggling around here tomorrow," he announced.

Just then, Emmeline noticed something on the far wall of the hut, something dark against the plywood background. The others turned to watch her as she went over to it. The object turned out to be a carved wall ornament—the head of a cobra, its hood spread wide. It was made of some dark tropical wood and looked very real, seeming to sway in the air over them.

"That's Senesha," explained Digby, chuckling. "Our friendly neighbourhood snake-god. All the snake charmers in India carry amulets with his likeness."

Emmeline, gazing up at Senesha, remembered the anaconda coming towards her in the water. She shivered.

"I like to think he's one reason for our success here," added Digby. "We're snake charmers, too, in a way. Okay, onwards."

Snake Town itself, like Lizard Landing, was a semicircle of cages and boxes in a grassy clearing. The residents were looped over tree branches or resting motionless in each other's coils. There were two red-brown Jamaican boas, and two young green tree pythons (they weren't actually green, being immature, but a brilliant yellow), and the two flying snakes that Digby was so proud of. "They don't actually fly," he explained. "They just glide. They've got these wing flaps on either side of their belly. Sometimes I take them out and let them glide around for a while. One at a time, of course."

They also peeked inside Willa's pen (by far the largest enclosure in Snake Town) and found her resting comfortably in her muddy pool of water, her snout in a pile of leaves. Emmeline scrunched up her nose: the snake's den gave off a slimy, fleshy smell—something like dead shark stewed in garbagey swamp water. Digby showed them where Willa had wriggled out under the wire lattice, and where he had lately sunk another section of fencing to make sure it didn't happen again.

"That is an amazing collection of . . . beauties," said Gran at the end of the tour.

Digby smiled. "I haven't shown you our most celebrated guests. We keep them by themselves, since they're a bit high-strung."

He led the way to a large wire cage, some distance behind that of the Jamaican boas, and stopped a good ten metres from it. "I must ask you to be very quiet," he said, lowering his voice. "In there are two of the rarest animals in the world—a pair of giant La Gomera lizards. They were thought to be extinct for five hundred years. Then scientists discovered them in a single valley on La Gomera Island, in the Canary Islands."

Emmeline and Gran peered inside the cage, but the lizards must have been keeping very still among the shadows, for they could see nothing.

"Nobody has ever succeeded in breeding them," continued Digby. "We've been trying for weeks now. Everything has to be just right. We've been monitoring the temperature and moisture level— you see the sprinklers there—and we've kept the cage free of ticks, and we've given them exactly the right kind of food . . . but so far nothing. They just ignore each other."

"I don't think they like each other personally," put in Tom.

"They're *lizards*, for heaven's sake," replied his uncle. "It's not as if they have to have the same hobbies. No, they keep on getting disturbed, that's the problem. We've had so many . . . bedevilments."

"What do you mean, bedevilments?" asked Gran.

"I mean, *bedevilments*. Ever since these lizards arrived, we've had problems. First we lost our assistant keeper, Pauline."

"Please don't tell me you lost her to Willa."

"No, no. She just left. Basic lack of character."

Tom piped up, "She was creeped out all the time."

"No!" said Gran.

"As I say, a basic lack of character," affirmed Digby. "Then there was the invasion of the turtles. Yes, *turtles*. We have a few native ones on the island—just small ones, no snappers. Very unadventurous little guys, generally. But for some reason, a whole bunch of them decided to explore the haven one day. We found dozens crawling everywhere, through Snake Town and Lizard Landing, even through the cottage. Craziness." He shook his head. "And then the inboard engine broke down on our trusty boat. I can't help wondering if something got in there, too, and chewed some wires. It's been problems like that, one after another . . . Well, look at the time! I'd say lunch is a better idea than tea."

They had lunch at a small cedar-shingled cottage that served as the island's living quarters and office. While Digby made sandwiches, Tom showed them around the house. The place was crammed with mementoes from Digby's travels and framed certificates from various zoos. Both Gran and Emmeline noticed that many of these recognized "Digby and Mara Larose."

"Aunt Mara, yeah," said Tom, when Gran asked him about it. "She started Reptile Haven with Digby. They divorced two years ago. Now they're like the La Gomera lizards—they can't stand each other." He lowered his voice, glancing back at the kitchen. "But Mara was really good with the snakes. Willa would never have gotten loose with *her* around."

"That's something I wanted to ask you, Tom," said Gran. "You say your parents are okay with you working here? Even with Willa?"

"Yeah, I talked them into it," said Tom casually. "It wasn't that hard—my mum is a vet and my dad is a biology prof." He lowered his voice again. "But actually, I don't think I'll tell them about Willa getting loose. They'll just get nervous. They don't know how serene she is."

They ate lunch on a real terrace, with flagstones and climbing flowers on a latticework. White butterflies busied themselves around the shrubs, frothing their small zones of space-time. Gran was surprised at how pleasant it was. She was beginning to enjoy herself, and she told her hosts the whole story of *Permanent Wants*. Digby listened politely, but it was clear he wanted to get back to his favourite topic—reptiles and the Reptile Haven. He had studied them all over the world, he said, and had never found a place like this island for breeding them.

"I like to think," he said, munching his sandwich, "that this is a patch of the great reptile kingdom that is now long gone—the place where Senesha and all the other cold-blooded gods came from."

"The other gods?" said Gran.

"Yes. There's a hierarchy of reptile gods, some more powerful than others. I hope to write a book on it one day." He shook his head. "But the children of the gods are having a hard time of it now. Ordinary snakes and lizards and other reptiles—they're under threat everywhere. That's why our island is so important."

"Dad said that if you stay on this island long enough," interjected Tom, "the reptile part of your brain will start waking up. We all have a reptile brain hidden deep inside us, you know."

"I guess for some it's not so deeply hidden," Gran remarked.

She was actually thinking about a landlord she had once known, but she laughed when Digby said, "Why, thank you!" and winked at her.

After lunch, Digby said he really should try to fix the motorboat, and Gran offered to help. (She wanted to learn a bit more about engines, in case she ever had to repair theirs.) Tom and Emmeline decided to explore the island, and spent the rest of the day together. They found some moss that looked exactly like a patch of miniature trees; it would have been a perfect spot to place toy soldiers. They stood in the pebbled shallows, where the water was the colour of the purest Baltic amber, and waited for minnows to approach their toes. They collected fossils (or what they thought were fossils) and skipped stones and swam underwater together. For Emmeline, it was one of the best days of the summer.

Now and then, thinking about Tom, her hands would move slightly, making images in her mind. She had already given him a name-sign: her index finger drawn straight down from her mouth and then curled. (It means *red* in Sign language, but of course the curling part nicely captured his curling hair.) He was both a talker and a listener. As she put it to herself:

> *round and around*
>
> > *redtalking*
>
> > > *words in air*

This was definitely true about Tom. He would chat away to Emmeline, talking "around and around," and then pause, as if listening to her reply—as if he could catch her unspoken "words in air." Then he would keep right on talking. He was one of those rare people who unconsciously soften the awkward edges of others around them.

It wasn't until late in the afternoon, when they were walking back to the cottage, that Tom wondered aloud, "How come you don't speak, Em?"

Emmeline gave him a dispirited glance. Would she ever be able to explain—*really* explain—what had happened to her? If she just took it very slowly, maybe she could do it. She had to remember the spaces between words, and the order, and little words like *the* and *of* . . . She stood still for a long moment, her eyes closed.

> *speakingbrain it might is there*
>
> > *not but*

doctors say back

yes and try try try

In the end, she just turned over her medical ID bracelet and showed it to him. Engraved below an emergency hotline number were three lines:

Emmeline has aphasia
(difficulty reading, writing, and speaking).
She has no drug or other allergies.

"Hmm," remarked Tom. "Aphasia." He had no idea what the word meant, but he took a stab at it. "So I guess it's your brain and not . . . your voice box or whatever."

Emmeline nodded glumly. If only her bracelet listed all the things she *could* do, and not just her problems. She could draw and paint quite well, everybody said. She loved to put two colours on her palette and blend them with her finger. She could do karate, too. Most of all, she could play the violin. In fact, she heard music everywhere—in dripping water, rustling leaves, distant traffic, and even the sound of someone tipping birdseed into a feeder. Music had become precious to her ever since she lost her language. Oddly, she could still read it not too badly, and she could hum *very* well. She knew nineteen and a half tunes on the violin, and about fifty or so to hum.

"Well," said Tom, "you seem just like everybody else. I mean, you seem pretty normal."

Emmeline gave him a look that said "Right." She wasn't normal to the kids who had once been her friends, that was for sure. For almost two years, she'd had to scrabble around in her mind, searching for words, while the kids around her would be fidgeting and looking away. Her friend Sonja, trying to be helpful, had given her some advice. "If you can't think of anything to say," she counselled, "just nod. And laugh a bit. Not too much, just a bit. Like it's not a big deal." Then she had added without thinking: "But if you get stuck, try to keep your mouth closed. Sometimes you look like a *fish*."

Emmeline sighed. Now she had something to ask Tom, but as usual she had to rack her mind for ways to get it across. She waved a hand, indicating the trees on the shoreline, and then cupped her hand to her ear. When Tom didn't understand, she tried darting and swooping her hand like a swallow in flight. Then she shook her head. She had to repeat these gestures several times before Tom caught on.

"Birds," said Tom. "I got you. Yeah, there are no birds here. Digby says it's because of our snakes. But you know what? There weren't any birds when we first came here, two summers ago. No chipmunks either, or rabbits." He picked up a stone and sent it skipping; they both watched it—*pap, pap, pap, plonk.* "Sometimes I think Digby is right: this is a bit of the old reptile kingdom. It was *waiting* for us. That's why the animals like it here. That's why Senesha likes it here."

Emmeline eyed him curiously. Tom, as usual, continued right on after a moment's pause.

"Mum's always teasing us about Senesha. 'Don't offend Senesha,' she says. 'He's the *Man*.' But you know, I get the feeling that he's not the Man on this island." He glanced down at Emmeline. "I know what you're thinking: Who *is* the Man here, right?"

Emmeline nodded.

"I don't know, Em," said Tom, looking out at the water. "Something bigger than Senesha, anyway. Maybe the whole island. That's the feeling I get sometimes." He turned back to her. "Hey, let's go and have a look at those python eggs."

Gran and Digby joined them at the snake nursery (the adults had managed to get the engine running), and they all studied the python eggs.

"If you want to stick around," said Digby, "I'm sure you'll be able to see some baby pythons in the morning. You're welcome to moor at the dock; it's very sheltered."

Gran gave a rueful smile. She had planned to spend only an hour on the island, and here they were, on the verge of making a weekend out of it. But she could see how Emmeline was enjoying herself, and besides, it *was* a bit late to find new anchorage. Still, she couldn't help being a bit leery of overnighting there. The image of Willa swimming towards Emmeline would take more than a day to fade.

Tom seemed to read her thoughts. "You don't have to worry about Willa. There's no way she can get out now."

"Well, thank you," said Gran. "Maybe we will stay here; it certainly is a nice little harbour." She glanced at her watch. "But it's getting late, and I think we should get back to the boat now. Our cat has been alone for most of the day."

"Right-ho," said Digby cheerfully (he had perked up at the thought that his visitors might stay). "We'll leave you to your own devices. If you need water or anything, don't hesitate to knock."

It was a two-minute walk from Snake Town to the small treed inlet on the other side of the island where both Digby's motorboat and *Permanent Wants* were moored. Lafcadio was *not* in a good mood when they got back. Once released from the cabin, he jumped onto the dock, head high and tail lashing. Em wanted to practise her violin—she hoped to play for Tom sometime—and Gran agreed to make dinner.

Em loved the warm tawny colour of her violin, the feel of it her hands, the graceful f-holes in the body that always reminded her of two swans facing each other. Now, on deck, she brought it to her shoulder and played a few scales to warm up. It was such a relief to let go of words, to rinse her mind clean with music. She played "Tarantella," "Flop-Eared Mule," "Swallowtail Jig," and part of "The Road to Lisdoonvarna" (that was the half song she knew). She generally liked to play when the crickets were cheeping, but for some reason, they were silent now. When she stopped playing, the birdless, cricket-less silence was even more noticeable. After listening for a moment, she put her fiddle in its case and went below to help Gran.

Lafcadio spent a few minutes prowling about the dock, but he was back on board before long.

"Yes, he feels something," said Gran. "It's a funny place, this Reptile Haven." She gazed out over the quiet shore. "Digby's got everything so organized and orderly and . . . domestic. It's almost as if he's trying to keep the wild out. But the wild is there—trying to get *in*."

Emmeline awoke in the middle of the night and lay listening to the stillness. She could hear Gran's breathing and the soft lapping of water against the hull—both comforting sounds. The crickets were silent, a rare state for them. She moved a bit closer to the wall; with her ear against the hull, she could hear the water better.

Then, from some distance away, she heard another sound—a faint scraping, like something heavy moving over stones. She sat up at once. The sound made her think of Willa slithering onto land, but somehow she didn't think that was right. It was more the sound of a boat being dragged up the shore. After a minute, she slipped on her jeans and felt around for her penlight. Again came the scraping from the shore, and this time Gran stirred in her sleep. Noiselessly, Emmeline opened the cabin door. Lafcadio was there at once, twining about her legs. She stepped from the stern onto the dock, and just then she saw, from thirty metres down the shore, a flicker of light. A flashlight.

Lafcadio, who was always active in the darkness, jumped onto the dock ahead of her. She wasn't sure she wanted to go walking around Reptile Haven at night. But she was very curious about the scraping sound, and anyway, with Lafcadio she felt safe; if there were any snakes out there, he'd let her know. And snakes didn't carry flashlights. It could have been Tom or Digby, of course, in which case she could go back to bed. But she thought she'd just make sure.

She stepped off the dock walkway and began making her way along the undergrowth of the shore. It was pitch dark, but she didn't want to turn on her penlight, in case there *was* an intruder on the island. She moved slowly, and Lafcadio, thankfully, stayed right at her feet, guiding her along. A half moon showed above the lake, and a few stars looked down on their pinpoint reflections in the still water. She walked with her hands out, feeling her way, and after a moment she touched something hard and smooth. A canoe. She was right: it had been dragged up here, where there was lots of cover. Glancing up the shore, she saw another flicker of light weaving through the darkness. Somebody was walking up the trail towards the reptile enclosures.

She turned on her own light briefly, just long enough to make out the trail, and then began moving through the trees. She couldn't see Lafcadio, but she sensed him just ahead of her. Snake Town was two minutes' walk up a rise. There were fewer trees here, and more moonlight. Just then, she spied a figure moving ahead through the darkness. She quickened her pace. It wasn't Tom or Digby, she was sure of that. Now she was among the collection of old stumps and pieces of driftwood that surrounded Snake Town. She crouched down among them, fingers outspread on the ground, like a sprinter.

The figure had stopped beside one of the snake cages. Emmeline heard the faint clinking of keys, and then the sound of the cage door swinging open.

She crouched down, straining to see in the darkness. Then she heard a low voice—a woman's voice—from inside the cage. She crept forward.

"Did you miss me, sweeties?" the voice was saying. "Don't hiss in my ear, now. Hello, Elvira, you old smoothie. Make room for Alvin. Come here, sweet cheeks. Are you two being good or bad? Bad, I hope."

Emmeline listened, fascinated. That was the cage of the Jamaican boas. The woman was talking to them as if they were babies!

Suddenly, she felt Lafcadio stiffen beside her. She reached down: he was making a low growl—a real growl, a *rrrouwah*. Then he was gone. One moment she felt fur, and the next, air. She heard a faint rustling as he sprinted up the rise.

The woman in the cage must have had very good ears. Her voice stopped, and there was absolute silence. The next minute, she was at the door of the cage, flashlight in hand, looking out into the darkness.

Emmeline held her breath. She wanted to go after Lafcadio, but she knew that if she moved forward into the clearing, the woman might see her. What had scared him? She began to back up very quietly, towards the collection of stumps and driftwood. The woman stepped outside the cage—Emmeline heard once more the squeak of the door—and now stood in front of it. The girl crouched down beside a large stump. Where *was* Lafcadio? The woman didn't seem willing to move; she was standing there in front of the pen, holding the door closed behind her.

"Who's there?" she said softly. Crouching beside the stump, Emmeline suddenly felt a chill of fear. Why on earth hadn't she woken Gran up? Now Lafcadio was gone and she was alone. In the moonlight, the pieces of wood beside her had strange, gnarled shapes. They could have been great lizards, standing still as statues. And then she became aware of sounds all around her, soft, rustling sounds. She froze. By themselves the sounds were tiny, but together they produced a vast, layered whispering, like monarch butterflies alighting in a huge flock. Emmeline turned her head and gasped. The stump beside her had become *alive;* the very bark seemed to be writhing and seething in the moonlight . . .

She bolted just as Lafcadio had.

Up the rise she raced, straight towards the figure standing at the door of the cage. The woman had just enough time to take a step backwards when Emmeline barrelled into her. "Oomph!" grunted the stranger, staggering. The cage door banged open. Emmeline tumbled in on top of the intruder, and for a second they rolled in a heap on the dirt floor. Then the girl heard a hissing close to her ear; that was too much for her. She screamed and covered her head.

"*Shh!*" said the woman, who had got the scream full force.

Emmeline could only lie shaking on the floor, her hands over her head, while the woman struggled to her feet. Fumbling for her flashlight, the intruder shone it around the pen.

"Drat!" she said, and moved to the door. "Alvin! Betty!" she called. She was panting slightly. "Great!" she whispered fiercely. "They got out!"

Emmeline must have been a sorry sight, gasping on the floor of the cage, for the woman bent down and said in a more temperate voice: "All right, kid. Take it easy. They were frightened of *you*, too."

But Emmeline wasn't thinking of the boas; she was thinking of what she had just escaped—a *nest* of snakes. That was why the stumps seethed like a hornet's nest, she was sure. Struggling to her feet, she banged the door shut and stood with her hands against it, her teeth clenched. No snakes were going to get in *there*.

"Look, dear, you've had a fright," said the woman. "Just take it easy." She shone her light outside the cage. "You can stay here if you want, but I have to go out and look for those snakes."

Emmeline shook her head furiously and grabbed the woman's arm.

"Let me out, kid," said the woman. "Wow, you have quite a grip."

Just then, Emmeline heard the most welcome sound in the world—Gran calling her name. From the bottom of the rise, a flashlight beam swept across the interior of the snake cage.

"Emmeline!" called Gran urgently. "Where are you?"

The intruder swore quietly.

Emmeline flung the cage door open and rushed out into her grandmother's arms. Gran had only a second to hug her before the girl seized her hand and began tugging her towards the snake pen.

"What is it, Em?" said Gran.

Emmeline just kept tugging. She had only one thought: *snakes*. Snakes everywhere; snakes of all sizes; snakes slithering in from everywhere to attack them. Her grandmother gave in to the tugging, and in a minute the two of them were inside the cage. Raising her flashlight, Gran illuminated the face of the stranger.

"Who are *you*?" she said in surprise.

"The pizza delivery girl," replied the other crossly. She was a wiry, compact, pony-tailed woman, about the same age as Digby. "Look, I'd love to stay for introductions, but there are two boas loose." Yet she hesitated. Her eyes were on Emmeline, who was now signing frantically to her grandmother.

"What's up with her?" said the woman.

Emmeline was making a certain sign over and over—two fingers crooked like talons and spiralling forward from under her chin.

"Snakes," translated Gran. "Where?"

Emmeline moved close to the cage wire and pointed down

the rise, towards the woodpile. Gran shone her flashlight in that direction.

"She says there's more snakes over there," said Gran. "*Lots.*"

Just then came voices from the direction of the cottage. Another light could be seen bobbing through the darkness.

"Who's there?" called Digby.

"Great," said the woman bitterly. "Here comes the old man. What a party."

Tom appeared just ahead of Digby; he was jogging down the path rather recklessly, wearing a headlamp. He seemed to be enjoying himself. Digby followed more cautiously, clomping forward in his rubber boots. When he saw the stranger, he stopped dead.

"Mara!" he exclaimed.

"Hi, Aunt Mara!" said Tom excitedly.

"Hey, Tommy," said the woman shortly, stepping outside the cage. "Yes, the gang's all here. And a good thing, too—we're going to need everybody. Digby, the Jamaican boas got loose, and this girl says there are more snakes down by the woodpile."

"What!" Digby was aghast. He came close, his mouth set. "This is *your* doing, isn't it, Mara?"

"Don't be an idiot, Digby," said Mara. "I don't let snakes loose. You know that." She turned to the boy. "Tom, go and get the snake gun. We'll check out the woodpile first."

"Chaos," said Digby brokenly. "Day and night, I'm fighting chaos."

Mara was already striding towards the woodpile. Tom flashed his headlamp around the clearing, maybe hoping to catch sight of the boas, and then raced away in the direction of the cottage. Digby just stood there muttering, his flashlight held limply at his side. Gran noticed that he was wearing pyjamas—striped ones—under a windbreaker.

Just then came an exclamation from Mara. "I don't believe this," they heard her say.

Digby, recovering, clomped off towards the woodpile. Gran and Emmeline followed, mainly because they were afraid to be left alone. Emmeline kept a tight hold of Gran's hand.

"My *Lord*," breathed Gran.

The woodpile was a mass of small snakes. They were dropping from branches and squirming in and out of fissures and stirring the pieces of bark that lay on the grass. None of them was longer than thirty centimetres, but together they produced that vast, dry, rustling sound. You could hear it only if you were perfectly silent (and all the onlookers were). Emmeline clutched Gran: to think she had been *crouching* there.

"They're garter snakes," said Mara in puzzlement, casting her flashlight beam over the woodpile. "Not ours at all."

"It's like a gathering," said Gran in awe.

"What is going *on* tonight?" said Digby, bewildered. "All we need is for Willa to get loose again."

At this, Emmeline and Gran flinched, but Digby said: "Don't worry, I checked her cage on the way here. At least *she's* behaving herself." He gave the woodpile a final sweep of his flashlight beam. "Okay, Alvin and Betty. We can start by checking the—"

Just then, they heard a thrashing, scuffling sound. It came from the cage on the outskirts of the enclosure.

"Oh, no!" moaned Digby. "Something's got in with the La Gomera lizards!"

That was a memorable night for Emmeline and Gran. Somehow the escaped boas had got into the cage of the temperamental La

Gomera lizards; perhaps it was the only warm, quiet place the snakes could find. They would have been quite happy to rest there, wrapped in each other's coils, if it hadn't been for the other occupants. The La Gomera lizards clearly considered the cage *their* territory. Fortunately it wasn't a real fight—just a kind of reptilian standoff, with much hissing and darting and rearing up. When Emmeline and the others arrived at the cage, the lizards were doing a kind of push-up with their front limbs, as if to limber up for battle. At any other time, it would have been amusing.

It is not easy to capture two large, annoyed snakes at night, especially when the bystanders are two large, annoyed lizards. First Digby slipped inside the cage, carrying the snake gun that Tom had fetched. (It wasn't actually a gun, but a long pole that ended in a pair of claspers; with this tool, Digby could catch a snake just behind the head without harming it.) He managed to pick up one of the boas and then carry the writhing snake back to its own cage. Once there, he had a bit of a problem, since the reptile had wrapped itself around the pole and wouldn't come off. Meanwhile, in the lizards' cage, Mara was trying to get the other boa to wrap itself around the handle of a canoe paddle. Just when it seemed to be ready to do that, Emmeline accidentally tripped the sprinkler system, and Mara could be heard swearing mightily as she got drenched. Unexpectedly, the soaking seemed to calm the animals down. Mara finally got the other boa onto the paddle and then carried it back to its home, with Emmeline and Gran giving her a wide berth. Once the two snakes were together, they slithered away into a dark corner. Mara and Digby sat down heavily on the bench near the cage.

"Those La Gomera lizards will be on edge for weeks now!" groaned Digby. "We can forget about any babies this year." He eyed his ex-wife balefully. "You and your night visits, Mara!"

"You know darn well I have a right to visit," snapped Mara, and she turned to Gran. "When he got this island, he figured he'd get away from me. No such luck, Digby!"

Just then came the night's first bit of good cheer: Lafcadio appeared. He came from the direction of the boat, and Gran suspected that he had gone back there to escape the ruckus, then come looking for them. Emmeline scooped him up at once. Usually Lafcadio didn't like to be held, but this time he consented, purring loudly.

"Too many snakes for you, Laf?" said Gran. Looking to the east, she noticed that the sky was starting to lighten. "Well, it's a new day," she said.

Digby and Mara exchanged looks of poison. Mara's denim shirt was still damp, and Digby had bits of twig in his hair.

"How about some breakfast on my boat?" said Gran. "I can give you some dry clothes, Mara."

This was wise: a meal on neutral territory is a good way to defuse tension. While Tom and his uncle went to change, Mara followed Gran and Emmeline to the boat. (Emmeline had come to like Mara, who seemed to have forgiven her for tripping the sprinkler. "It was just another ring to the circus, dear," she said.) Emmeline started scrambling some eggs, and Gran got their visitor some dry clothes. It was then that Mara opened up, a bit grudgingly, about herself and Digby.

"It's the old story," she said. "Digby and I got divorced, but the judge recognized that I had built the haven, too. So he gave me visiting rights with the reptiles."

"I see," said Gran. Having been on Squamish Island for twenty-four hours, she was no longer surprised by such a notion.

"People think it's weird," Mara conceded. "But I don't care. Reptiles are amazing creatures, especially the snakes." She shrugged. "Anyway, Digby moved the haven out here two years ago, thinking he could get away from me. Ha! I just rented one of the cottages on the shore and started paddling over here at night. He never changed the locks on the cages, and I still had my keys. Easy."

"Then *you* were behind those bedevilments?" said Gran.

"What bedevilments?"

"I mean the chaos that Digby talked about. His assistant keeper left, and his motorboat broke down, and—"

Mara gave a harsh laugh. "Look, I'm not above causing that man trouble—he's caused me plenty. But I would never stoop to sabotage. The work of the haven is just too important."

"So you didn't by chance set loose any . . . er, turtles?"

"You've got to be kidding."

Just then, they were interrupted by the shouts of Tom and Digby, who were running down the path towards the dock.

"What is it?" called Gran, coming out on deck with the others.

"The La Gomera lizards!" exclaimed Digby. "They're together! They're sunning themselves cheek to cheek!"

"Yeah," affirmed Tom. "At least they're *talking* to each other now." He glanced up at Digby, then at Mara. His aunt caught the look, but his uncle was too excited to notice.

"When will I learn to ignore the zoo experts!" exclaimed Digby. "Here I was thinking that those lizards had to have everything nice and quiet. No surprises, no disruptions—no danger. But maybe that's exactly what they were missing. Having to fight off those boas did it for them."

"Well, all's well that ends well," said Gran. "Maybe we have Senesha to thank."

"Or at least the wild," added Mara. "*That's* what is missing from the haven, if you ask me."

Wild, thought Emmeline. She knew that word. Yes, there was a wild here—a *very* wild. Wilder than Senesha. Wilder than the wild.

Emmeline has a natural sense of the dramatic. When telling me this story, she paused right at this point, hands held up. (Gran had already told me a lot of it, but she wanted to tell the ending.)

"A *wild*?" I prompted.

She rested her hands in her lap, looking tired. As usual, I had to read between the lines—or the signs. Something very wild . . . some kind of Presence, I guessed. And apparently, this Presence had many *children*. (Emmeline was signing again.) A Presence with children? Now she made the sign for *sad*—both hands moving down her face, fingers apart, to imitate tears. So this Presence was wild *and* sad? I wished Gran was there; she usually was, to help me out. The Presence was sad because it was losing its children, maybe?

Yes. Emmeline nodded in relief. I knew what it cost her to try to describe her experiences.

Anyway, this was what I came up with:

If you spend any time on Squamish Island, you might be able to sense it—some vast and powerful Presence. It is very old, much older than Senesha, who I think is one of its children. It has *many* children, and it's always making more of them. Maybe it wants to populate the world with itself. And maybe it looks out over Creation and sees what is happening to all its children—the snakes and lizards and other reptiles—and that makes it mad with grief. And so it *pushes*. It pushes harder and harder.

I couldn't help asking Emmeline, "But what does this Thing look like? Does it look like anything at all?"

She sat pondering a long moment. I was always hoping she would try a word or two, but she just made a few quick hand movements, a jumble, a flurry—one hand above the other, and both hands turning in opposite directions. Was it just that she was fed up? No. She made the sign again. And suddenly I knew what she wanted to say.

It looks like chaos.

Fifth Tale

A Patriot of the Night

When the history of Euphalia, Ontario (population 1,140), is finally written, the man known as the Great Zucchini—lover of magic, darkness, and Tim Hortons donuts—will surely get lots of respectful attention.

Not that he was much appreciated for most of his career. In fact, a lot of people thought him a nuisance. He travelled from town to town along the Rideau Waterway, doing his magic tricks for anybody who would stand still, and collecting handouts to allow him (as he explained) to continue his studies in hypnotism and brainwashing. He hadn't had a day off in twenty-three years, he told Gran and Emmeline as he attempted to demonstrate the Knot That Unties Itself. Gran gave him some change for his efforts and asked him—as she asked every local character—if there were any interesting cultural attractions in the area.

The Great Zucchini slipped his pinkie under the rim of his ear and scratched vigorously. He was a short, heavy man, roughcast and seamed like an old factory wall. His face put you in mind of the grainy, world-roughened face of a ship's figurehead that has sailed through all kinds of weather—except that they generally have straight, noble noses, while the nose of the Great Zucchini was big and shapeless and criss-crossed with little cranberry-tinted veins. He wore a Blue Jays baseball cap, Bermuda shorts, and an old striped sports coat (probably because he needed sleeves for his tricks).

"Cultural attractions?" he repeated. "Here?" He chuckled. "Well, there's *me*. And Smitty's got a set of wind-up chattering teeth at his garage—he'll wind 'em up for you at no charge. But aside from that, you got to go to Perth. They got that monument to the Mammoth Cheese there." He looked out across the river—they were standing beside a picnic table at the Euphalia lockstation— and rubbed his chin. "But here's a thought. You like lookin' at stars?"

Both Gran and Emmeline liked looking at stars.

"You drive thirty miles north from Euphalia," he said, "down County Road Eleven, and you'll get to Hathaway Flats. There's absolutely nothin' there. No houses, no farms, nothin'—just bare rock and moss and scrub trees. It's beautiful. And at night, it gets dark as pitch. I mean *really* dark—folks are always surprised at how dark it is. There's no lights around anywhere, see; no towns or gas stations or anything. I hear it's a reserve now, like a park for the stars. You sometimes get astronomers from Ottawa comin' out there to set up their telescopes."

"Well, it sounds very nice," said Gran. "But we don't have a car."

"Oh, you can rent one at Smitty's," said the man. "He always has one or two clunkers out back. Just tell him I sent you."

"Well, thank you," said Gran. "And are you staying around Euphalia for a while, Mr. . . . er, Zucchini?"

"Oh, I guess so," he said wearily. "Weekend's coming up, and there'll be a few tourists travelling through. They're always good for a bit of the old wampum. I mean, a bit of the old coin."

In the sag of his voice, the rawness of his gaze, Gran and Emmeline glimpsed a life of doing cheap magic tricks for tourists, of sleeping on park benches, of picking up beer bottles for the deposit money—a life of husk and rind. Emmeline suddenly made a quick sign to Gran and scampered off to *Permanent Wants*, moored a few paces away.

"Your first mate doesn't say much, does she?" remarked the Great Zucchini.

"No," agreed Gran, who didn't want to go into details about Emmeline's condition. "But I believe she's gone to get you something, Mr. Zucchini."

Emmeline had remembered that among their stock was a book of stage magic. She knew it by the cover picture of a female magician in tails and a top hat. Its title was *Wonders on a Shoestring: Making Great Magic Out of Slender Means*. It was just the book for the Great Zucchini—his means were the only thing slender about him.

In less than a minute she had rejoined the other two. "A present, Mr. Zucchini," said Gran, when she saw the book.

They were both surprised to see how touched the man was. His face got as red as his nose, he brushed at his eyes as if they had something in them, and finally he swept off his baseball cap. "Well, well," he mumbled. "I can pick up a few dodges from this, for sure." He studied the cover photo and gave a chuckle. "The old magic-cabinet routine. Haven't done that in a while."

The cover showed the top-hatted woman magician standing beside a large magic cabinet that was divided into moveable sections. A man was inside the cabinet; you could see his face in the top part. The magician had slid aside the middle section of the box and was waving her magic wand in the empty space. It looked as though the man's middle had completely disappeared. His eyes were wide in alarm.

"I used to have one of them magic cabinets myself," said the

Great Zucchini. "Smitty's got it in his garage somewhere. I'll have to get it out and dust it off." He looked from Emmeline to Gran. "You're a pair of apple fritters, you two."

Gran smiled. "Well, I guess we should be going if we want to get a berth at the marina," she said. "Nice to meet you, Mr. Zucchini."

The Great Zucchini tipped the peak of his cap. "You check out Hathaway Flats, now. In fact, why not take a tent and camp there? It's very safe." He looked out at the river. "We need more darkness, don't you think? That's where we went wrong, if you ask me— we got rid of darkness. We *banished* it. That's why it's so hard to do magic these days. You want my opinion."

The next evening, after hiring a car from Smitty's Garage (and marvelling at the man's wind-up clacking teeth, which he introduced as the mayor of Euphalia), they drove out to Hathaway Flats.

The countryside was certainly lonely. After a while they didn't see any houses, just a few ruins and once or twice an old barn with a collapsed roof. Some large, solitary oaks could be seen on ridges, but most of the trees were of the small, wispy kind—wind hermits, Gran called them. They would have missed the flats if they hadn't got very careful directions from Smitty. He had told them to watch out for an old rusted hoe in a roadside field—it was just past the junction of Latchford Lane and the county road—and to take the next left. After bumping down three kilometres of the worst road Gran had ever seen, they came to a modest hand-painted sign:

Hathaway Flats Conservation Reserve
Part of the southernmost edge of the Canadian Shield,
Hathaway Flats is a place of rock, moss, water, and stars. Here

you will find old time underfoot and very old time overhead. Please help keep our flats natural and leave only footprints.

There was a cleared dirt space to park the car, and an outhouse nearby, but that was all.

"Well, it's very *elemental*," said Gran as she locked the car.

They walked through the scrub brush to the edge of the flats. Around them were "whalebacks"—long ridges of worn rock dotted with puddles of rainwater and patches of lichen. Here and there, they could see boulders that had been left by the glaciers in their long, slow mumbling across the land. The sense of space was wonderful; because of the low, sparse trees they could see from horizon to horizon. The air was as pure as wintergreen.

"*Very* elemental," said Gran. "I like it."

They found a nice mossy spot to set up their tent and then got some water from a stream two hundred metres away. For dinner they rustled up potato soup and rye bread sandwiches. Dessert was blueberries, Emmeline's third-favourite food (after blueberry pancakes and blueberry smoothies). Their only visitors were a few chipmunks; they didn't hear a single car pass on the road. By nine-thirty, a sickle moon had appeared, along with a few planets. Emmeline saw with delight that one of the planets—Gran thought it might be Jupiter—was reflected in a puddle of rainwater in a rock hollow; it sat like a white opal in the dark pool. After a while, they spread out their sleeping bags and lay down. The sky fell away from them, a vast candled continent. Emmeline felt her mind swimming into it and turning around easily, like a resting dolphin. Shooting stars rode the lanes of the night, as fluid as chloroplasts in a leaf cell. They lay there on a patch of moss at the edge the Canadian Shield, on the curve of a darkened hemisphere, in the Orion Arm of the Milky Way galaxy, and knew where they were.

Emmeline wondered if her friend Madison was doing anything as exciting as this right now. Probably not, but that wouldn't matter to Madison. Whatever she was doing, she would make it into an opera later. That's what Emmeline's mother liked to say. Madison's favourite subject was herself, and her words always flowed like schooling salmon, or shooting stars, or the tiny rainbow-coloured bubbles that popped out of the Fruit and Veggie Soak bottle on *Permanent Wants* when somebody shook it. And she never let facts get in the way of the flow. Once (years before, when Emmeline could still speak), she had told Emmeline to eat all the food on her plate, because there were children in Africa who got only one meal a year. "But they'd be dead, then!" Emmeline had protested. "No, they get used to it," Madison had replied calmly. They'd argued about it for the rest of the meal; that was the nature of their friendship.

And now, without her best friend to challenge her, Madison was a walking fountain of exaggeration. Emmeline could almost feel sorry for her.

"Well, the Great Zucchini was right," said Gran, her hands behind her head. "It gets pretty dark here."

The darkness had a wonderful richness to it. They heard an owl and a whippoorwill, and saw bats crookedly carousing the starry spaces between trees. Once, when Emmeline got out her sketchpad, she scared up a big moth that flickered away like a windblown maple seed in the beam of her flashlight. Shrimp! she said in her mind, pointing.

"Yes," said Gran. "Hopefully there aren't any skunks here."

Just after eleven o'clock, Emmeline—whose ears were sharpest—caught a rustle in the scrub brush behind them. She stood up quickly, peering into the darkness.

"What is it?" said Gran, raising herself on her elbow.

For a moment they both waited, motionless. The neighbourhood owl hooted again, and from across the flats came the soft murmuring of the stream. A breeze stirred the larch trees by the road. After a minute, a figure emerged—a figure even darker than the surrounding night. It came a few cautious steps closer, rustling the bracken, and then stopped, showing pure black against the midnight blue of the sky.

Gran was now wondering if she'd been very rash to camp there, with just herself and Emmeline. She switched on her flashlight but kept the beam directed at the ground. "Good evening!" she called out firmly.

"Good evening," said the figure, and Gran and Emmeline knew it was a woman. There was another silence. They couldn't see the figure now because she had moved to a patch of absolute darkness under the trees.

"A wonderful evening," she said.

"It is," said Gran amiably. "You're here for the stars, too?"

The stranger took a step closer, and her silhouette became visible again. To Emmeline, she was like a human shadow that had escaped its body and was now exploring—carefully, warily—on its own.

"I am here . . . for the darkness," she replied. Her accent was strange—not European, not South American, but something even more remote. "Pardon me, friend," she continued, "but would you mind to *distinguish* your light?"

"Sorry," said Gran, and switched off her flashlight.

"Thank you," said the stranger with relief. "I came here to escape light, you see."

"Well, you've come to the right place," said Gran. "Are you from Euphalia?"

"No," said the stranger. "I am from far away." She was now a few metres from them, though they could barely make her out. "We are the only humans here?" she continued.

"I think so," replied Gran. She guessed from the voice that the stranger was quite young. "We didn't hear your car," she added.

"I come by feet," was the reply. Before Gran could ask her how she had made it out to the flats, the stranger said: "I will not keep you, good people. I have important work to do, and I must—Ah!"

Her gaze had lit on the planet that lay reflected in the puddle of rainwater. She strode over to the whaleback, walking as confidently as if it were broad daylight. Gran and Emmeline followed more cautiously. The planet was a tiny arrowhead of light in the black pool; it had the vivid, hallucinatory stillness of something seen under a microscope. At the puddle, the stranger stood still for a second, and they heard what sounded like a pocket being unsnapped. Then she crouched down beside the puddle. The bright opal of the planet swirled and eddied in the darkness; the woman had obviously dipped something into the water. An odd thought struck Emmeline: Was the stranger trying to *scoop up* the planet? After a second the woman straightened, and once more the planet rested serene and still in the pool. Then came the rustle of a garment, followed by the snapping sound again.

"There," said the stranger with satisfaction. "A good beginning to the night." She faced them. "I will leave you now. I have much to do before the sun shows. You do not know how lucky you are to have a place like this." She turned, but then hesitated. "I . . . I must ask a boon."

"A what?" said Gran, who hadn't quite got used to her old-fashioned way of speaking.

"A boon, a favour." The stranger came a step nearer. "If anybody else appears, please do not speak of me. I ask with a great need that you follow your business and say not a thing about me. Please."

Her tone was quiet, but Gran could sense the urgency behind it.

"That's fine by us," she said.

"Thank you. I see you are patriots of the night—like me." With that, the woman turned and disappeared into the darkness.

Gran and Emmeline went back to watching the stars, but they were both thinking about the stranger, and every once in a while, they would stand up to scan the flats. But they saw no sign of the dark woman, and after a while, they drifted off to sleep under the stars, Gran still wearing her glasses. Both of them woke up a lot during the night. Slowly the night sky changed above them. The constellations migrated across the sky; the Milky Way faded like a wisp blown from a snowdrift. Dawn had barely arrived when Gran got up to make herself some tea. Emmeline was still soundly sleeping, tucked deep into her sleeping bag, so only the top of her head showed. Gran got the Whisperlight burner going and began making breakfast, and eventually Emmeline wriggled out of her bag and started across the flats to get more water from the stream. The land was flooded with the delicate honeyed light of early morning. The girl was on her way back when she saw the stranger approaching.

The visitor looked young—maybe twenty or so—and wore a bulky bomber jacket, stretchy slacks, and a beret. Everything but the slacks seemed a bit too big for her. No spot of colour could be seen anywhere from head to toe; from her ankle boots to her beret, she was clothed in jet black. She might have been a Goth except for her face, which was pretty but a bit soft, with cheek-bones well hidden and candle-flame eyes. Her hair, a very pale blonde, was cut pageboy-style. To Emmeline, she looked and moved like someone who had dressed for a movie part—that of a World War II spy, say—and had been given cast-offs from the wardrobe department.

"We were just about to have breakfast," called Gran. "Would you like to join us?"

The woman looked around furtively. "Well, perhaps for a short while," she said. "The truth is, I didn't eat for a long time."

"Then please," insisted Gran. "My name's Teo. This is Emmeline."

The stranger inclined her head. "I am Tenebrio," she said, taking off her bulky bomber jacket. It seemed unusually heavy from the way she handled it.

"And where are you planning to go today?" asked Gran, handing her a slice of multigrain bread and nudging the jar of Nutella close.

The woman named Tenebrio sat cross-legged beside her coat. Her shirt was a lightweight turtleneck—black, of course. "I would love to stay here," she said, "but I must return to my home."

"Oh?" said Gran. "Where's that?" She still wasn't able to place the stranger's accent.

"Very far from here," said Tenebrio, just as she had the previous night. She slathered Nutella on her bread and tackled it with gusto. "This is a very savoury and *opulent* food," she said, her mouth full.

"It's called Nutella," said Gran. "Dig in. We've got plenty."

Tenebrio's eyes, Emmeline noticed, were very much like Lafcadio's—same black, almond-shaped iris; same feathered green pupil. They almost seemed to have smoke curling inside them. She remembered how easily Tenebrio had moved through the night, and wondered if the woman could see in the dark.

"Since I was very young, I have wanted to see this place," remarked Tenebrio, accepting a cup of tea from Gran.

"Really?" said Gran curiously. "Is it known in your country?"

"It is known to us partisans," said the other mysteriously. "We call it Lasha in my tongue—'the Cradle.'"

Slowly, with pauses, Emmeline signed to Gran: *What does she mean?*

Tenebrio smiled at Emmeline. "You use your hands to speak," she observed.

"Emmeline prefers to talk that way," explained Gran. "So do I, sometimes."

Tenebrio nodded. "Like the trees. They use their hands to talk, and never hide their thoughts. I like to observe their observations."

Emmeline tilted her head, amused. Whenever people saw her using Sign, they almost always wanted to know what her problem was. Tenebrio just seemed to accept it. The girl was starting to warm to the black-clad stranger.

"Emmeline wants to know why you call this the Cradle," said Gran.

The stranger studied them briefly. "Some of my compatriots would counsel me to be silent now. But you are kind to me, and I think you are also partisans in your roots, so I shall explain."

Again she looked out across the landscape, taking in the whalebacks, the puddles of rainwater, and (barely visible through the scrub trees) the cheerfully painted outhouse at the entrance.

"What do you see in the darkness here?" she asked in a low voice.

"What do I *see*?" repeated Gran, puzzled. "I'm not sure I understand. It seems very rich and . . . high-quality darkness, if that's what you're getting at."

"That is just what I am stating," said Tenebrio. "As rich and high-quality as . . . I don't know. *This*." She held up her bread and Nutella. "You see, this place is the primordial well of night. Under the rock firmament here is a reservoir of darkness so inky black, so powerful, that just a bit on your fingertip will blot out a small nation. All the darkness in the cosmos comes from here. This is Lasha, the Cradle. This is the pool of night out of which the universe was created."

Gran and Emmeline blinked. Tenebrio took another sip of tea.

"Interesting notion," said Gran. Emmeline raised her eyebrows. Gran gave her a look that said: *Let me go my own way on this.* Sometimes they really didn't need Sign.

"The Lasha darkness has always been with us," continued Tenebrio, "but for a long time it had no home. Then, when the planets formed, it joined with the cosmic dust and became part of the earth—part of your country."

"You're saying this darkness is *underground* here?" pursued Gran.

Tenebrio nodded solemnly. "When the sun goes down, the darkness begins to seep out at certain places. And one must be able to read the land to find those places."

In her bewilderment, Emmeline suddenly remembered how, the night before, Tenebrio had dipped something into the puddle that contained the reflection of the planet. Was *that* one of the places? She was about to ask (or sign) a question when they all heard the sound of a car on the dirt road.

The young woman tensed. She waited, eyes narrowed, but the car must have belonged to a local farmer, for the sound of its engine soon faded.

"I cannot stay here," she said. "In daylight, it is dangerous to me."

"Why?" said Gran, but Tenebrio was hastily putting on her bulky coat.

"I must go," she said. "Thank you, friends."

"Wait, wait," said Gran, getting to her feet. "Let us give you a ride back to Euphalia. You *are* going back there, aren't you?"

Tenebrio bit her lip. She looked no longer like a Resistance fighter out of an old movie, but like a frightened girl.

"Very well," she said. "But we must hurry."

"We'll be ready to go in a moment," replied Gran. Emmeline was already pulling up tent pegs.

In ten minutes, they were bumping along the dirt lane towards the county road. Gran tried to get Tenebrio to say more about herself, but the young woman was too tense. With every car that passed, she would slump down low in her seat, pulling her beret over her eyes. They drove to Euphalia without exchanging more than a few words. Once in town, Tenebrio got even more nervous; she put on a pair of cheap dollar-store sunglasses and slumped lower still.

"I say we have some lunch on our boat," said Gran. "It's very private there. After that, you can decide what you want to do. We can give you a lift somewhere if you want."

Tenebrio seemed more at ease on *Permanent Wants*. Though the day was fine, they ate lunch inside the cabin, since she obviously preferred it. They had bagels, cheese, and iced lemonade. The latter was a completely new experience for Tenebrio; she said it was like frozen sunlight.

"Well, you can have as much as you want," said Gran. "We've got four bottles in the fridge." She hoped that their visitor would relax enough to open up to them, but Tenebrio still seemed unwilling to talk about herself.

"Your country is beautiful," she remarked, looking through the cabin doorway. Across the way, the glittering river flowed by stately oaks.

Emmeline put down her bagel and signed: *Your . . . country . . .* Then she opened her hands in a questioning gesture.

Gran asked it aloud: "What is your country like?"

"My country," replied Tenebrio, closing her eyes.

Her face seemed paler than before, her eyelids slightly bluish. She looks *bushed*, thought Gran.

"It used to be beautiful," continued Tenebrio, opening her eyes. "It used to be the most benighted country anywhere. But then we became *enlightened*."

"That doesn't sound good," said Gran.

"Lights everywhere," said Tenebrio. "Street lights and factory lights and security lights and . . ." She shook her head. "We no longer have a night, just a *watering-down* of the day. Indeed, in some of our cities, the night is brighter than the day. And the government says it's progress. Away with the old, they say, and welcome to the new. Welcome to the factories and steel towers and everything else with lights. Go away with the darkness, away with the stars. Nobody can see them now, with all the light. And all the night creatures are dying off. They grow sick from the light. People, too, though they don't speak of it. They have ailments they cannot name. They don't sleep well; they don't dream. How can they? The world is but glow and glare."

"I can see why you didn't want to leave the flats," Gran remarked.

"I could easily have spent my whole life in Lasha," said Tenebrio emphatically. "Think of it! The great inn of the stars, the moon soft as a bee's wing, the hunched and olden-faced trees, the creatures— owls and wildcats and night birds and the sweet wolfkin bats—and the drenching, *drenching* darkness!" Her face was filled with a fierce longing. "Yes, I could have made it my home for ever. Death would not have caught me alone if I'd had my friend, my *husband*, the darkness with me!"

She closed her eyes once more and then, rubbing a hand across her brow, drank her lemonade as if parched.

"I must rest," she said.

"Of course," said Gran. "I have a feeling that you generally sleep during the day."

"You will stay on your vessel?" Tenebrio asked anxiously. "You are not going away?"

Gran assured her that they would remain close by, and in a few minutes, Tenebrio was sound asleep on Gran's bunk, her arms around her coat.

"I'm *very* far from figuring that girl out," said Gran in a low voice, once they were out on deck again.

Emmeline was scanning the grounds of the marina. After a moment, she signed: *Where's Lafcadio?*

They looked for Lafcadio until evening, never straying far from the boat, but the cat was nowhere to be found.

"Well, he's gone off on one of his explorations," said Gran irritably. She glanced inside the cabin; Tenebrio was still asleep. "Let's start dinner anyway. It's after seven. I'm sure that stupid cat will come back when he's hungry."

Twenty minutes later, Emmeline was on top of the cabin, having a final look around for Lafcadio, when she saw two strange men approaching. She jumped down, giving a rap on the cabin door, and Gran (who had been stirring the spaghetti sauce) came outside. The strangers wore cheap off-white suits that seemed somehow medical. One had a shaved head, while the other had wispy reddish-blond hair, fine as the silk on ears of corn. Each wore sunglasses and carried something like a cellphone on his belt. What was most remarkable about them was their skin, which was unnaturally pale—the colour of the raw boneless chicken you buy in supermarkets.

The men were nearing the dock when they did something very odd. A big oak tree threw some shade over the lawn, and instead of walking under the oak, they made a detour—as if they didn't want to walk through shadow.

"Good day, compassionate people," said the one with the hair. His voice was as thin and washed out as the rest of him. "If we could disturb your leisure."

He smiled a strange, effortful smile, and Gran and Emmeline

got a shock: his teeth were the same unhealthy raw tint as his skin. They almost seemed to be made of flesh. He was like one of those mummified men who have been drained of colour by being in a crypt for two thousand years.

"Yes?" said Gran suspiciously.

"We spoke with the colourful personage called Smitty," said the pale man, "and he said that you went to the place of—" he hesitated, as if he found the words hard to say—"darkness. The flats."

It wasn't so much that he had a foreign accent; he actually had *no* accent, no geographical flavour to his voice. It was a *null* voice. Gran suddenly decided that she would tell him nothing.

"It is . . . very *dark* there, no?" pursued the man. Both he and his partner were looking over *Permanent Wants*, and the bald one tilted his head slightly, obviously trying to see inside the cabin. Now that they were up close, Emmeline could see that they wore large flowers in their lapels—plastic flowers. You could tell they were plastic from five metres away.

"Perhaps you saw a friend of ours," continued the man. "A lady in black costume. We thought she might have visited the flats when you were there."

Gran looked the man straight in the eye—or rather straight in the sunglasses—and said, "Sorry, I can't help you."

Again the man's eyes moved over *Permanent Wants*. "Ah. That is unfortunate. We are looking for her because . . . well, she is not right in the mind, speaking with charity. Her thoughts are broken and shadowed. She is disordered in her precepts. Her clothes are a wailing, her brain is old smoke, and her talk is a stringy nothingness. We have been sent by her family to bring her back home."

"As I say, we didn't see her." Gran's gaze was unwavering.

The man sighed. "Well, perhaps it is better that you did not meet her. She is a sad and slanted citizen. She looks crimes at others. Her understanding is a stump. She frightens children and elderlies. We need to find her and take her back to her family. Loving attention is the only thing that can help her."

They both launched themselves into a smile. It was hideous to watch. Their thin lips parted; their mummified teeth appeared. The edges of their mouths twitched upwards. It made Emmeline think of all those horror movies about corpses being animated by a single jolt of electricity. They stood stiffly for a moment, their smiles like scar tissue.

"Excuse me, we are about to eat dinner," said Gran.

"Oh, please, we must not prevent you," replied the leader. "But, compassionate lady, one more thing I may mention. There is a reward for this person we are seeking."

Emmeline was staring at the pale men as vacantly as she could. She hoped to make them uncomfortable, but they took no notice.

"Sorry, we're not interested," said Gran.

"Not interested?" The man seemed surprised. "Well, then, perhaps there is something else, besides money, to make you happy and pump you up. Something you *treasure*—"

"For the last time," said Gran, "we can't help you. Now *goodbye*."

She said this so fiercely that the men backed away a step. With a last glance over the boat, they withdrew in the direction of the marina office. Emmeline watched them go with a look of disgust.

Just then, they heard a sound from the cabin. Tenebrio had opened the door a crack.

"Can you still see them?" she whispered.

"No, they've gone," said Gran. "Who are they?"

"Dangerous men," replied the other. "They are covered in guile."

"You're going to have to tell us more than that, Tenebrio."

The young woman sighed and opened the door a bit more. Her hair was mussed and flyaway from sleeping on it.

"They are agents of my government," she said. "I didn't think they would come to Lasha—they detest darkness. But I was sure they would come after me when daylight came."

"But why are they chasing you?"

"I am against everything they stand for." She raised her head just high enough to look across the dock. "I am afraid I have put you in danger; I have put this town in danger."

"Listen, this is ridiculous," said Gran. "I'm going to call the police right now."

Tenebrio shook her head. "Your police cannot protect me, Teo. These men will only retreat and wait for a better chance. But I do not think they will try to take me by force—not with people around. They will hold their time. For now I must remain hidden." She ran her hand through her hair. "I must think of something."

"I *have* thought of something," said Gran. "We leave by boat, right now. We'll be miles out before they know we're gone. I just have to tell Mrs. Lehmann we're leaving."

Mrs. Lehmann was the marina owner, a cheerful, sun-darkened woman with orange hair. She wore black-and-white running shoes with semi-high heels—a fashion novelty that Emmeline envied.

"I wish it were that easy," said Tenebrio, and raised her head again. "Can you see them now, Emmeline?"

Emmeline jumped up on the dock and, after scanning the marina grounds, signed to Gran.

"Emmeline says they're getting into their van," said Gran.

"I don't like this," muttered Tenebrio.

"Now's our chance," said Gran decisively. "We'll leave and settle the bill later— Wait, we won't even have to do that. Here comes Mrs. Lehmann now."

The marina owner was coming towards the boat in her sneaker-heels, clearly not in her usual good mood.

"Creepy, very creepy," she said.

"You're talking about the pale guys, of course," said Gran.

"Who else?" said Mrs. Lehmann. "That's the second time they've been here today. They left you this just now." She handed Gran a folded-up piece of paper.

Gran unfolded it and gasped. The others crowded around to read.

We have your cat.

At 9:30 p.m., we shall call the coin telephone at the back of the marina. Prepare your compassionate selves to follow our instructions.

"I'm *so* sorry," Mrs. Lehmann was saying. "They came around asking about you earlier, as I said, and Lafcadio happened to be walking by, and they said, 'Oh, is that *your* animal friend?' And I said no, it's not, and would they please just leave, but I guess they had a look at Lafcadio's collar afterwards."

Gran nodded grimly. At the start of the summer, somebody had gotten Lafcadio a joke collar that said "Chief Mousing Officer, *Permanent Wants.*"

The daylight had almost gone, and they were all sitting on the deck of the boat. The spaghetti remained uneaten on the galley stove. The white van had vanished—Emmeline had crept up to the edge of the dock to check—but they all had the feeling that the pale men were not far away.

"They were wearing these fake plastic flowers on their lapels," said Mrs. Lehmann. "Did you see that? I think there were little bulbs inside them, like Christmas lights! That is *beyond* tacky."

Tenebrio nodded. "Those flowers hide powerful lights that can be switched on in an instant. Darkness is the only thing they fear; before it, they become helpless as children."

"Well," said Gran, looking at her watch, "we've got less than ten minutes to—"

Just then, there came from the dock a voice that Gran and Emmeline recognized.

"Hi, folks!" it said. "So you're back from the flats."

Tenebrio got to her feet at once, alarmed, but Gran said: "Don't worry, that's just our local street magician. Come on board quick, Mr. Zucchini."

"Don't mind if I do," said the Great Zucchini, who wasn't used to being invited aboard people's boats. "Hey, Cap'n, that book you gave me has some real nuggets in it. I got out my old magic cabinet from—"

"Listen, Mr. Zucchini," interrupted Gran, "you may be able to help us. This is . . . a foreign visitor, Tenebrio."

"How do," said the Great Zucchini cheerfully as he stepped into the boat. "Tenebrio—that's a nice name. Sounds like an Italian soft drink."

Despite her anxiety, Tenebrio managed a smile. "It is not my real name; it is—"

"Let me guess," said the Great Zucchini. "Your *stage* name. I figured you might be in the magic line, too, just from your duds. So what brings you to—"

"Mr. Zucchini, we don't have time for this," said Gran. "Tenebrio is in danger from foreign agents."

The Great Zucchini whistled softly. "No kidding. That's got to be a first for Euphalia."

"They've kidnapped Emmeline's cat and they're holding him for ransom," put in Mrs. Lehmann breathlessly. "And Tenebrio is the ransom price. It's *despicable*."

The Great Zucchini turned to Tenebrio. "But why are they after you, kid? You a spy or something?"

Everybody looked at Tenebrio, who—despite the warm evening—was wearing her bomber jacket.

"I guess it is time I told you all," she said gravely.

She slipped off her coat and, holding it up, showed them the interior; the dark material bulged in places.

"*This* is what they are after," she said.

"Your coat?" said Mrs. Lehmann in confusion.

"No, the *darkness*," replied Tenebrio.

"Oh, the darkness," said Mrs. Lehmann, with a puzzled glance at the others. She was having a rough day.

Tenebrio slipped her arm into one sleeve, then the other. "In the secret pockets of this garment," she said, "I carry ten containers, all filled and sealed. It is enough darkness to restore the night we knew in my grandfather's time. Indeed"—she shrugged on her jacket and looked around at them—"I have enough darkness here to start another *universe*."

Everybody stared at her open-mouthed except the Great Zucchini, who chuckled.

"Kid," he said, "if your act is as good as your patter, then I'm in for some real competition."

"I'm sorry, Tenebrio," said Gran in bewilderment, "but I just don't . . . You *collected* darkness?"

Tenebrio nodded, smiling again. "At Lasha, yes. I can see in the dark, Teo."

"But for heaven's sake," objected Gran, "darkness isn't a substance. You can't collect it; you can't put it into a *container*."

"That's true of darkness today," said Tenebrio. "But this is the *old* darkness. Read the holy books of this world, the old books that speak of Creation; they all talk of the first darkness as a palpable thing."

Gran still looked bewildered, but the Great Zucchini nodded.

"That's kinda true, you know," he reflected. "In Genesis, Teo, remember? God *divided* the darkness from the light, just as he divided the earth from the heavens. It sure sounds like he was working with . . . *stuff*, like."

Again Tenebrio smiled at him. "You seem to understand these things well, Magician."

The Great Zucchini looked a bit embarrassed. "Oh, well. That was my hobby as a kid—cosmogony."

"Let me get this straight," said Gran to Tenebrio. "Your secret weapon is *darkness*? That's what you're taking back to your country?"

Tenebrio nodded. "We cannot hope to defeat the government with acts of sabotage. At most, we might be able to *disabilitate* a power plant. But with the primordial darkness . . ." She touched the interior of her coat. "In the daylight it is harmless, just a seed. It can take root only in absolute night. Any truly dark place will do—a lonely valley under a moonless midnight sky, or an underground cave, or even a root cellar. Plant the Lasha seed in such a bed, and the darkness will spread like wildfire." She shook her head. "But even such small pockets of night are fast disappearing from my country. I *must* get the Lasha darkness home before—"

Just then, from the back of the marina office, came the ring of the pay telephone. Everybody jumped.

"It's the pasty guys!" exclaimed Mrs. Lehmann.

"Listen, Teo," said Tenebrio quickly, "agree to their conditions. Tell them I will give myself up."

"Absolutely not!" said Gran.

"Please trust me," urged Tenebrio as the telephone rang again. "I know they will consent to meet us only in a well-lit place, so you must insist on the village square. With many people around, it will be safer for you. Now—quickly."

"I just hope you know what you're doing," said Gran tightly. "All right, then—you stay here, out of sight. Mr. Zucchini, you stay with her. Make sure *nobody* comes near the boat."

The Great Zucchini saluted as the others jumped onto the dock and began racing towards the phone. Gran picked up the receiver on the sixth ring.

"Is this the compassionate lady?" said a silken, washed-out voice.

"No," said Gran, panting slightly, "this is the crazy axe-wielding lady out for revenge. What have you done with our cat, you creep?"

"Your animal friend is perfectly safe."

"How do I know?"

There was a pause. Gran was holding the receiver so that Emmeline and Mrs. Lehmann could hear, and after a moment, they all caught the sound of loud purring.

"Lafcadio!" said Gran sharply.

The purring stopped, and there was a guilty-sounding meow.

"Lafcadio," said Gran, "stop fooling around and get home *now!*"

The pale voice came back on the line. "You see, your cat is safe. In fact, he is now enjoying a good dinner, which we kindly provided. I'm sure you don't want it to be the last meal of his life."

Emmeline gritted her teeth. Gran gritted her teeth. Mrs. Lehmann did the same, but she also cast a glance around for a concealed camera. The thought had struck her that maybe they were all being filmed as part of some idiotic TV show.

"Listen to me," continued the voice on the telephone. "We know you are helping the dangerous criminal who calls herself Tenebrio. She must give herself up, along with the . . . contraband she carries in her coat. We shall come to your vessel in exactly ten minutes, with the cat."

"No!" said Gran. "We make the exchange in the village. At the town square, near the Tim Hortons."

There was a pause. Gran and Emmeline waited fearfully. Then the voice continued: "Very well. But do not think that the presence of innocent Tim Horton people will stay our hand if you try a deceit. The village square in fifteen minutes. Do not be late. Once we have the criminal, we will release your cat."

There was a click. Gran looked at the receiver, her face grim, and then hung up. "We have not yet begun to fight," she said.

In a minute they were back on board *Permanent Wants*.

"Well, you got what you wanted," said Gran to Tenebrio, and she related the gist of their conversation. The young woman nodded.

"I think that was Number One you were talking to," she said. "He makes very few mistakes." She pulled on her beret. "Well, let us go."

"Listen, Tenebrio," said Gran, "this has gone far enough. I'm calling the police."

Tenebrio put up her hand. "Teo, you must let me do this my way."

"But the police can be here in a matter of—"

This time it was the Great Zucchini who spoke. "Cap'n, I don't pretend to understand what's going on here, but the kid seems to know more about it than we do. Maybe we should follow her lead."

"Well, it makes my blood boil," fumed Gran. "Who do they think they are? With their stupid plastic flowers."

"I have a feeling they might be more of a force than they look," said the Great Zucchini. "Anyway . . . um, ladies." He tipped his baseball cap and turned towards the dock.

"Wait a minute," said Gran. "Where are *you* going?"

The Great Zucchini looked at her in mild surprise.

"I'm going to do what I do every Saturday night," he said. "My magic."

He hitched up his pants, climbed laboriously onto the dock, and was off at a rapid shuffle. Gran and Emmeline stared after him.

"Thanks for rallying round, Zucchini!" called Gran hotly. She shook her head. "I knew that man wasn't a tower of strength, but really!"

"He is very devoted to his magic," said Tenebrio calmly. She picked up her coat, which had been lying across a deck chair. Gran and Emmeline exchanged glances.

"Are you going to let us in on your plan, Tenebrio?" said Gran. "Because we know you have one."

"It is a rule among us partisans," said Tenebrio, "that we share only necessary information. That way we are all safer. Just be ready to follow my lead."

"You know what I say, girl?" said Mrs. Lehmann aggressively. "I say we give those pasty guys what for. At home I've got a shotgun, a twenty-two, three flare guns, and a harpoon. What if I plant myself in front of Tim Hortons with a few concealed weapons? I know the manager, see—"

"I thank you for your offer, friend," said Tenebrio. "But you would only put our lives and your own in danger. The best thing you can do is go straight to your home and stay there."

"Now?" protested Mrs. Lehmann. "But I'll miss out on the fun!"

"I think the fun will seek you out," said Tenebrio grimly.

Night had come by the time they reached the town square, but the centre of the town was well lit. A lot of the shops were still open, and out-of-towners continued to wander through them, unable to shut off the tourist circuits in their brains. In front of the Tim Hortons, the Great Zucchini was in his summer sports coat, trying desperately to impress a trio of hard-eyed kids who were robotically licking ice cream cones. He had set up his old magic cabinet—plywood and black cardboard patched here and there with duct tape—but for the moment, he was trying to levitate a salt shaker using a concealed toothpick. The kids were as silent as a jury.

Tenebrio looked around in disgust at all the street lamps, illuminated signs, and spillover light from the store interiors. "I can see why Number One consented to meet us here," she remarked. "What do they have to fear from darkness here?"

The pale men were standing apart from the tourists, at the back of the town square. There were three of them now. The new one (who looked just like the others) held a pet carrier—one of those white plastic cases with a wire-lattice opening. Their white van was parked at the other end of the square.

Tenebrio stopped three metres away from them, looking defiant.

"So we meet again, Tenebrio," said Number One with a clammy smile.

His assistant set down the pet carrier, and from the interior came an audible meow. Emmeline's face showed her relief. She took a step forward, and the pale men tensed, their hands going to their lapel flowers.

"Give the child her cat," said Tenebrio sternly.

"Certainly," said Number One. "But first—your coat."

Without a word, Tenebrio slipped off her coat. Number One took it gingerly, holding it at arm's length. Again his companions brought their hands to their lapel flowers, their faces taut.

"Hmm," said Number One, hefting the coat. "Heavy. You have been busy, Tenebrio." He touched a bulge in the interior lining, and the other two men stood perfectly still, faces averted—as if afraid of a blow.

"We will dispose of this later," said Number One, handing the coat to the man beside him. The latter took it in both hands and set off towards the van, holding the garment as if it housed a colony of sleeping bees.

"But perhaps you have kept some for yourself?" said Number One to Tenebrio. "Open your hands."

Tenebrio did so, palms out. Her expression didn't change.

"Put them on top of your head," said Number One. He stepped forward with the other man so they stood on either side of her. At the van, the other agent slammed the back door on Tenebrio's coat. In the silence that followed, they all heard the Great Zucchini's irritated voice from across the street: "It's the humidity, I'm telling you. Houdini himself wouldn't have been able to levitate a salt shaker in this weather. Okay, moving on . . ."

"The cat," said Tenebrio, looking straight at Number One.

Number One smiled his petrified smile. "You may take your cat, child."

"*I'll* take him," said Gran, putting a hand on Emmeline's shoulder. The pale men watched her warily as she scooped up the pet carrier.

"We wish that you will leave now, compassionate lady," said Number One, keeping his eyes on Tenebrio.

"Not yet," said Gran tightly, handing the pet carrier to Emmeline. Tenebrio turned slightly, her hands still on her head, and gave Gran a warning glance down the length of her elbow. Gran ignored her.

"I don't think I've seen another white van in this town," said Gran. "You'll be absurdly easy to catch. And believe me, we *will* catch you."

Number One just smiled. "You do not know us, compassionate lady. You do not know where we come from."

"What's that got to do with it?" said Gran, suddenly uneasy.

From the other end of the square came the Great Zucchini's voice: "You want a real trick, eh, you brats? I'll give you a real trick."

"Where *do* you come from?" pressed Gran.

Emmeline's attention was divided between Gran and the Great Zucchini. What was he doing? The girl watched him rip off a length of duct tape that lined the door of his cabinet. Then, his hand on the latch, he said in a great voice, "For my last trick, I summon the power of . . . *darkness!*"

And he flung open the door.

The blackout that hit the counties of Lanark, Frontenac, Leeds, and Grenville on that night was (the authorities agreed) one of the strangest on record. All through the Rideau Corridor, it caused panic and chaos—and wonder. In the town of Burritts Rapids, Mrs. Mylene Gaffney, the retired town librarian, was driving home from her quilting guild meeting when suddenly the entire street went dark. Her car jumped the curb and crashed into the storefront yard of Dreskin's Lawn and Garden Store, ploughing through birdhouses and plastic flamingoes and flowerbed windmills. She managed to get out of her car and then run five blocks to her own house, where she found her Pekinese dog, Fausto, barking hysterically. "I figured it was either a terrorist attack or the end of the world," she was later quoted as saying, "because Fausto doesn't get excited easily." Forty kilometres to the northwest, in Perth, Oren Wehl and his wife, Pipilotti, were watching David Attenborough's *Life of Mammals* on their big-screen TV when a "tsunami of darkness" (Mr. Wehl's words) swept through the house. Strangely, their TV did not go off. It flickered and dimmed to the point where David Attenborough became "faint as cigarette smoke," but they still heard him explaining clearly the remarkable family life of the Pygmy shrew. Sixty kilometres southwest, in the late innings of a softball game, the local home-run king, Manny "Cruise Missile" Cruz, had just connected with a pitch when the darkness obliterated the scoreboard, the surrounding town, and even the lighted telecommunications tower fifteen kilometres away. Everybody stood still in awe. Several spectators later reported that for a second or two, they were able to follow the path of the batted softball, as it arced like a dark meteorite against the backdrop of stars.

In all these incidents, remarkably, no injuries were reported. Even the local hospitals managed to cope.

But everybody in the Euphalia town square knew that this was no ordinary blackout. Astonishingly, the power had *not gone off*— some of the streetlights still hummed faintly—but all illumination was completely overwhelmed by the darkness. The huge neon sign on Smitty's Garage was reduced to a bit of pale acne on the night's complexion. People gasped and cried out. The pale men seemed more rattled than anybody: they made choking sounds and could be heard scrabbling for their flower lights. But when they turned them on, they were just pinpoints of light, faint as distant stars. You couldn't even see the pinpoints if you looked straight at them; you had to use the corner of your eye.

Gran and Emmeline were as startled as everybody else, but they heard Tenebrio's voice near them. "Quick, friends," she said. "Put your hand out, both of you. On my shoulder—there. I will lead you." In a few seconds, Gran and Emmeline were guided away from the chaos of the square.

"What on earth?" whispered Gran. She and Emmeline had to move at a rapid walk to keep up with Tenebrio.

"Do not be afraid," came Tenebrio's voice. "It was the magician. He seeded the darkness."

"He *what*?"

In the starlight they could faintly see the glimmer of stopped cars, some with engines still running. The bewildered drivers were outside, peering at their headlights; they couldn't understand why the lights weren't working when their engines were.

"I *knew* he could do it," said Tenebrio. Noticing that Emmeline was struggling to keep up, she reached over to take the pet carrier from her. "From the beginning I thought he understood me, understood my mission. So when you left to take the call from Number One, I told him that I had indeed a weapon beyond imagining—the Lasha darkness. But as a mere seed, it was unusable; I needed a well of absolute night in which to plant it. He thought about it for a moment, and then—he got very excited, and his face got very red—he offered his magic cabinet. It wasn't very big, he said, but he could make it completely dark with . . . I believe it was duck tape."

"That's crazy!" said Gran. "That's completely—The Great Zucchini did *that*?"

"So I gave him a tiny bit of darkness," continued Tenebrio, "smaller than a . . . I don't know how to say it in your language. *Very* small. I thought he would be sure to lose it, but he had a clever idea. He got out some chewing gum and chewed it with great rapidity, then put the bit of darkness in the gum, and finally wrapped it all up in paper. He said that a magician must always be ready with such devices."

They had reached the marina now. Starlight swam in the water like flecks of saffron in dark Middle Eastern tea. Once they were safely beside *Permanent Wants*, Tenebrio put the pet carrier down and undid the latch. Lafcadio slipped out; they couldn't see him, but they felt him curling around their legs.

"Farewell, good magician," said Tenebrio. From the tone of her voice, they could tell that she was facing away from them, towards the town centre. "You are a true patriot of the night." Then she turned back. "Teo, earlier you offered your boat to escape. I think now I must accept your offer."

"But I can't see a thing!" exclaimed Gran.

"I can. We will go slow; I shall guide you." They heard her jump lightly into the boat. "The magician had only a small space to seed the darkness, so the night he made is only a hint of what it could have been. But it is enough. Number One and the others will be helpless until morning."

"But your coat," said Gran. "They've got your coat, with your containers, and your—" Even after what had happened, she couldn't bring herself to say it: *your darkness.*

Tenebrio laughed. "No, they don't have my containers. They have your lemonade bottles." They heard her opening the cabin door and knew from the echoing sound of her voice that she had slipped inside. "I also did that when you were talking on the phone—switched the darkness for the lemonade. I hope you don't mind, Teo. I guessed they would not open up my coat to check, such is their fear of the Lasha darkness. I put my containers right here in a little space under . . ." Her voice got even smaller. "Yes, all safe. Now, let me help you into your boat."

After that night, as you might imagine, the Great Zucchini's reputation went way up. Several people in the Euphalia town square had heard what he said just before the darkness descended. The police scoffed at the idea that the Zuke (as they called him) could have had anything to do with creating the blackout, but still, word got around. Now he has part of Smitty's Garage as an office. He gets asked to perform at various events, like the agricultural fair and the Christmas Kiwanis party. And he has influence, too: he's even managed to get the town council to take down a lot of the "infernal" lighting in the village. But when I met him, he was standing, as always, in front of the Tim Hortons, trying to pull an egg out of an empty hat.

I had to find him, you see. When I first got this story from Emmeline and Gran, I didn't know what to think. Emmeline herself still didn't quite believe the story, even though she had *lived* through it. I decided I had to get it all again from the man at the centre of things.

At first he didn't want to admit anything. "The night has its own secrets," he observed, rather grandly. But when I pressed him, he admitted that it was all true—and no, he *couldn't* add anything more to the story.

"But what about this Tenebrio?" I continued. "Did you ever see her again?"

He shook his head. "She asked Cap'n Teo to drop her off on the shore at dawn, and she disappeared. The pale guys, too, eventually. But I tell you, for a while there they were in a sorry state. Looked like death warmed over. Although I guess they *always* looked like that. Anyway, I like to think that Tenebrio gave 'em the slip and made it home—with her darkness."

"And where *was* her home?"

I was very curious about this. *You do not know where we are from,* Number One had said to Gran. It had sounded like both a boast and a threat.

"Mr. Zucchini?" I prompted. "Where was Tenebrio from?"

"Can't say, really," replied the man, avoiding my eye. "Hey, do you know the Torn Ten-Dollar Bill That Repairs Itself? This stupid egg isn't co-operating."

But I think now that he could indeed have added something more to the story. When I asked him about Tenebrio, I'm sure I saw his eyes flicker upwards, to the sky.

Sixth Tale

The Witches of Timberquinn

Timberquinn is as old as any of the villages along the Rideau Waterway, and pretty in a faded way. It has a grocery store, a diner, a home furnishings store, a "dairy emporium," and two-hour complimentary parking on Main Street. It has a dentist and a doctor who between them have almost sixty years of practice. It has a detailed town map mounted on the wall of the old town hall, which carries the notice "Please Note: This Map Is Only an Artist's Impression." It has never won the Communities in Bloom Award or been described as "a unique shopping experience," but that's okay with the townspeople. They've only recently begun to welcome visitors.

The fact is, people used to stay away from Timberquinn. There was something missing from the town, something as vital as sunshine or love or laughter. Sure, it *seemed* normal enough—at first glance. If you'd dropped in there any Sunday morning, you would have seen all the usual sights of a Rideau Valley town. At the old swing bridge, kids would have been jumping and diving into the clear water beside the sign that said "No Jumping or Diving from

Bridge." Outside McMillan's Dairy Emporium, people would have been solemnly eating fresh cheese curd; if you went close, you would have heard them making tiny squeaking sounds. You would have heard the murmur of prayer from the United Church, or the occasional clack of a ball at the lawn bowling club, or a dozen other peaceful summer sounds. And yet, after half an hour in the place, you would have felt a greyness, an emptiness stealing into your soul.

Not long ago, a reporter from a Toronto paper dropped in to talk to the citizens. He was curious to find out what the town thought about the waterway being named a United Nations World Heritage Site. And everybody he talked to liked the idea. "It's great to be recognized," said an old man listlessly. "It's what we've been waiting for," said a lady tiredly. "Respect at last," said the chip-wagon man hopelessly. And all of them asked the reporter, "Are you staying long?" in a way that meant "Are you leaving soon?"

One conversation stood out in the reporter's mind. He was at the dairy emporium, talking to the owner, a grey-haired man with a drooping moustache. The radio, tuned to the CBC, was playing behind the counter. "Hello," drawled the voice on the radio. "I'm Stuart McLean, and this is *The Vinyl Cafe*." When the shopkeeper heard this, his eyes registered a look of fear. He bolted behind the counter and switched the radio off just as it had begun to play the old-timey guitar theme that kicks off every show.

"Don't you like *The Vinyl Cafe*?" asked the reporter in surprise.

"Oh, of course," said the owner nervously. "Dave and Morley—they're like old friends. It's just that"—and he glanced around furtively—"I don't like the music."

Yes, there was something not quite right about Timberquinn. And it would have remained that way if Gran and Emmeline hadn't shown up there one August day, in the company of the man known as Johnny Rover.

Waterways sometimes have hitch-hikers, just as highways do, and Johnny Rover was the Rideau's. Every June, guitar in hand, he would leave his job as a high school guidance counsellor in Kingston and travel up and down the waterway. He could sing lamentations and funny songs; he could tell ghost stories; he could make jokes in several accents. His singing and guitar-playing had actually made dogs howl, but that was part of his appeal. "Music is the ground-water of the universe," he would say. "It flows like this river. I'm not a musician; I'm just a spout where the waters come together and burst up and everybody goes, 'Take a picture, quick!'" He liked to sing about new-rigged ships, tramp steamers, Barrett's Privateers, Bonnie Prince Charlie, the Rights of Man, the mist-covered mountains of home, and setting off for Dublin with a stout quarter-staff in hand to banish ghost and goblin.

Gran and Emmeline met him at Chaffeys lockstation. He invited them to sit down at his picnic table and share some of his strawberries, which they did. He was a short, stocky man with clip-on sunglasses (the kind you could flip up) and a reddish-blond Abraham Lincoln beard. His face was like the worn spruce top of an old guitar, grainy and lined but sun-kindled. His Hawaiian shirt filled the landscape with strange and exotic tints. When he heard that they were a floating secondhand bookstore, he was delighted.

"Just what the Rideau needs," he said. "Hey, do you have any songbooks?"

"One," said Gran. "*Songs of Two Rivers*."

Johnny Rover flipped up his sunglasses. "No kidding! Rory McPhail's *Songs of Two Rivers*? That's a classic."

"Well, come and have a look at it," said Gran. "We're moored right over there."

"I will," he promised. "But now . . ." He picked up his guitar. "My public awaits."

They didn't really see the awaiting public he referred to, but a few minutes later, back on *Permanent Wants*, they heard the jangling of his guitar and his scratchy voice.

"Now I know why they call him Bob Dylan without the vocal range," commented Gran.

Em wasn't sure who Bob Dylan was, but she smiled anyway. It didn't matter if Johnny wasn't the greatest musician; if he loved music, he was okay by her. Music was something she didn't need words for. Words were clumsy, hairy creatures; they grunted and waddled. But music—that was a flock of brilliant birds that flew straight to her and ate out of her hand. And the music in *Songs of Two Rivers* was wonderful; she had been dipping into it for weeks, trying the fiddle pieces. (If you play the violin, you will know that a fiddle is just another name for the instrument.) Her favourite piece was "The Roaring Boy," about an orphan with "hair of tow and wildshore eyes," who slept under the stars and ate what he stole, a boy "all lynx and barefoot lightning" (as the lyrics said). And that's what the tune was like—lynx and lightning chasing each other over twelve measures.

It wasn't long before Johnny Rover was sitting in the galley of *Permanent Wants*, poring over *Songs of Two Rivers*. The two rivers, it turned out, were the Ottawa and the Rideau—Johnny's favourites.

"What a treasure chest," he said, turning the pages. "Look at this: 'Adieu to Tommy Drew,' 'Shanty Days,' 'The Roaring Boy.' And gosh, here's 'The Witches of Timberquinn.' Haven't played that in years." He looked thoughtful.

"Timberquinn," said Gran. "Isn't that right around here?"

"Just up the river a bit," said Johnny. He rubbed his rusty-blond beard. "It's funny you should come across one of the old songs about the place. There's no songs coming from the town now, that's for sure."

"Why not?" asked Gran.

"Nobody really knows," said Johnny. "The townspeople won't say a word on the subject. But I can tell you that you'll never hear any concerts in Timberquinn—or hymns, or guitar-playing on the porches, or even whistling. It's as though they've *banished* music."

"Why would they do that?"

Johnny shrugged. "It's one of the great mysteries of the Rideau. I call it tragic, because the place used to be a fine musical town. For a hundred and fifty years, they turned out ballads like cheeses."

"How old is *this* song?" asked Gran, peering over his shoulder.

"One of the oldest, I would say." He read from the introduction: "'This ballad dates from the building of the Rideau Canal and tells of an Irish witch triumphing over a witch of the Protestant variety.'" He looked up at them, chuckling. "Those witches sure liked to mix it up back then. You know, I think the last time I played this song was right in Timberquinn itself—at the folk festival there. That must have been twenty-five years ago. The next year, they stopped having the festival."

Emmeline marvelled at his flow of words—but then, she marvelled at *anybody's* flow of words. Where did they all come from? What a strange thing: puffs of air that meant things. She could not keep them in her mind no matter how hard she tried. But she had noticed that if the people speaking really *felt* the words, the pictures created in her mind could be very rich . . . almost holograms (if you know what they are).

"But there must be a reason for it all," said Gran.

Emmeline signed to her: *Let's go there.*

"Yes, we should," said Gran. "What do you say, Johnny?"

Johnny suddenly looked awkward. "Oh, I don't know. It's not really my kind of town now, without any music."

"But you of all people must be burning to solve the mystery," said Gran. "Aren't you the musical spirit of the Rideau?"

Johnny coughed. "Well, the thing is . . . I played there that one year at the festival, and the next year they stopped having it. Sometimes I think they associate *me* with the drought or the curse, or whatever it is."

"Nonsense," said Gran. "This town needs musical healing, Johnny, and you're the man to do it."

Johnny shifted uncomfortably. Maybe, for the first time in his life, he was wondering if his music *was* healing.

It took them barely half an hour to see all of Timberquinn. They strolled through the little park and read all the plaques on the four benches, which told them who had donated each bench. They looked at gently used clothes, gently used books, and gently used wooden duck decoys. They read the city hall tribute that celebrated the fallen labourers, known as navvies, who had built the Rideau Canal. Afterwards, they sat on the front patio at the local cafe, wondering just what was up with this town.

"Feel like you're on vacation among the living dead?" asked Johnny Rover cheerfully. "That's Timberquinn." He was dressed in a flat cap, sunglasses, and a faded Mariposa Folk Festival T-shirt.

Gran and Emmeline, who both felt drained, didn't bother to respond.

Johnny pushed his coffee cup away. "I say we go back to your boat and you can give me a ride downriver. I told you this was a lost cause."

Emmeline, who had finished her Coke, signed to Gran that she was going over to the park again.

"Okay, sweetie," said Gran, and turned back to the folk singer. "Why are you *disguised*, Johnny?"

"I'm not disguised," protested Johnny. "It's the sun. I'm fair-skinned, you know. Just like—"

"I know. Bonnie Prince Charlie."

Emmeline had already slipped away, knapsack in hand. Inside it was a water bottle, the book *Songs of Two Rivers*, and something she had put in when the others weren't looking—her violin. (Being three-quarter size, it was just small enough to fit inside her knapsack.) She was determined to find out what was going on in this town.

Reaching the park, she chose a large oak tree and sat down on a bench that had been donated by "Theatre Night in Timberquinn." A few townspeople were strolling past the shop windows, but nobody paid her any attention. The whole park seemed to be drowsing in a bed of cut grass and summer dreams. A gentle breeze came in from the river, and the trees swayed and rippled like underwater things, like sea kelp or the sails of sunken ships. The place was quiet enough to practise telepathy. But as Emmeline took out her violin, she felt a slight chill; it almost seemed as if the park had come awake. She hesitated, watching the shifting patterns of sunlight around her. Some sparrows hopped through the grass, their heads moving in quick mechanical jerks, as if they had been filmed and badly edited. She didn't feel the chill again, but she definitely felt an alertness, a watchfulness, around her. Bow in hand, she brought the violin to her shoulder. The sparrows suddenly flew away and she watched them go, wondering, What *was* it about this place? But after a moment the soft silence returned, and she launched into "The Roaring Boy," the rollicking tune from *Songs of Two Rivers*.

And at once she stopped, wincing. Her violin was making an awful off-key sound.

She drew it away from her shoulder, puzzled, and squinted down the strings. Everything looked okay. She tightened her bow and tried again. But again the strings went *skreck* and *squee,* like chalk on a blackboard. What on earth was wrong?

Looking up, she saw that she was attracting attention. A mother with a baby carriage was staring at her with a mixture of fear and disapproval. Another woman in a sweatshirt was shading her eyes, trying to find the source of the noise. A heavy man in overalls had stopped as he was getting out of his pickup, his hand on the open door. From his look, he might have caught Emmeline breaking into his house.

She tried her violin once more—with exactly the same result. It was too much for the man in overalls: he left his truck and lumbered across the park.

"Here!" he said roughly. "What do you think you're doin'?"

Emmeline stood up, alarmed. Behind him came the woman in the sweatshirt; the mother had picked up her crying baby and was trying to comfort the infant.

"You know you ain't supposed to do that here," said the man in overalls.

Emmeline held her violin and bow away, thinking he would try to take it from her. The woman in the sweatshirt now reached them, breathing hard, and the man in overalls turned to her.

"She's got some kinda violin thing," he said, "and she's *playin'* it."

"Well, she's obviously not from here, Clem," said the woman in the sweatshirt, who looked a bit more sympathetic than the man. "What's your name, dear?"

Emmeline could only shake her head. She couldn't understand what was happening with her violin; it seemed possessed. Once again she raised it to her shoulder. Both the man and the woman said, "No!"

"That does it," said the man, holding out his hand. "Let's have it."

Emmeline shook her head again, looking fierce. Nobody was going to take her violin away.

"She's an outsider, Clem," said the woman in the sweatshirt. "She doesn't know."

Emmeline, wondering if she should just bolt, looked across the street to the cafe. To her relief, she saw Gran and Johnny Rover approaching.

"Emmeline?" said Gran breathlessly as she came up. "Are you all right?"

Emmeline made the sign for *problem*, or *trouble*, and pointed to her violin.

"Oh, she's deaf," said the woman in the sweatshirt. "We didn't know—"

"No, she's *not* deaf," said Gran. "What's the problem with your violin?"

"It's not her violin," said the woman in the sweatshirt. "It's . . . the *town*."

"Hettie," said Clem warningly, but the woman named Hettie waved her hand dismissively.

"I think these folks have a right to know," said Hettie. "They look trustworthy."

"No, they don't," said Clem, staring hard at Johnny Rover, who (uncharacteristically) had said nothing so far.

"Why don't you all come to my house," said Hettie, addressing Gran and the others, "and I'll explain. Not you, Clem."

Clem glowered. "Hettie, you start talking about it and we're going to have all sorts of kooks comin' here."

"Kooks!" said Gran. "What do you mean, kooks?"

"I mean, *kooks*," said Clem. "Psychics and ghost-busters and . . . *psychologists*." Again he eyed Johnny Rover in his flat cap, sunglasses, and Mariposa Folk Festival T-shirt, which had a picture of a smiling sunflower playing a ukulele. "Is that what you are, bud?" he said suspiciously. "A psychologist?"

Johnny Rover smiled wanly. "No, no, friend. I'm just a folk singer."

Clem shivered and took a step back, studying Johnny with narrowed eyes.

"You aren't the guy from *On the Road Again*, are you?" he asked fearfully.

"Come with me, folks," said Hettie briskly. "My place is just over there, near the church." She shooed them across the lawn, and Clem was left under the tree, grumbling loudly.

"You'll have to excuse Clem," she said once they were out of earshot. "He gets only one channel on his TV set, and his brain has shrunk to nothing. He's like everybody else here—he wants to hush it all up. But I say it's time we talked. After twenty-five years, it's *time*."

They accompanied Hettie across the park, down a little side street, and around the town church. Just past the church was a little frame house with hanging flowerpots on the porch. Hettie gestured them inside, telling them not to bother about their shoes, and then led them to the bright, airy kitchen at the back.

"So you're a folk singer, are you?" she said to Johnny, putting on the kettle.

For a second Johnny hesitated; clearly, his profession was out of favour in this town. But his pride won out.

"That's what I am," he said stoutly. "Johnny Rover, they call me. Roving the Rideau all summer long."

"Johnny Rover," mused Hettie. "I *thought* I knew you from somewhere. You were here at the last music festival we had, twenty-five years ago."

"So what happened?" said Gran curiously. "Why did you stop your festivals?"

Hettie shook her head. "I wish I could tell you. Something changed that summer, but we don't know what. All we know is that ever since then, nobody has been able to play music here. It always comes out all screechy and scratchy." She nodded to Emmeline. "I'm sure you can play real well, dear—when you're not in Timberquinn. This town *kills* music."

"I've never heard of anything like that," said Gran. "Have you had it investigated?"

Hettie shrugged. "Of course. We had the municipal engineer in and a psychologist and even a guy from the Psychic Research Society in Toronto. They had different explanations, some of them pretty wonky. Electromagnetic disturbances, bad auras—you name it. But none of them could tell us how to *fix* the problem, and after a while, the townspeople just got rid of their guitars and their pianos and even their record players. I hung up my own fiddle—you can see it on the wall there—and haven't touched it since. A whole generation has grown up without music. It's sad."

"Sad!" said Johnny Rover, suddenly passionate. "I'll say it's sad. It's a *travesty*."

Hettie eyed him for a moment. "Yes, I remember you, Johnny Rover," she said, in a voice that wasn't exactly admiring. "I was only fifteen that summer, but I remember thinking that I'd never heard anybody play and sing like *that*."

There was an awkward silence. Johnny's musical abilities were the stuff of legend.

"It almost sounds," remarked Gran, "as if your town is cursed, Hettie."

At this, Hettie became very still. "There it is. We don't like to say it—we don't want to be *backward*—but that's what it is: a curse."

"Sure it's a curse," said Johnny Rover enthusiastically. "This happens all the time in folk songs. We just have to go back into the history of this town and find out who cursed it. Has there been any strife here?"

"Are you kidding?" said Hettie. "It's been strife since day one. You just have to listen to the old songs from around here. Catholics fighting with Protestants, the Irish with the English . . ."

"And witches with witches," put in Gran.

Hettie smiled. "You're talking about 'The Witches of Timber-quinn.' That's a barn burner."

Emmeline had already dived into her knapsack and drawn out *Songs from Two Rivers*, which she opened to "The Witches of Timberquinn."

"Everyone knows this one," said Hettie, taking the book. "Or used to."

"I've got a funny feeling about that song," said Johnny pensively, "and I've had it for twenty-five years. What's the story again, Hettie?"

"Well, it's supposed to be about two local women," said Hettie, turning. "One was the infamous Amenia Hughling. She wasn't a witch with spells and so on; she was just very . . . insensitive."

"How so?" said Gran.

"Well, she was the wife of one of the officers under Colonel By, the man who built the waterway. A bobcat in a bonnet, they called her. Not bad looking, by all accounts—light ginger hair and fierce blue eyes—but a real flamer. She never liked people to have a good time, and she outlawed music and dancing. But the Irish families who worked on the canal *loved* music and dancing. So there was some friction."

"Curses," said Johnny with relish.

"Lots of them," affirmed Hettie. "And it all came to a head one summer day when the Irish labourers held a wedding celebration. People were playing lots of music and dancing their heads off. And right into the middle of it comes Amenia—with a few beefy soldiers from her husband's regiment. She tells the revellers to stop because she can't get any sleep, and they tell her to get lost. I guess she flew into a rage and ordered the soldiers to start breaking fiddles and pipes. *Big* mistake."

Once again, as she had in the park, Emmeline felt a sudden chill in the air. Looking through the window, she saw that the wind had risen and clouds were flowing across the sky. Though the sun was still bright, she had the strange feeling that a storm was coming.

"What Amenia didn't know," continued Hettie, "was that one of the wedding party really *was* a witch. Or at least, a girl with Irish fairy blood. Nessa, she was called. White Nessa because of her silver-blonde hair. A wonderful harpist, they say. She was filled with righteous anger at Amenia, and . . . well, it's in the song here."

And she read from the lyrics:

"You are air, you are melody,
Let your blood and flesh be song."
Thus Nessa spake to the raging one
And Amenia the witch was gone.

Nessa took up her harp
And the fiddlers played along
And young and old were dancing
To fashion the cage of song.

"'To fashion the cage of song'?" said Gran. "What does that mean?"

"That is priceless!" exclaimed Johnny. "Nessa changed Amenia into *music*!"

Hettie nodded. "Into *this* music."

"So there's a witch imprisoned right here," chuckled Johnny, pointing to the notes on the page. "I told you this was a treasure chest, Teo!"

Emmeline was wonderstruck. A woman changed into *music*? She tried to imagine a woman as "air and melody"—as notes and the spaces between notes, as harmonies and silences, as the little *plink-plink* tones (pizzicati, they are called) that she made when she plucked the violin strings instead of bowing them. She *had* to tell her violin teacher, Mrs. Benjamin, all about this.

"But what does this last verse mean?" asked Gran, and read it out loud:

> *Said Nessa, "I have made this music*
> *Out of my craft and art.*
> *Be true to its weft and weave*
> *Be true its iron heart."*

"I used to wonder that myself," said Hettie. "Then I asked old Mrs. Melusine—she used to be the choir director here, back when we had a choir, and knows all the old songs. She believes that Nessa was telling people not to *change* things. 'Be true to its weft and weave'—be true to the melody and rhythm. Nessa wanted people to always play the tune as *she* played it."

Johnny waved a hand. "But you know what, Hettie? Folk songs *don't* stay the same. People change them as they play. I do that myself. I simplify things, or I change the rhythm, or—"

Suddenly he stopped, as if something had just come into his mind. Hettie was watching him intently. The room became so silent that they could hear the ticking of the wall clock. Then, outside, the wind rose again. They heard a faint mournful sighing—the telephone wires? the clothesline?—and the house creaked ominously around them.

Before they left Timberquinn that afternoon, Hettie took them to the empty lot beside the churchyard, where (legend had it) the whole episode had taken place. They stood there in the shade of the waving oak trees, all of them occupied with their own thoughts. Gran, as always, thought that there had to be some natural explanation. Emmeline remembered the chill she had felt inside Hettie's bright kitchen. As for Johnny, it was hard to know *what* he was thinking; he hadn't said a word.

"I think we should be scientific about this," said Gran finally. "Starting tomorrow. I want to know how far this effect extends. A mile out of town? Two miles? We'll tackle it in the morning."

"No," said Johnny Rover heavily.

The others turned to him.

"What do you mean, no?" said Gran.

"I mean there's no point," said Johnny. "Hettie's right." He shook his head. "All these years I've felt in my bones that something went wrong at that festival. And I can remember exactly when I got that feeling—the afternoon of the last day. When I played 'The Witches of Timberquinn.'"

Hettie nodded to herself, but Gran looked exasperated.

"Johnny," she said, "you can't really believe that you set loose a hundred-and-fifty-year-old spirit just because you mangled an old song?"

"You don't know folk music, Teo," said Johnny earnestly. "That's *normal*." His normally cheerful face was slack and anxious. "It makes sense, doesn't it? Nessa told everybody not to fool around with the melody. Why? Because the melody was a *cage* of notes. If you changed things too much, you'd weaken the cage." He shook his head. "Amenia has been taking her revenge on the town for the last twenty-five years. She must be in some weird form of sound waves now."

"But why would she would take revenge on the townspeople of today?" Gran asked. "They never did anything to her."

"I think," said Hettie, "you'll find the answer in the local phone book." She gave a half smile at their bewildered looks. "Lots of Irish names. I bet most of the town is descended from the people at that wedding."

"Are there any descendants of Amenia's around?" asked Johnny.

"None that we know of. She had no children with Corporal Hughling; that's a matter of record." Hettie was silent a moment, looking out at the empty lot. "But rumour had it that years before her marriage, as a teenager, she had to give up a baby boy for adoption. I think Amenia had a harder life than most people know. But come with me. I want to show you something."

She led them across the empty lot to the back of the church, where they followed her down a sunken stair to an unlocked door. Hettie pushed it open, nudging aside a carton with her foot. A musty smell met their nostrils. Hettie switched on the bare bulb overhead, and they all stood still. The room was chock-full of musical instruments—guitars with stained and streaked tops; fiddles of various sizes; a ukulele that must have once been a brilliant blue but had faded to a dull lilac; a piano draped in an old blanket. The carton that Hettie had nudged aside held half a dozen tambourines. In the shadows, Emmeline could see even more instruments, carelessly piled like old garden tools. They were as shadowed and sunken and forgotten as instruments on the *Titanic*.

"Here they sleep," said Hettie. "It was our choir director who collected them—old Mrs. Melusine. I think she believes that one day there will be a kind of resurrection. The townspeople will take up their guitars and violins and spoons, and there will be music again in the town. One day."

Emmeline was thinking that it would take a lot to wake up these guitars and fiddles and spoons. Any musician will tell you that when an instrument is not played for a long time, it stops being an instrument and becomes just wood and strings and glue. It returns to its elements, like a long-dead tree. All the instruments in the room were like that. They slept the decaying sleep of last year's leaves.

Johnny Rover sighed heavily; he probably felt that this was his doing.

"Listen," he said, "all this happened because of a dispute in the nineteenth century. It seems so crazy. Couldn't we just gather the townspeople in the churchyard and . . . well, have a kind of ceremony?"

"You mean an *exorcism*?" asked Hettie.

"No, no. I mean a ceremony of reconciliation. You can all say that you're sorry about what happened to Amenia, then ask her to forgive you. And *me*."

"I guess it's worth a try," said Gran doubtfully. "But I still say—"

"I know, I know," interrupted Johnny. "You think there's a natural explanation. But maybe ghosts *are* natural, Teo."

"Well, let's sound out Reverend Pat on it," said Hettie. "He'd try anything to shake off the curse. He used to play in a punk rock band—that's his electric guitar over there—and I'm sure he'd love to take it up again."

They turned to go—all except Emmeline, who glanced back at Gran with her hand up, five fingers outspread. *Just five minutes.* Gran nodded.

"Can Em and I look around for a bit?" she said to Hettie.

"Sure," said Hettie. "Johnny and I will be at the front, in the church office. But remember—"

"I know. Don't play anything," said Gran. "But do you think your vengeful spirit is down here, too?"

"She's *everywhere*," said Hettie.

With the others gone, the room breathed out a dusty, airless, left-behind smell.

"That part I'm starting to believe," said Gran with a cough.

Emmeline was moving around the room, touching the instruments, blowing the dust from them. Strangely, in this dead and empty place, she was hearing a lively fiddle tune inside her head—"The Roaring Boy." She felt the skylarking energy, the sixteenth notes tumbling over one another like his racing heart (he never stopped running, that boy). *Fol-de-diddle-oh, fol-de-day-oh* . . . That's what the boy sang. Not even her dad would sing something that old-fashioned now, but it felt right for the song. A longing came over her to get out her violin and play the song right here and *wake everybody up*. Surely Amenia would not be listening here, underground? Emmeline had set down her knapsack and was reaching for her violin when a voice sounded behind them.

"I thought I heard somebody down here," it said.

Emmeline and Gran turned. Before them was a bent white-haired woman.

"I'm Mrs. Melusine," she said, smiling.

Outside, the wind rose, and the windowpanes in the church basement rattled uneasily. Emmeline couldn't see any trees from where she sat, but their mournful sighing came through even there.

"You hear it, don't you?" said Mrs. Melusine. "Amenia was not a happy woman. But that's folk music: behind one sad story, you'll find another."

The three of them—Gran, Emmeline, and Mrs. Melusine—sat sipping tea in the church basement. Mrs. Melusine was a tiny woman with hair in a bun and small, veined hands. But you could tell from her clear, fine-grained voice that she had once been a singer, and her eyes were young—spring-fed eyes, Sea of Cortez eyes.

"Is it true what Hettie said?" asked Gran. "That Amenia had to give up a baby boy for adoption?"

Mrs. Melusine nodded. "It was the times, you see. She wasn't married, and back then it was shameful to raise a baby without a husband."

"Do we know what happened to the boy?" said Gran.

Mrs. Melusine shook her head. "We just know that Amenia searched for her son all her life. No wonder she could be a wildcat sometimes. Behind the witch's rage was a mother's heartbreak."

"Well, they're hoping to have some kind of reconciliation ceremony," said Gran, and explained Johnny's plan. Mrs. Melusine looked doubtful.

"If you ask me," she said, "a spirit that comes out of music must return to music. If we had a powerful minstrel in this town, somebody with the *know*, maybe he could get the spirit back into the song. But we don't have any real minstrels anymore."

"No, we just have Johnny," said Gran. "But maybe if we gave him all the—"

Suddenly she stopped. Emmeline was humming a tune very quietly—so quietly that even a spirit would have had to be very close to hear it. Gran moved closer. She was sure she had heard the tune before.

"Shh, child," said Mrs. Melusine, looking around uneasily.

Emmeline was looking at Gran, her eyes alight. Now she knew why "The Roaring Boy" had been in her head ever since she came to Timberquinn. A motherless boy who haunted the countryside, a boy like a wildcat, with "hair of tow and wildshore eyes." She remembered Hettie's description of Amenia: a "flamer" with light

ginger hair and fierce blue eyes. She didn't know the story behind
the song; she didn't know who the real Roaring Boy was. But she
had the strongest feeling—the strongest *musical* feeling—that he
was Amenia's lost son.

Reverend Pat was all for having the reconciliation ceremony the
very next day (he really missed his punk rock years) and was quite
sure he could round up enough townspeople to take part. People
were desperate for the end of the musical drought, he said. And
so, the following morning, Gran, Johnny, and Emmeline showed
up at the churchyard—Johnny with his guitar, Emmeline with her
violin, and Gran with a tambourine. Reverend Pat was at the head
of a small group of townspeople, along with the former members of his punk rock band—Lou, the dentist, and Wally, the town
pharmacist. The punk rockers had got out their old electric guitars
from the church storage room and stood holding them awkwardly,
like shy teenagers waiting their turn at a talent show. Touchingly,
their guitar cases still bore old stickers that said "Destroy!" and
"Anarchy in the U.K."

After a few minutes, the small crowd grew quiet, and Reverend
Pat cleared his throat.

"Friends," he said solemnly, "our town has been without music
for too long. It's been twenty-five years since Planxty Irwin Public
School had a band. Twenty-five years since our last hymn-sing.
Twenty-five years since Wally, Lou, and I were threatened with
reform school for playing power tools on stage. Friends, we want
our musical traditions back. And for that we must ask forgiveness."

Em looked at Gran, who looked at Mrs. Melusine, who looked
back at Em. At first, back in the church basement, the girl had

despaired of ever explaining her idea to them. But after she had got out *Songs from Two Rivers*, and after a lot of pointing and signing on her part, they had understood that she wanted them to accompany her on a particular fiddle piece—Mrs. Melusine on voice, and Gran on something not too challenging. ("How about one of these things?" Gran had said, picking up a tambourine from the carton. "I've seen it done on television.") They had practised all day yesterday on *Permanent Wants*, which, they discovered, was moored outside the town boundaries—and so was outside the witch's influence. Em wasn't sure she had the fast fiddle parts down really well, but that was okay. It was the spirit of the song that mattered.

"Forgiveness is the beginning of change," continued Reverend Pat. "We must ask forgiveness of . . . er, the entity, Mrs. Amenia Hughling."

He nodded at Hettie, who now stepped forward, holding her violin and bow.

"Amenia," she said clearly, "you were wronged. We acknowledge that. Nobody should have to spend an eternity as a fiddle tune. We want to say how sorry we are, Amenia. We hope you will let bygones be bygones."

There was another silence. Far off came the faint drone of an airplane. The daisies nodded encouragingly in the breeze.

"Are you there, Amenia?" said Revered Pat in a louder voice. "We want to reach out to you. Let there be peace and harmony and . . . *melody* once again in this town."

After a moment, Hettie put her fiddle to her shoulder, took a deep breath, and began to play.

For a second—just a second—they thought it had worked; the fiddle tone came out clear and strong. But then the tone suddenly slid into a tinny, jagged screech. A fiddle string snapped, and everybody winced. Hettie put her bow down with a grimace.

"I knew it," she muttered. Then, drawing herself up, she called angrily, "C'mon, Amenia! Let it go!"

Reverend Pat was clearly shaken. "We can't undo the past, Amenia!" he called. "We can only say we're sorry."

The breeze suddenly rose, creakily turning the old weathervane on the church shed. The trees muttered and whispered. Wally looked down at his guitar; the strings were sounding faintly, tunelessly, in the wind. There was no note of forgiveness in all this rustling and sighing. The people, their hands on their hats, listened with grim faces.

All except Emmeline, Gran, and Mrs. Melusine. An unspoken signal passed between them. Emmeline put her violin to her shoulder and took a deep breath. She had "recital nerves," but she wasn't going to back out now. Gran held up the tambourine, and Mrs. Melusine stepped forward with her copy of *Songs of Two Rivers*. The townspeople, wondering, drew back to give them room.

"Amenia, you've been seeking all your life for your lost son," said Mrs. Melusine clearly. "Well, your search is over. Listen."

And they did a pretty good job of "The Roaring Boy," considering that they had only practised it for an afternoon. With all eyes on her, Emmeline did flub a few notes in the fast passages, but for most of the song, the people around her were nodding in appreciation. Gran followed Emmeline's lead, beating time on the tambourine, and Mrs. Melusine sang as she had never sung before.

Where did you come from, O Roaring Boy?
Where do you go when the night draws near?
Do you dream of a home and a feather bed
And a heart that holds you dear?

The townspeople listened, rapt. In fact, the whole church-yard seemed to be listening; the trees barely moved and the old weathervane rested motionless. Cars stopped on the street, and children ran across the lawn to join the crowd. It was real music. Gran occasionally lost the rhythm, and Mrs. Melusine's voice cracked once or twice, but it was *tuneful*—the first tuneful music in the town for a quarter century.

And after each fiddle part, as Emmeline lowered her instrument, she could feel the strange breathless quiet behind the music. She knew then that the spirit was also listening—listening with an ecstatic yearning.

Eventually Emmeline drew out the final flourish, and the song came to a close. Gran stood with the tambourine at her side, slightly flushed. Mrs. Melusine seemed to be listening to the echoes.

"Go in peace, Amenia," she said.

Hettie brought her own fiddle to her chin and drew experimentally on her bow. Yes—real music. She played a few notes, cautiously, and then repeated a bit of Emmeline's fiddle theme from the song. Johnny, guitar in hand, joined in with some soft strumming, and it *still* sounded good.

"Yes!" breathed Hettie.

"You did it, gals!" said Johnny excitedly. In his mind, his musical reputation had been restored.

Reverend Pat bowed his head for a few seconds, then turned to Wally and Jim.

"Right, you guys," he said eagerly. "Let's set up in the church hall and make up for lost time."

Emmeline could sense in her very bones the changed atmosphere. Around her was an emptiness, but a good emptiness—an escape, a release from pain.

Old Mrs. Melusine sat between Gran and Emmeline, regarding me with twinkling eyes. She had made the trip here at my invitation; when I told her that I wanted to collect all the stories from the summer of *Permanent Wants*, she readily accepted. She had already sung for me "The Roaring Boy," with Emmeline accompanying her on the violin.

"Timberquinn is almost back to normal," she said. "Almost." She shook her head. "Sometimes I'll be walking down the street, with church bells and wind chimes and everything sounding so beautiful—so *on-key*—and then it will all be drowned out by a hideous screeching."

"So the spirit is still around," I said in surprise. "Maybe you'll have to think about exorcism after all."

"Oh, it's not the spirit," replied Mrs. Melusine. "It's Reverend Pat's band. And yes, maybe we *should* think about exorcism." She chuckled. "But Amenia has gone, bless her heart. We're quite sure of that."

"And where did she go?" I wondered. "Where do musical spirits go?"

"I think Amenia is with her son now," said Mrs. Melusine simply. "Thanks to Emmeline."

"That's the part I can't really get my head around," said Gran. She couldn't quite bring herself to believe that there ever *was* a spirit.

Mrs. Melusine shrugged. "Out of music she came, and to music she has returned. One kind of life energy has become another. I don't find it so hard to believe, Teo." She shook her head ruefully. "You know, I'd always wondered what had happened to the baby Amenia had to give away. I looked everywhere for him—in hospital records and town archives and church registers—but I was looking in the wrong places. He wasn't in those old records; he was in a *song*." She and Emmeline exchanged a smile. "My great-great-grandmother would have said that a song was the first place to look."

"Your great-great-grandmother?" said Gran.

"A wonderful musician herself," said Mrs. Melusine.

I saw in my mind's eye a wedding celebration of long ago—the women in long dresses, the men in buckskin and breeches, and all of them swinging one another around in the lantern light. In the middle of it was White Nessa of the silver hair, dipping and swaying as she played her harp. And then, looking at white-haired Mrs. Melusine, I remembered what Hettie had said: that almost everybody in town was descended from the people at the wedding.

"I have to admit I've always liked a good fiddle tune," said Mrs. Melusine. "I've got musical blood in me that goes way back."

Seventh Tale

Her
Living
Echo

It was close to noon on a hot August day, and Emmeline was walking by herself on a wooded trail not far from a small lock-station near the town of Merrickville. Her eyes ranged from the trees to the ground, watching for anything interesting—oddly shaped pine cones, seed cases, ants battling other ants, and small, round stones for her slingshot. So far she'd seen nobody on the trail, although she'd heard a dog barking not far away. She hadn't found much in the way of forest treasures either—just a long piece of dead wood that she now carried. It bowed out at the end, but otherwise it made a pretty good wizard's staff.

They were on the return leg of their journey. A week earlier they'd reached Kingston, spent a few days sightseeing with Emmeline's mum and dad, and then began retracing their route along the waterway. The return trip had gone much faster—until this morning, that is. The engine of *Permanent Wants* had decided to conk out not far from the town of Merrickville. At the moment, Emmeline's father and Gran were back at the boat, tinkering, and Emmeline had decided to go for a walk. (Gran was easier in her mind about letting Em go off on her own now; the girl had shown more than once that she was perfectly able to handle herself.)

She hadn't seen any really good places to practise karate (she liked hidden glades where people couldn't see her), but she did try a few kicks here and there. She wondered how long it would take to get her black belt. Her sixteen-year-old cousin, Shelby, was trying for her black belt in the fall. To get your black belt, Shelby said, you had to fight off four other black belts for two hours, and there was always an ambulance on call. Emmeline wondered if she'd be ready to try for her black belt when she was thirteen. While she practised her karate moves along the trail, she imagined four black belts trying get past her defences, and so punched and whirl-kicked in every direction. Maybe when she actually fought them, she thought, she'd lose a tooth or get knocked unconscious. And then all the black belts, feeling terrible, would accompany her in the ambulance; they might even award her the black belt right there. Yes, she'd be ready by thirteen—maybe even by twelve.

She was on the point of retracing her route back to the lockstation when her eyes caught something in the undergrowth beside the trail. The white trim of a photograph was just visible through the leaves. She stepped off the trail (looking around for poison ivy first) and stooped to pick it up.

She gasped. The photo was of *her*.

She was quite sure of that. Even with the washed-out colours, she could recognize her own face. And yet the Emmeline in the photo looked so . . . *abandoned*. Her hair was like straw, her face was streaked with dirt, and one sleeve of her tattered jacket was coming off. She looked like one of the children in those famous pictures of the Depression era—children who appear even more hopeless than the adults. In the background of the photo was a cityscape of some kind, but it didn't look like Ottawa. Emmeline wasn't even sure it was North America.

She turned the photo over. There was writing on the back—about ten lines. The writing looked odd; she didn't think it was English. She tried spelling out the first word but didn't get very far. It *couldn't* be English.

She shivered. Of all the strange things that had happened that summer, this was the strangest. She had never had her picture taken dressed like that. And how did the photo get *here*? She poked around a bit with her "wizard's staff," but finding nothing more in the undergrowth, she stepped back onto the trail. Had she been meant to find the photo? Of course she had—after all, it was a picture of her. And yet it had been lying off the trail, barely visible in the undergrowth. It was pure luck that she had seen it at all.

She would have liked to keep this all to herself, but there was the writing on the back of the photo. Somebody would have to help her with that.

She closed her eyes in frustration. Was that going to be her *life*? She suddenly decided that she would solve the mystery on her own, and not tell Gran or her father or anybody else. Tucking the photo in the pocket of her jeans, she glanced up and down the trail. She was quite sure that someone had dropped the photo recently; it wasn't wrinkled or faded from the damp. And this someone might still be around.

She began retracing her route, scanning the trailside as she did so, but found nothing more until she reached the lockstation. Beyond the white clapboard house that served as headquarters she could see *Permanent Wants* moored in the holding area. There were a few other boats there, too, waiting to go into the lock. She came to a stop beside the plaque that marked the trailhead. From this point, the trail went off in two directions, tracing out a loop through the forest.

She got out the photo again. *Was* it her? She thought she saw tear streaks on the dirty face in the photo, and she touched her own face. What she needed was another picture of herself, to compare. Her dad carried one, she knew . . .

Just then, from farther down the trail, she heard the barking of a dog. A sharp bark with a whine at the end. She was quite sure it was the same dog she had heard earlier.

She began walking quickly along the path, still carrying her wizard's staff. Maybe the dog had nothing to do with the dropped photo, but she thought she'd investigate anyway. She passed a few benches and a little stream that flowed through a culvert and an old fence that was woven like a wicker basket. The barking grew louder. Turning a corner, she suddenly stopped.

Before her was a very tall woman and a black dog—a dog stocky and blunt-headed, though not big. The dog was barking its head off.

The stranger looked as if she could easily have wrung the dog's neck. She was well over six feet tall, lanky and raw-boned, with a face like a flint axe and long, limp hair. But she was clearly afraid, and she stood with her back to a tree, her large jaw outthrust. Over her shoulder hung a satchel, like the ones worn by mail carriers, and she was holding it away from the dog.

The dog was certainly putting itself into its work, throwing its head out for each bark. Emmeline took a fresh grip on her wizard's staff. She generally steered clear of barking dogs, but she sensed that this one wasn't vicious, just an aggressive yapper. Holding her staff in front of her, she took a step towards it. The dog sidled away from her but continued to bark, its head down, its front feet spread out in front of it. Emmeline thumped the ground with her staff, and the dog backed away even more. By then, Emmeline had got between it and the woman.

"Festus!" came a man's voice from down the trail. "Come here!"

The dog wavered. To help it make up its mind, Emmeline lunged at it with her staff. It gave a few last barks and then bounded away. The tall woman adjusted the strap of her satchel, breathing hard.

"I really have to get some of that pepper spray," she said, wiping her brow with her sleeve. "Anyway, thanks, kid. I've faced bandits in India and a hurricane in the Caribbean and snowstorms in the Yukon, but for some reason, yappy dogs just get under my skin."

She undid a military-style canteen from her belt and, tilting back her head, took a long drink.

"I already had one run-in with that mutt today," she continued. "I was on my way to my favourite swimming hole and suddenly there it was. Dogs just don't like me. Drink?"

But Emmeline had her eyes on the woman's satchel. Slowly she withdrew the photo from the pocket of her shorts. The woman, seeing it, exclaimed.

"Drat that dog!" she said. "I *thought* I might have dropped something."

She took the photo, glanced at it, and shook her head wearily.

"You know," she said, "I sometimes wonder if I'm even necessary. If I mess up, the thing gets delivered anyway." She handed the photo back to Emmeline. "Here. It's yours. It would have got to you eventually."

Emmeline, determined to get to the heart of things, tapped the picture impatiently and pointed to herself. The woman took another gulp of water, nodding as she swallowed.

"Yep," she said. "It's your doppelgänger."

Emmeline must have looked even more confused, for the woman said, "I guess you deserve an explanation, since you rescued me. Let's go and find a bench, and I'll tell you everything."

They walked in silence back down the trail, past the little stream that flowed through a culvert, and soon came to one of the benches.

Lifting the strap off her shoulder, the tall woman set her satchel beside the bench and sat down, stretching her long legs in front of her. She wore red knee-length cotton shorts with a drawstring and a light-coloured cotton top, both very loose. On her feet were red Converse All-Star running shoes, the kind that basketball players wear. Emmeline could see that under her top, she was wearing a sports bra.

The girl sat down beside the stranger, still holding the photo. She couldn't get over the size of the woman's feet.

"What you got there," said the woman conversationally, "is a picture of your doppelgänger. That's a German word meaning double goer, or double walker. You see, everybody in the world has a double—a natural twin, a living echo. Another *you.*" Her smile was as awkward and angled as the rest of her. "Doppelgängers aren't supposed to meet," she continued, "and I guess there are good reasons for that. But there's no reason they can't *communicate.* That's the way I see it, anyway." She detached her canteen and took another swig of water. "And they can't communicate without a middleman, a go-between. That's me. I deliver messages between doppelgängers—DGs, for short."

Emmeline had been listening very carefully to the explanation, but it really hadn't helped her much. She frowned at her photo. She wanted the tall woman to explain it all again, using *simple* words this time.

"My name's Iseult, by the way," added the tall woman in the same amiable tone. "Iseult Consolata LeGrand. Pretty fancy name for a plain Jane like me, I know. And you?"

But Emmeline, growing ever more impatient, just turned the card over and tapped the writing.

"You want me to read it, eh?" said the woman named Iseult. "Sure."

But instead of actually reading it, she held the photo to her forehead. "'Dear Doppelgänger,'" recited Iseult, her eyes closed. "'How are you? I am fine. This is the only photo I have of me, and I would like you to have it. I want to know everything about you. Do you have a pet? Do you have a refrigerator? Babu wrote this—'" Opening her eyes briefly, Iseult interjected, "I think Babu is another street kid." Then she went on: "'Babu wrote this because I can't write that well. Please, please write back. Love, Emyla.'"

She glanced at the writing on the photo and handed it back to Emmeline.

"It's in Russian, by the way," she added.

Emmeline's head was swimming. *Russian?* Now she wished she *had* enlisted the help of her dad. She gazed hopelessly at the photo. One thing was clear: the girl in the picture was very poor. She had asked if Emmeline had a *refrigerator*. Now Emmeline wondered if the dirt flecks on her double's face might have been scars or scabs.

Iseult showed no curiosity as to why Emmeline didn't speak; she just seemed to go along with it.

"If you want to write something back," she offered, "I can take the message right now."

Emmeline shook her head and held up her wrist with the medical ID bracelet. The woman took the pendant in her large hand and studied it.

"Oh," she said. "Sorry, I didn't know." She was silent for a moment. "But you sure have a way with dogs, Emmeline. They should put *that* on your bracelet."

She gave her spindly smile, a smile that was just a stretching of her face—the smile of someone who had lived a hard life.

"You don't have to send your doppelgänger a letter," she continued. "You can send her a photo, or just a souvenir. If it's small enough to fit in my bag, I can take it."

Emmeline shrugged helplessly. She knew she wouldn't be able to get anything from the boat without the adults asking her what she was doing. They *always* did that.

"But there's no rush," said Iseult, who seemed to sense the girl's frustration. "I have a few more things to deliver. I can meet you later today at the trailhead. How about in an hour?" She stood up. "And if that dog is really gone, I think I'm going to have my swim. Do you think it's really gone?"

Hutterson's Illustrated Encyclopedia of Paranormal and Occult Worlds— that was the book Emmeline wanted. She found it after a few minutes of rooting around in the hot, airless storage hold of *Permanent Wants*. As always, she knew the book by the cover illustration: a pyramid with a human eye on top of it, like the engraving on the American dollar bill. She had dipped into it often during the journey, reading the pictures. One illustration she particularly remembered showed two men in old-fashioned clothes—top hats, walking sticks, and long coattails—staring at each other in astonishment. They had good reason to be astonished: one man was the exact double of the other, right down to the black ribbon on his pince-nez. Facing the illustration was a page of print that might, she guessed, shed some light on what Iseult had talked about. She would have to get somebody to read it to her. She needed badly to understand.

Her father and Gran were both kneeling around the engine well, looking hot and oily. Gran was definitely not her usual cheerful self. She wished Picardy Bob were there—he was good at fixing things—but he wasn't due to arrive until later that afternoon. And anyway, Picardy Bob was *always* fixing things for them. If they didn't have any success with the engine, Gran figured they'd have to enlist the help of the only boat mechanic around: a loud, fat man named Dexter Nervish, who'd been at the lockstation several times that afternoon. He had already made a mocking comment about *Permanent Wants*, and Gran didn't want to give him any business if she could help it.

"What have you got there, Em?" said Emmeline's dad as the girl emerged from the cabin.

Emmeline's dad was a tall, soft-spoken man with glasses like Clark Kent's. He almost never lost his temper, unlike the other members of his family.

Emmeline opened the book at the illustration, signing that she wanted him to read it out loud.

"In a little while, Emmeline," said Gran. "Once we're finished here."

Emmeline shook her head impatiently at Gran, and gestured again at her dad. *Important,* she signed.

Gran looked up. "I said when we're finished."

Emmeline flushed. She made a brushing-away motion, as if insects were bothering her. Gran's eyes narrowed.

"I'll ignore that," she said.

Emmeline glared. She had a glare like the mouth of a live volcano, since she couldn't express her anger in words.

"Well, maybe it's time for a break anyway," said her dad, wiping his oily hands on a rag.

Gran took a long breath.

"We might be able to make some progress," she said evenly, "if we didn't stop for breaks all the time."

Emmeline suddenly decided she'd had enough. She tossed the book down, jumped up on the roof of the cabin, crossed it in two strides, and then leapt from there onto the dock. When she was angry, Emmeline could be more gale than girl.

"Emmeline!" called Gran, but the girl was already off in the direction of the trail. "Now what was *that* all about?" she said.

Emmeline's dad was looking at the rag in his hands, wondering if it was too dirty to wipe his brow with. He would give his daughter a minute or two to calm down and then go after her. His eye caught the book that Emmeline had tossed away, and picking it up, he flipped through the pages until he found the illustration the girl had showed him—the man in the top hat, looking at his mirror image.

"Doppelgängers," he said in puzzlement, reading the entry title.

It took only twenty minutes for Emmeline to find Iseult. The tall woman was sitting on the shore of her swimming hole, which looked lovely—green and tree-shaded, with a sandy bottom where sunlight wove a rippling pattern. The pond must have been fed by a creek, since Emmeline could faintly hear running water. Iseult had just finished her swim, and her long hair hung damp over her shoulders. Her Converse All-Stars were beside her, with her white athletic socks stuffed inside them. On seeing the girl, her face lit up.

"Hullo, Emmeline! I didn't expect you so soon."

Emmeline sat down, her face red from running, and slipped off her sandals. With the calming sound of the water and Iseult's friendly face, she felt her mood lightening already. She dabbled her toes in the water and flashed a small smile at Iseult.

"I delivered my other messages," said Iseult, "and now I'm . . . on holiday." She sighed, as if this were a real challenge. "Did you find something to send to your DG?"

Emmeline shook her head. She had planned to bring a newspaper article about *Permanent Wants*, which had a picture of her, but it was too late now. Just then, her eye fell on her medical ID bracelet.

Emmeline has difficulty reading, writing, and speaking. . . . It was time for it to go, she decided.

"It's very pretty," said Iseult, taking the bracelet from Emmeline. "But . . . um, are you sure you want to part with this?"

Emmeline nodded firmly. Iseult shrugged, put it in her bag, and closed the flap.

"It's peaceful here, isn't it?" she said. "I hate beaches. People are always gawking and dogs are barking and children . . ." She shook her head. "Sometimes children can be the worst."

Emmeline nodded; she knew that herself. She plucked a piece of grass and began chewing it. She had the feeling that if she let her companion talk, all her questions would be answered after a while.

"I'm so glad I have the name Iseult," said the woman presently. "That's a *strong* name, don't you think? A strong, beautiful name. I've often felt that my name is the only beautiful thing about me."

She said this without a trace of self-pity, as if she were commenting on the scenery. Emmeline stretched out on the grass, her eyes on Iseult. The woman's toes were oddly small, little girl's toes, though her feet were probably size eleven.

"I guess you're wondering how I got into this racket in the first place," Iseult continued. "I mean, being a messenger for the DGs. I'm a wanderer. I've always liked to travel, especially the rough edges of the world, and I've always liked to *read* about travelling. And once I was reading this old book, called *Sailing Alone Around the World*—"

Emmeline sat up in excitement. She knew that book well; it used to be a favourite of Grandpa Silas's.

"Oh, you know it, do you?" said Iseult. "Well, there's a part where old Slocum—he's the author—talks about this sea captain he knew. The captain used to sail a regular route past an island that served as a kind of post office. Ships would leave letters there, and the captain would stop and pick up the letters and make sure they got delivered. He didn't get paid for it; he just *did* it." She smoothed her damp hair. "I wanted badly to be like that captain. In a way he was holding civilization together; hundreds of sailors depended on him. And I decided I would do the same thing—only I would deliver messages from the whole *world* to itself. Because I knew by then that doppelgängers exist. I knew that very early on."

Iseult fell silent, as if this was as much as she cared to say on the subject. Emmeline was thinking about her double, the girl in the photo. If she understood right, this girl was *her*. Emyla was Emmeline in another life. Did that mean this girl had language problems, too? Emyla said she didn't write very well, but maybe that was because she didn't spend a lot of time in school. And—Emmeline was dying to know—could she speak?

"One thing I learned very early on," said Iseult, "is that DGs are not clones. Each DG has something that her twin lacks. And I thought: Why *not* let them communicate?" A note of defiance had entered her voice. "If they could somehow share thoughts, their lives would be better. They'd *complete* each other. And above all, they'd know they were not alone. And that's how—"

Just then, a voice came floating down the trail behind them: "Emmeline! Em!" It was her dad.

Iseult stood up hastily. "Somebody's looking for you," she said, flustered.

Emmeline sighed; someone was *always* looking for her. She got to her feet and turned to face her dad, hands on her hips.

"There you are!" said her dad, hot but relieved. He stopped short when he saw Iseult.

"Hello, sir," said Iseult quickly.

Emmeline gestured to Iseult and signed *friend*, hooking her right index finger over her left and then reversing her hands so the left index finger was on top. She did this very emphatically, holding up her hands for her dad to see. Her dad wasn't very fluent in Sign, but he knew that hand shape.

"She's a very good listener," continued Iseult earnestly. "Sorry if I kept her."

"That's okay," said Emmeline's dad, still wondering. Emmeline could guess why Iseult felt ill at ease: people probably reacted harshly towards her because . . . well, she *did* look different. The girl repeated the sign for *friend,* and her dad nodded. He tended to trust his daughter's instincts.

"We were just going to have some lunch," he said. "Would you like to join us?"

Emmeline looked at Iseult enquiringly.

"Oh, thanks for the offer," said Iseult. "But I think—"

Emmeline seized the woman's hand, to Iseult's embarrassment.

"You'd be welcome," said Em's dad. "We've got enough for all."

Emmeline nodded vigorously. Iseult looked down at her bare feet. "Well, maybe I could," she said hesitatingly. "You don't have a dog, do you?"

"No, just a cat," said her father. "And two crickets."

"Two crickets!" said Iseult, glancing up with her grimace-smile. "Like old Josh Slocum. Well, I guess I can handle crickets."

Back at the boat, Gran and Emmeline eyed each other warily. Gran had given up on the engine and decided that for her own peace of mind they would have to get in the boat mechanic, Dexter Nervish—though he *was* a prize jerk. But first she wanted a bit of lunch; she was making sandwiches when the others arrived. She warmed to Iseult at once when she found out that the latter was a big fan of Joshua Slocum.

Emmeline's dad had just finished setting up an extra deck chair for their guest when he noticed the copy of *Hutterson's Illustrated Encyclopedia.*

"Hey, Em," he said, "you wanted me to read something from this, right?"

Emmeline glanced quickly at Iseult, wondering if the tall woman wanted her story revealed. Iseult was looking around awkwardly and didn't seem to be paying attention.

"This bit, wasn't it?" said Emmeline's father, opening it to the picture of the two men. "About doppelgängers."

Now Iseult was alert. "That sounds interesting," she said easily, taking her seat.

"Believe me," said Emmeline's dad, "we've got a wealth of out-of-the-way knowledge on this boat. Let's see." He began reading: "'Every human being on earth is said to have a double, also known as a doppelgänger. This belief is very ancient and has appeared in some form all over the world. In British and Irish folklore, the double is called a *fetch;* in Swedish the word is *vardøger.* Some versions of the legend hold that these doubles are no more than ghostly replicas of people. According to this view, it is unlucky to catch a glimpse of one's doppelgänger. However, doppelgängers are also considered good and even necessary influences. Some people believe that every person on earth exists as two selves, and that these selves live out their own lives in different parts of the world. The universe is so arranged that these doubles never meet.'"

"Good thing, too," said Gran, coming out with the plate of sandwiches. "Could you imagine the mix-ups?"

"'But it sometimes happens that they catch glimpses of each other in dreams and visions. There is an interesting minor legend associated with this idea that the doppelgänger is one half of a single self. Very rarely, the legend goes, someone appears on the earth who does *not* have a doppelgänger. Such people are called *Einzelgängers,* or lone-walkers. These solitaries know themselves to be a single soul, unique and alone, and are often the unhappiest of humans.'" Emmeline's dad looked up, chuckling. "The stuff you learn on *Permanent Wants*! How come you were interested in doppelgängers, Em?"

Emmeline sat still in her chair. She wondered if Iseult would answer for her, but the latter was looking away with an odd expression on her face. The woman looked both weary and hopeless. It was as if the passage had somehow brought home to her that her life was pointless. Emmeline's dad noticed it, too, and was just about to say something when they all heard an angry voice coming from the dock. They glanced up to see the local mechanic, Dexter Nervish, bearing down on them, waving a card of some kind.

"You!" he said, glaring at Iseult. "What's your game?"

Dexter's head was shaped like peanut, the lower half bigger than the top half. If you looked at him from a certain angle, he seemed to be all jaw. He had bad teeth and a sleeve of wine-coloured tattoos on each arm, but he was a good mechanic.

"What are you on about, Dexter?" said Gran.

"I'm talking to Pippi Longstocking here," said Dexter, his fiery gaze fixed on Iseult. "I got this postcard in the mail—from *myself*." He held up the postcard; on the front was a photo of a man who looked exactly like Dexter. "And *she* delivered it."

Everybody looked at Iseult, who calmly took a bite of her sandwich.

"Don't deny it!" said Dexter. "The guys at the marina saw you."

"I'm not denying it," said Iseult.

"Is this how you get your kicks? Hey?" said Dexter.

Iseult put her sandwich down.

"Maybe you might read that bit about doppelgängers again," she said to Emmeline's dad.

"I'm talking to you, Stretch!" said Dexter.

"Just the first paragraph will do." Iseult looked up at the angry mechanic. "Listen carefully, Dexter."

Emmeline's dad read the passage again. Dexter tried to interrupt several times, but Gran shushed him. At the end of it, he stood there with arms folded.

"So you see, Dexter," said Iseult. "It's not a photo of you. It's your doppelgänger."

Dexter looked from Iseult to the others. "Who are you guys, the Addams Family? Cut the crap and tell me where you got that photo."

"Okay, Dexter, okay," said Emmeline's dad. He turned to Iseult. "Where *did* you get this photo of Dexter, Iseult?"

"It's *not* Dexter," said Iseult patiently. "It's his doppelgänger."

"That's a lot for us to believe," said Emmeline's dad.

"Ask your daughter," said Iseult mildly.

They all looked at Emmeline, who took a deep breath. *Another* situation she would have to manage. After a moment, she drew out the photo of her doppelgänger and handed it to her father. Gran leaned over to look. She and Em's dad had exactly the same reaction, as if they had rehearsed it. They stared open-mouthed at the photo, then at Emmeline, then at Iseult.

"These sandwiches are *delicious*," said Iseult.

For almost ten minutes, Iseult talked and they listened. Her awkwardness fell away quickly; she was passionately keen to tell them about her life mission. Dexter, who saw that the others were just as bewildered as he was, joined them in the cockpit. At the end of the ten minutes, there was a long silence. Iseult offered the last sandwich around, but the others shook their heads dazedly, so she finished it.

"And you just travel around delivering these messages?" asked Emmeline's dad. "That's your . . . *job*?"

"Well, I don't get paid for it," said Iseult. "I usually get work on a ship; I love the sea. I've been everything from cook to engineer's assistant."

"And you know *Russian*," said Gran, still bewildered.

"Just a few words," said Iseult. "But I don't really need to know the languages of the messages. I seem to be able pick up the emotions anyway. That's the part I don't understand myself. It's like a resonance."

"Malarkey!" said Dexter, getting angry again. "Listen, you know what my *doppelgängster* wanted from me? Money. Does that sound on the level to you?"

"Well, he *is* your double," said Iseult dryly. Gran smothered a smile.

"Where did he write to you from, Dexter?" asked Emmeline's father curiously.

"Never mind that," said Dexter. "The point is—"

"Mongolia," said Iseult.

"Dexter's doppelgänger is *Mongolian*?" said Gran in astonishment.

"British," corrected Iseult. "But he lives in Mongolia."

Dexter glowered. "Hey, that's *private* information."

"What he wrote to you is private," said Iseult, "but his situation is not. He told me all about it. Yes, he's in Mongolia, working on a housing project there. I would guess that's why he's asking for money." He looked from Dexter to Emmeline. "You're both wondering how your doppelgänger learned about you. Probably in a dream: that's the usual route. And by the way, it is *not* bad luck to see your doppelgänger in a dream. That gets into a lot of books, but I don't know why. Dreaming of your doppelgänger just means a change—maybe a big change. Because a doppelgänger is the *rest* of you, in a way."

"Question!" said Dexter mockingly, raising a beefy hand. "How do these doppelgängers find *you*? You in the Yellow Pages?"

"I find *them*," replied Iseult simply. "If the need is great enough, I always find them."

"Bah!" said Dexter, just like a villain in a book. Emmeline's dad decided it was time to steer the conversation into other channels. "You say you've worked on a ship, Iseult," he said. "Do you know anything about diesel engines?"

"I can take a look," said Iseult.

"You're not going to let *her* fool around with your engine?" exclaimed Dexter.

"You don't have to watch," Gran told him. "Better go and report this Mongolian postal fraud."

"I'm afraid we might have made things worse than they were," said Emmeline's father to Iseult.

"I bet you did," said Dexter, rolling up his sleeves. "Okay, let's have a look."

"We didn't ask for your help, Dexter," Gran put in.

"I'm giving it anyway," returned Dexter. "You people seem pretty helpless. Let's get that bloody engine cover off."

"And we *don't* use coarse language on this boat," said Gran sharply.

"No wonder you can't fix your engine," said Dexter.

The two of them—Dexter and Iseult—spent more than an hour on the engine, tinkering, banging, and arguing. Gran and Emmeline's dad stood by, handing tools to the workers, but both of them were still turning over Iseult's story in their minds. At one point, Gran went over to the copy of *Hutterson's Illustrated Encyclopedia*, picked it up, and gave the doppelgänger passage a quick read. Emmeline's father joined her.

"*Doppelgängers?*" he said in a low voice. "Is this for real?"

"Believe me," said Gran, "the whole summer has been like that. Hasn't it, Em?"

Emmeline nodded emphatically. Pirates, anacondas, reptile gods, musical spirits, creepy pale men who hated darkness—her scrapbook was full to the brim with "notable attractions," as the tourist brochures put it. She went back to comparing a photo of herself to Emyla's photo. It was spooky how alike they were. Her doppelgänger looked exactly as she had for an entire year—when she was struggling and raging to hold on to her language.

Eventually Iseult put down her screwdriver and tried the starter, and the engine sputtered and caught. They all sat back, looking relieved, and even Dexter grunted in satisfaction. He got to his feet, wiping his face with his shirt tail.

"I got one question for you all," he said. "Just one question."

"Yes?" said Gran.

He glared around at them. "Where *is* Mongolia, anyway?"

Trying not to smile, Gran told him. "The capital city is Ulan Bator," she concluded. "It's supposed to be the coldest national capital in the world—right in front of Ottawa."

Dexter shook his head in wonder. "What kind of *loser* would go there?" he said, and stumped off.

Now that the job was done, Iseult seemed at a loss. She rubbed her bare knees, which were red from kneeling on the pebbled deck, and bent to pick up her satchel.

"Well," she said, "I guess it's time I was going."

They all looked at her in dismay.

"We owe you dinner, Iseult," said Emmeline's father. "At the very least."

Iseult avoided his eyes. "Maybe some other time. I've got miles to go before I sleep, as the man said."

Gran said, "Can't you take a day off?"

Iseult's face was suddenly raw with emotion. "I *dread* my days off," she said. The way she was standing, her rangy frame seemed to be thin and fragile, as if it might be taken apart any moment by a gust of wind, like a badly constructed scarecrow.

"You don't know how lucky you are to have doppelgängers," she blurted out.

"What do you mean?" said Gran. "Doesn't *everybody* have a doppelgänger?"

Iseult shook her head. "That book you read from—it was right. There are some people who are born without doppelgängers. *Einzelgängers*, lonewalkers, nomad souls—call them what you want. I'm one. I knew I was one from a very early age. And that's the real reason I do what I do. How wonderful it must be to know that there is someone out there who is *you*, but also more than you. Who knows exactly what you're battling in your life . . ."

Emmeline rushed close to Iseult and took the woman's hand. This was exactly how she felt about her own doppelgänger. Emyla wouldn't just talk unceasingly, as Madison did, but would listen to her. She'd listen even if Emmeline couldn't *say* anything.

"But maybe," said Gran, "there are *other* lonewalkers."

Iseult, suddenly angry, drew her hand out of Emmeline's grasp. "Do you know how rare they are?"

"No," said Gran quietly. "How rare?"

Iseult gestured hopelessly. "One born every generation. Or every *century*. I've read different things, but I can tell you they're *rare*."

"Maybe not so rare," said Gran in the same even tone. "I think Em and I met another one this summer."

Iseult blinked, the tears clearly visible in her eyes. Emmeline was staring at Gran.

"You said that the books were not always accurate about doppel-gängers," continued Gran. "I have a feeling they're not always accurate about lonewalkers."

Just then, from beyond the dock, they heard the sound of tires on gravel. Picardy Bob had arrived in his battered Honda Civic.

"And here's the man who knows every lonewalker for miles around," said Gran.

The boat was crowded that evening. Iseult seemed to take up more space than anybody, with her lanky frame and big feet, and as the night wore on, she got more and more animated. Picardy Bob was very keen to hear Iseult's story, and the others were glad to fill in the details. They ate a long, leisurely dinner and talked far into the night, about doppelgängers and other mysteries, about all the strange and wonderful things that had happened to them that summer. And Gran told Iseult a bit about the other lonewalker they had met on the waterway.

"He's a bit eccentric," said Gran. "He's a pirate, and he believes his bay is a portal to . . . um, a pirate world."

"He does?" said Picardy Bob.

"But I don't think he's big on vacations either," said Gran to Iseult.

"I like him already." Iseult smiled.

She was too tall for the bunks on board, so she spread out a big beach blanket on the upper deck. The others protested, but she didn't mind; she was used to sleeping outdoors. When Emmeline came up that evening to make sure she was comfortable, she got out the girl's medical ID bracelet. "I don't know when I'll be over to see Emyla again," she said, "so I'd better give this back to you."

Emmeline made a firm gesture: *keep it.* Iseult nodded sympathetically.

"Well, at least you know that Emyla is there," she said, "and she knows that you're *here*. So now I guess it's up to you two."

Picardy Bob and Emmeline's dad spread out sleeping bags in different areas of the boat, and soon silence fell. The night had fruited impressively with stars, and they all drifted off on the great branching river of sleep. Emmeline saw in her dreams all the places they had visited and the people they'd met, and as usual she tried to find words, to chip them out of the granite of her mind and hand them around. *Good luck, Captain Lillwyn. Fight on, Mr. Drake. Goodbye, Tenebrio. Tom, be seeing you again.* She didn't find the words, but all her friends smiled goodbye to her, and she woke up with "The Roaring Boy" in her head.

The morning was clear and fine—a grand soft day, as they say in Ireland. They all parted ways in late morning, with Iseult and Picardy Bob driving upriver to Slackwater Bay, and Emmeline's dad going in the other direction to Ottawa. And then it was just Gran and Emmeline, as it had been at the beginning.

"Well, sweetie," said Gran, "we'll be back in Ottawa soon."

It was then that she noticed Emmeline's bare wrist. "Where's your bracelet?" she asked.

Emmeline signed that she had given it to Iseult. She expected Gran to be angry, but her grandmother just said: "Well, I always thought it was a bit clunky for you. We'll get you another one."

Emmeline didn't react; she just kept looking out at the trees.

"Or maybe not," said Gran, watching her.

Emmeline was off by herself, as she often was, inside her own mind. How she wished she could write something to Emyla! Something of her *own*—something that went from her mind right to the paper. That was the worst of it, having a broken language: you could never send your thoughts out to the world by *yourself*. Emyla would understand this, for she couldn't write. Whether she could speak, Emmeline didn't know, and maybe she'd never know. But she knew that her doppelgänger could help her somehow. Iseult had said that your doppelgänger was you, but also *more* than you . . .

She turned to Gran and began signing. She did it slowly, laboriously, as if her hands held a great weight. Though she didn't know it, her face looked exactly like Emyla's in the photo.

speak

awayfar

ever?
ever?

Gran went close and put her arms around her granddaughter. Maybe we're all lonewalkers at different times in our lives, she thought, and Emmeline had been one for two years.

But as it turned out, Emmeline saw her doppelgänger in a dream not long afterwards, when they were moored in Merrickville. It was such a vivid dream that it stayed with her for years.

In her dream she was walking down a badly lit alley at night— a dirty, rain-soaked alley, with garbage everywhere and plastic bags blowing about in the wind. Under a streetlight, she came to a small form wrapped in a torn blanket, sitting on layers of plastic and cardboard. She knelt down beside the form, and a grubby face peeped out at her. Emyla looked as sad and broken as she had in the photograph, and Emmeline wanted desperately to cheer her up. So she raised her violin to her shoulder—her violin was suddenly there in her dream—and plunged into the happiest, most rollicking tune she knew: "The Roaring Boy." At first, Emyla just listened quietly, peering out from the blanket, but then she started beating time on her knee, at first weakly and then more strongly. Soon, shrugging off the blanket, she stood up and was moving to the music.

For Emmeline, it was like watching herself in a mirror; Emyla's dance moves were exactly hers, right down to the arm-weave (very popular in the sixties). And then all at once, Emyla was singing. Emmeline was overjoyed: her doppelgänger could *speak*. She didn't understand any of the words—there seemed to be a lot that ended in sounds like *osht* and *ansk*—but she badly wanted to sing along. At first she just hummed loudly, but soon she was imitating the sounds Emyla made, and Emyla was laughing at her pronunciation, and they kept playing and singing and laughing together. Emmeline didn't find it hard to make the sounds; they weren't words to her. They came out of her just as the notes came out of the violin.

And then suddenly the music stopped, and they hugged each other and Emyla said clearly: "*Spaseebah*, Emmeline." (Later, Emmeline found out that *spaseebah* meant "thank you" in Russian.) The word was in Emmeline's head when she woke up, the three syllables as bright and distinct as three hummingbird eggs in a nest: *spa-SEE-bah*. She carried them around all day, and the next day afterwards—which was odd, because usually she forgot words as quickly as she learned them.

The Book
of the
Jewelled
Net

Picardy Bob used to say that in all the years he had known Josephina Fitch, her hair had never lacked drama. For a while it was in pigtails; then it was in dreadlocks. Now it was just high and wild and natural, like an osprey's nest. Josephina Fitch was a secondhand bookseller.

"I can say of bookselling," she liked to tell her customers, "what Henry David Thoreau said of being a hermit: I would recommend it only to those with large funds of sunshine within themselves." Picardy Bob agreed that she did generate a lot of light, like the sun and other large balls of gas. She wore bright smocks of banana and rose and lemon, with vivid snake-tongues of embroidery—green and gold and sometimes golded green—on the sleeves. Her bookstore, which specialized in New Age subjects (lots of titles like *Astrology for Economists* and *God Drives a Flying Saucer*), had little piles of coloured stones everywhere. She said these gave out different wavelengths of energy. At night she would decorate the porch of her Merrickville cottage with rows of scented candle-lanterns, to the wonder of passing bats and boaters. Through the grey and shabby world of secondhand bookselling she moved like a torch, or a torch song.

And with so much radiant energy, she was hard to resist. That was why, when Josephina stopped by *Permanent Wants* one afternoon to ask a favour, Gran and Emmeline couldn't bring themselves to say no.

"I'm trying to get the hop on your man Bob," explained Josephina, who was dressed in her work clothes—embroidered relaxed-fit jeans, gigantic hoop earrings, and a blouse like a peach squall. "I'm sure you'll help me out for such a worthy cause." She grinned: she and Bob were long-time rivals. "I've got three cartons of old books from an estate sale, and I'm on my way to another sale right now. I'm going to have a ton of stock to sort through, unless—"

"It's Sunday, Jo," observed Gran.

It was indeed a beautiful Sunday, and Gran and Emmeline were still thinking about how to spend it. They could have picked fresh blueberries for a pancake brunch. They could have motored down the river a short distance and taken some turns on the swing rope they had seen overhanging a bay. And they could have taken Lafcadio and the crickets to the Blessing of the Animals service at the local church, which included an optional sprinkle of holy water. (Gran thought they might pass on the sprinkle.) Doing work for Jo, however, was not on the agenda.

"I hear you, Teo," called Josephina, who was already fishing out a carton of books from the back of her station wagon. "But time and tide wait for no woman, as I'm sure I don't have to tell you two sailors. I'm on my way to Toronto tomorrow to see dealers, and I need a list of titles, publication dates, and . . . well, you know the drill, Teo." She set the carton down at their feet. "Of course, if you see anything you like, you're welcome to it. We help each other out in the book business, right, girls?"

Gran sighed. It was true that Josephina had donated a number of books to *Permanent Wants*, including *Teach Yourself Relativity!* and *The Totem Animal* (about the psychic powers of pets).

"So we can keep anything we want?" she said.

"Well, everything except first editions," said Josephina. "Could be some interesting stuff here. It comes from the estate of my neighbour on the river, Prospero White. An absolute loony, but rich as all get-out. He wanted to collect every book ever published. Can you imagine?" She plunked down the last carton. "I'll swing by in a few hours. And Lafcadio—take the rest of the day off, child. You've been working too hard."

Lafcadio, who was lying with half-closed eyes on the sunny deck, acknowledged the suggestion with a lazy flick of his tail.

After Jo had gone, Gran fetched paper and pencil and they made themselves comfortable on the settee of the cockpit, each with a carton of books before her. Most of the volumes were hardcover, large and heavy and not suitable for *Permanent Wants*. But halfway through the first carton, Emmeline came across something interesting.

It was a thick, overstuffed book like an old photo album, bound in black leather, with no cover illustration or title. It turned out to be a scrapbook of sorts—the weirdest scrapbook she had ever seen. Inside were photos, cartoons, ink drawings, pasted-in squares of print, bits of embroidery, pressed flowers, old stamps in transparent strips, pop-up illustrations that unfolded as you opened the page, and tiny coins taped to cardboard inserts. There were even cunning miniature models—a two-centimetre Eiffel Tower, a tiny Mona Lisa in a matchstick frame—tucked inside cloth pockets or dangling from threads. She was amazed that all these things hadn't been lost. The paper was some dark, soft material like linen, and altogether the book had the feel of something handmade, fashioned by a mad old collector who loved both trivia and trinkets.

"What have you got there, Em?" said Gran.

Together they opened the book to the title page, which contained a passage in flowing, old-fashioned handwriting, like that of ancient manuscripts that are kept under glass. Gran read out loud:

Reader, welcome to the Book of the Jewelled Net, which like the legendary net of the Buddhist god Indra, stretches to the farthest edges of the universe—and beyond. What will you find here? Every magic trick ever performed. Every movie poster ever produced. The contents of every *National Geographic* ever published. Every proverb and fable in every language. The life histories of every man, woman, and child who went down on the *Titanic*—plus an illustrated catalogue of everything they had in their pockets. Every galaxy, every comet, every moon, every planet, real or imagined, is charted and described here. This is the Book of Alpha and Omega, the Libris Ultima, the Unsoundable Book of Everything!

Gran chuckled. "Everything you always wanted to know about everything. Just what we need."

In a few minutes, they had completely forgotten the other cartons of books.

Never had they seen a book with less rhyme or reason to it. Every page was a hodgepodge of illustrations, found objects, and pasted-in bits of text—all seemingly unrelated. Gran, reading the text fragments on a single page, found that they were about medieval angels, Inuit throat singing, early primitive humans, and international city streets with odd names (she liked Logic Lane in Oxford, England; Emmeline liked the Street of the Four Winds in Paris, France).

"It's not so much a book as a museum," said Gran. "Or maybe a landfill site. Get away, Laf."

Lafcadio was mewing and nosing at them; he even raised a paw to bat at the book, and Gran had to pull it out of the way.

"Something tells me we're going to have a hard time keeping this from Jo," said Gran. "Now what's this?"

Em had noticed a black elastic thread running through the book, snaking across one page and up another. As they went deeper, they found that it described different patterns and trajectories. Once, they discovered it stretching across the space between the opened pages, and Emmeline gazed in wonder: on the thread was a tiny acrobat, no larger than a chess pawn, hanging from the thread with wire arms. Gran flicked it with her finger, and it spun around.

Emmeline suddenly knew what the book reminded her of. At the end of her street was a big stone house, the former home of an old woman who could not throw anything away. She just kept hoarding and hoarding; it was a disease, Em's father said. Apparently you could barely get inside the house, it was so crammed with junk; and once inside, you had to walk down a narrow little aisle, with magazines and newspapers and clothes and books stacked beside you to the ceiling. It was not a healthy place to live. *That's* what this book was like, Emmeline thought: an old house stuffed to the ceiling with junk.

A horn sounded from the dock, and a familiar station wagon rolled down the gravel lane. "So how did it go, girls?" called Josephine, getting out.

Gran and Emmeline looked up dazedly.

"Back already?" said Gran.

"Not rushing you, I hope," said Jo. "I did say a couple of hours."

Emmeline turned Gran's wrist over and looked at the latter's watch. Noon already! They had spent two hours looking at the book; the other cartons of books hadn't been touched.

"Um, we got sidetracked," said Gran guiltily.

"I'd say you did," said Jo, stooping to retrieve Gran's list of books; it contained only eight titles. "You're definitely in Sunday mode, aren't you? What's that?"

Emmeline opened her arms wide, to express the idea of *everything*, and Gran nodded.

"Just what we're missing on *Permanent Wants*," she said, handing Jo the book. "The Book of the Jewelled Net. The Unsoundable Book of Everything. Quite a find, eh?"

Jo, book in hand, had become very still.

"This was in one of the boxes?" she said.

"What's the matter?" said Gran.

Jo, who had turned noticeably pale, was flipping through the pages when suddenly she let out a yelp and dropped the book. Gran and Emmeline jumped up, and Lafcadio stretched himself into his hunter's stance. Gran bent to retrieve the book and, turning it over, gasped: on the page was a huge ash-coloured moth, motionless, with dark wing markings like eddying smoke. They all stared at it for a moment before realizing that it was *painted* onto the page—but painted with such skill, its wings shadowing a section of print, that it looked alive.

"Oh, my spirit guides, it's *true*," breathed Jo. She had her eyes on Lafcadio, who was now growling. "Teo, you don't want to keep that book. Believe me."

"Why not?" said Gran.

"Somehow that old fool White got a hold of it," muttered Jo. "No wonder he went crazy at the end." She made an effort to calm herself. "That book destroys, Teo."

"What on earth are you talking about?"

"I don't know much about it—nobody does. But I do know that the title is deadly accurate. It *is* the Book of Everything. You've got everything in the universe between two covers. You could read it every day of your life and never get to the end, never even scrape the surface. People have been driven mad by it."

"Come on, Jo," said Gran. "This is me you're talking to, not one of your credulous customers."

Jo looked from the girl to the grandmother. "How much have you read in it?"

"Nothing," said Gran shortly. "We've barely dipped into it." A suspicion had begun to grow in her mind that the book was valuable, and that Jo was putting on this act just to get it back. "Look, Jo," she said, tucking the book under her arm, "you said we could keep what we wanted, and we want *this*. Now, if you give us another hour or two, we can finish these other cartons for you."

Jo, glowering, suddenly seemed to abandon the argument.

"All right," she said in a voice of forced calm. "You put the book aside and look after my cartons. In the meantime, I'm going to find out everything I can about it. Keep an eye on them, Lafcadio." She strode up the dock path and opened the door of her station wagon. "Trust old White to leave me in a lurch," she declared. "First his septic tank, and now *this*."

Flaps and pockets and envelopes inside envelopes . . . really, the book was hard to resist. Each page was like a cluttered desktop where things lay layered and hidden and half-obscured. Even the larger trinkets, like the miniature Mona Lisa, could rest unnoticed in cloth pouches that were sewn right into the page. Reading the book was like taking part in a scavenger hunt. When Gran and Emmeline sat down with it again after lunch, they found a few things in the first pages that had initially escaped their notice—a watermark, a tiny seashell on a thread, and even a small blue envelope inside a pocket.

"I thought I checked inside there," said Gran, pulling out the envelope, which was decorated with sparkly stars and moons.

Inside they found some fine grey dust, along with a printed card. Emmeline sprinkled a bit of the dust on her palm while Gran read:

This is surface dust from a moon that orbits the planet HD 188753 A (c), which orbits the star HD 188753, which is found in the Cygnus constellation of our Milky Way galaxy, approximately 150 light-years from earth. At one time, the moon was home to a primitive form of microorganism that died out because of an asteroid collision. But if you put this dust under a microscope, you can still see the tiny silica "houses" that are the only remains of this plucky life form. (Find the connections! Follow the thread to learn more about ancient microorganisms in the Milky Way!)

"This book is a *treat*," chuckled Gran, but then, suddenly looking thoughtful, she dipped a finger into the dust. "Cygnus," she said. "The Swan. My favourite constellation." She studied the dust abstractedly while Emmeline turned the pages, following the thread, which seemed to weave and radiate through the entire book.

But it was odd, thought the girl, that they hadn't found that envelope the first time.

Gran put out a hand to stop Emmeline from turning the pages. Before them, tucked inside a flap, was a folded sheet of white paper that bore the words "Rainbow Rider." Gran, her eyes bright and curious, opened up the paper; it was criss-crossed with dotted lines.

"Now let me see if I remember," she said in a strange voice. She folded the paper down the middle, following one dotted line, and then turned the corners in towards the centre. After holding the paper up to squint down its length, she did more folding and tapering, always following the dotted lines. Wings appeared, and a sharp nose. At length, she held up an elegant paper airplane; the name *Rainbow Rider* appeared on a wing.

"Do you remember how Grandpa Silas used to make these planes?" she said.

Em looked up; Gran's eyes were moist. The girl moved closer to her grandmother, gently taking the proffered plane.

"It's nothing," said Gran briskly. "It's just—" She shook her head and looked away. "The first time I met your grandpa, he made a Rainbow Rider for me out of a page of my lab report."

But now Emmeline was looking down at the book; the piece of paper had been hiding a picture of a great cloud-like tree on a grassland. She recognized the place at once, though she couldn't remember the name—the Kenyan savannah.

"We finished your cartons," said Gran when Josephina showed up again in mid-afternoon. "We also finished the Book of Everything."

"You *finished* it?" said Jo.

Gran nodded. "It's not a long book, just overstuffed. And I'm disappointed, Jo. You said it contained the entire universe. Nope. Not even close."

Jo looked from Gran to Emmeline as if they had just escaped from quarantine.

"Where's Lafcadio?" she asked suddenly.

"We put him inside because he was being such a pest," said Gran. "Here's your list of titles. Now, Jo, if you'll excuse us, we want to spend a little hang-time together—on a river swing."

Jo tucked the list of books into her jeans without even glancing at it. She may have been wearing hoop earrings and a peach blouse, but her eyes had a steely look.

"You may be interested to know," she said slowly, "how old Prospero White died. In a fire. It destroyed most of his house. The fire chief told me that it looked like Prospero started the fire himself. And I bet he was trying to destroy this book."

"Really?" said Gran. "Then he must have done a pretty bad job of it. Not a page has been singed."

"Yes, that's odd, isn't it?" said Jo. "Maybe the book *can't* be destroyed."

"Jo," said Gran, "you are a walking argument for avoiding the kinds of books you sell."

"Prospero White was all skin and bones when he died," said Jo emphatically. "While he devoured the book, *it* devoured him."

Again Emmeline thought of the big stone house on her street and the old woman who had once lived there; *she* had wasted away, too, people had said. The girl glanced at Gran, who just said kindly, "Let me help you with your cartons, Jo."

"Give me the book, Teo," returned Josephina.

"No," said Gran.

"Then come stay with me," said Jo. "Bring the book. We'll read it *together*, all three of us." Her eyes were fierce and imploring. "If the book contains everything in the universe, then it has to contain *itself*. Somewhere in its pages is a passage about the book and its origin. And maybe we can discover something about . . . breaking the spell."

"Jo," said Gran, "I keep telling you, we've *read* it. Haven't we, Emmeline? And I can tell you that we're not any crazier than we were before. The only warning label you have to put on that book concerns swallowing hazards. Now let's drop the subject and enjoy what's left of the afternoon." Gran stepped off the boat onto the dock. "Here, pass me one of those cartons, could you, Emmeline?"

As Gran carried the carton to the parked station wagon, Jo bent close to Emmeline.

"Em," she said, "keep your eye on your grandmother, please. I may be wrong about that book, but Lafcadio doesn't like it, did you notice? Don't read it at night, and don't let your gran read it by herself."

Em was bewildered. She couldn't really believe that a book could be evil. And she certainly couldn't believe that a scrapbook of barely fifty pages could contain the entire universe.

"People think it's the ultimate book of knowledge," said Jo. "But maybe there are some things we *shouldn't* know. Like our future . . . like how we will die. Am I right?"

Emmeline glanced up sharply. Did Jo really believe that the future was in there, among all that pointless stuff? It was just bits and pieces of somebody's life. Or maybe *everybody's* life—that's what it seemed like sometimes. She wasn't frightened of the book, but there was something about it . . . She nodded to Jo. After all the summer's adventures, she felt ready to be the level-headed one, the one people trusted.

"Good," whispered the bookseller, and raised her head. "All right, Teo," she called. "But maybe you could let Lafcadio out now. A fine totem animal like that, all cooped up?"

Emmeline lay wide awake in bed that night. The picture of the great cloud-like tree had resurrected buried memories. She travelled again through the hot grasslands of Kenya—she remembered the stale, burlapy smell inside the Land Rover, and the faint scent of gas—and out the window strange animals appeared: a giraffe floating, half deer and half sunflower, over the sunburnt plain; the cheetahs with their spearhead minds, watching lazily from the top of termite mounds; and a huge butterfly, a leaf of molten violet, fluttering gamely against the breeze. And then she was driving back to the camp in the afternoon, feeling hot and achy, and later the night turned red and the scorpion materialized—on the wall, on the ceiling, on her bed . . . After that, she didn't remember anything until she woke up in a hospital bed, surrounded by people she didn't know. She had tubes coming out of her nostril and forearms, her neck felt stiff, and she felt numb everywhere, including her mind; the only feeling she had was a small soreness where the tubes came out. She didn't know where she was, or who the people were who cried and laughed at the same time. And she couldn't speak a word. She didn't even know there was such a thing as language.

Over the next few weeks, she had to be taught her own name again—it took her that long to learn it—and even when she finally came back to Canada, she would sometimes forget it. At the hospital in Ottawa they put her inside big machines to see what her brain looked like, and gave her pills and injections, and asked her endless questions . . .

"Emmeline, here's a boy named Jim who gets all A's on his report card. How would he feel? You choose the word: happy, sad, afraid, or sorry."

Well, of course she knew how he would feel. But *saying* the word, or finding it on a card, or writing it—that was another thing.

"Okay, no problem, Emmeline. Let's go on to the next one."

Sign language helped a bit, but only a bit. It was the same with signs as with words—she had only a few dozen, while other people had thousands. And speaking remained a mind-breaking chore. Putting words into a sentence was like wrestling cement blocks into line. It was easier to be silent and use Sign only when she needed to. Slowly she let go of words—except in her dreams, where she was always trying, always looking. Now her dream of Emyla came back to her, and she felt the lightness on her wrist where her medical ID bracelet used to be. *Spaseebah*, Emmeline . . . She smiled; she still remembered the word. *Spa-SEE-bah.*

She turned over in her bunk. The doctors had said she was bound to get her language back—kids generally did, because their brains were young and adaptable. But most of the time, her brain sure didn't feel young and adaptable. Sometimes, when her brain felt particularly *inadaptable*, she would imagine herself in the future, as a completely normal teenager. She saw herself going to PG-rated movies (or even R-rated movies) by herself, and dying her hair different colours, and maybe even getting a tattoo—not a big one, but just big enough to make her mum mad (that never took much). And then her friend Madison would have to listen to *her* on the phone. And she would have lots of other friends, too, and they would all get together and talk like crazy, and she would speak as quickly and outrageously as they did.

She was drifting off to sleep among these pleasant images when she remembered what Jo had said: that the book contained the future. Well, if it was the Book of Everything, then it certainly would. The future, past, and present of every person, including her. But it wasn't the Book of Everything—that was ridiculous.

And yet . . . what if it *was*?

The next morning, while Gran was making breakfast, Emmeline slipped the book off the cabin shelf and sat down with it in the bow. Lafcadio followed her, meowing insistently, but she ignored him and began at the first page again. She opened all the fold-outs and explored every pocket. She took out every miniature from its pouch, turning it over in her fingers. She followed the black thread in all its intricate twisting. And she soon realized that they hadn't finished the book after all. Now she was uncovering something new on almost every page. Most books have only length; this one had *depth*. It was like an old house with hidden cellars and passageways; you might live in it for years and be unaware of the secret spaces beyond the walls.

You could indeed spend a lifetime reading this book, she thought.

They had a dozen things to do that day—getting groceries, washing the deck, setting up the bookshelves for the afternoon—but Em managed to snatch a few minutes here and there with the book. It wasn't easy, though. Lafcadio wouldn't let her browse in peace, and Gran asked her several times to come and help with something. But of all the books that had come their way that summer, she felt that this one was *hers*, and she was determined to make time for it.

She didn't find anything about herself or her future, however, and it was evening when she came again to the picture of the great cloud-like tree. She wondered now if it *was* Kenya. Well, she thought with disappointment, she could pick up the book again tonight; dinner would soon be ready. She was just about to close it when she noticed that the page was wrinkled and bumpy at the bottom. She moved her fingers over it—yes, there was something inside. Taking out her Swiss penknife (a Christmas present from her dad), she cut a slit in the clothlike page and then worked out six wooden letters— Scrabble letters, she saw in surprise.

She had loved Scrabble before the trip to Kenya.

She laid the six letters on the deck before her. Did they spell anything? She sighed; a letter puzzle like this was beyond her. She would have to give them to Gran after supper. Idly she turned the page, and at the bottom corner she found a colour photo of a sail-boat on a blue sea.

Now *that* (she was absolutely sure) wasn't there the first time they had read the book.

The boat was sailing in a strong wind; the sail was taut, and the little wind pennants on the mast streamed out horizontally. Two people were aboard, but the boat was too far away to make out their faces. Emmeline could see the image of a big blue swan on the side of the boat. She studied the picture in growing bewilderment: she had seen the boat before. It was the swan; she knew the swan . . .

Then it came to her: this was the sloop that had belonged to Grandpa Silas. He and Gran had sailed it halfway around the world.

Emmeline closed the book, trembling. This book wasn't about the universe; it was about *them*—Gran and her. It started out being about everything, everything and nothing, but now—

"Em," said Gran behind her, "could you leave that book just for one minute?"

Then, noticing the look on her granddaughter's face, she came close and saw the Scrabble letters on the deck.

"What have you got there?" she said.

Emmeline held up the book, showing the slit in the page. Gran said not a word about the damaged book; she just sat down and put an arm around the girl. Maybe she was remembering all the Scrabble games they had played together.

"I'm amazed at what's in here," she said finally, holding up the book and peering into the cut page. "But let's leave it for now, Em. We've been reading it for two days, and—"

Gran was staring at the Scrabble letters on the deck. Four of them were facing up; they spelled *cygu*. Reaching down, Gran turned over the other two—*n* and *s*—and then arranged them with the others. Emmeline couldn't read the resulting word, but Gran could.

"Cygnus," she said faintly. "The swan."

Now Em remembered: that was the name of the sailboat that had belonged to Grandpa Silas.

They were both so quiet that Em could hear her grandmother breathing. Then Gran turned the page and saw the picture of the actual boat, and her eyes widened. For half a minute, she sat in stunned silence. She seemed to have grown older before Emmeline's eyes; little lines had appeared at the corners of her eyes and mouth. Lafcadio came close to them, meowing softly, and from across the river came the sound of a boat engine. At length, Gran closed the book and scooped up the Scrabble letters.

"You know what?" she said, trying to keep her voice calm. "I say we take a run up to the house of this guy Prospero White. I'm not sure what we'll find, but I'd like to know more about him and this book of his."

The evening light was fading as *Permanent Wants* motored into the private bay of Prospero White. His enormous house, with one wing gutted by fire, could be seen through dark pines. But there was no dock, and the bay was choked with deadheads; Prospero White was clearly no boater. Gran throttled down and stood on tiptoe to look out over the water.

"You'd better go up front, Em," she said.

Emmeline didn't like the look of the bay, and the house had a hunched, skeletal presence. But she moved forward to the bow, Lafcadio at her side. She smelled marsh smells and saw clumps of algae drifting like black smoke under the surface. The bay was darker than the rest of the river; motoring up, they had enjoyed the last of the light, but now the sun was behind the trees.

"Okay," called Gran, "you two are my guides."

The boat moved in among the deadheads. Em pointed now to the left, now to the right, and Gran followed her granddaughter's lead, straining to see above the roof of the cabin. The bay seemed like a drowned wood, with mired stumps and root clusters and whole logs scattered everywhere. Usually such a place would attract a lot of birds at twilight, but Em heard none. In the poor light it was hard to see the logs that floated just under the surface, and she was constantly crouching to peer into the water. It occurred to her that they were going a bit faster than they should. Gran must have really wanted to get to the house—and to the bottom of things. Emmeline raised herself, intending to signal "slower" to Gran, but just then the house caught her gaze. What kind of man would live in a huge, *cadaverous* house like that? She remembered what Jo had said about Prospero White: that he wanted to collect every book ever published. And maybe, she thought, the Book of Everything was the answer to his dreams, since every book would be in there . . .

Just then came a jolt, and she was flung forward against the railing of *Permanent Wants*. Lafcadio, too, lost his footing but recovered at once, looking outraged. Em picked herself up dazedly; if the railing hadn't been there, she would have been thrown right overboard. The boat kept chugging forward.

There was no sign of Gran.

Em scampered back to the cockpit. Lafcadio dodged ahead, meowing frantically, and now she saw why. Gran was lying face down against the cockpit wall, unmoving.

Emmeline let out a cry and dropped to her knees beside the slumped form. Gran was out cold—she must have banged her head against the console. The girl suddenly became aware that the boat was still moving forward; reaching up, she pulled the throttle right back. The engine sputtered and stalled. In the silence came the soft sound of the bow wash as the boat lost momentum. Emmeline shook her grandmother gently.

pleasegran
please!

Panic seized Emmeline. She raised her head and gave a cry—a wordless, desperate cry. If anybody had heard it, they would have thought it was some night animal. But there was nobody in the deserted bay that Prospero White called home; the half-gutted house echoed her cry impassively.

She had to calm herself. Closing her eyes, she took a deep breath. A deadhead—they had struck a deadhead. And *she* was supposed to be the navigator! She stepped to the gunwale and peered down the side, looking for damage. No, it seemed okay. *Permanent Wants* had a good, thick hull. She looked to shore: no lights showed anywhere, and only silence met her ears. Even the crickets, Cass and Nova, were silent. Had she knocked them out, too?

She had to bring Gran around. Darting into the galley, she scooped up a damp cloth. With an effort, she turned over the inert form and brought her face close: she thought she could feel breathing. While Lafcadio nosed at them both, Emmeline dabbed Gran's forehead with the cloth. But the other did not stir, and Emmeline knew she had to get help immediately. There was no sense in going ashore here; nobody lived on this bay. Where could she go for help?

Then she remembered: Jo's house. The bookseller was Prospero's neighbour. Gran had said the house would be lit up with all kinds of candle-lanterns, and they had seen nothing of the kind on the way here, so it must be farther along the river. Emmeline would have to take Gran there in the boat. She would have to drive it herself.

Lafcadio, comfortingly, had grown quiet, stationing himself beside Gran while Emmeline did the tough work. The girl peered at the dashboard, trying to remember the procedure. There were two levers: the throttle (for making the boat go faster) and the gearshift (for switching into forward, neutral, and reverse). She was about to press the starter button when she realized the boat had to be in neutral. Fear knotted her stomach; she had never driven the boat before by herself. She pushed the gearshift lever forward until she felt it click. Okay, neutral. She pressed the starter button and held it. Yes! She caught a whiff of oil smoke, felt the familiar guttural vibration from the engine well, and heard the bubbling in the water at the base of the transom. Something was rattling behind her—the stern lamp. The casing must have been jarred when they hit the deadhead. Never mind! She had more important things to think about.

She put the boat into reverse, and the engine changed tone as they chugged backwards. Lafcadio hopped up on the cockpit settee for a quick look, then hopped down to his spot beside Gran. Em clutched the steering wheel, legs braced. Slowly, slowly . . . deadhead right there . . . okay, turn now . . . no, *wrong way* . . . yes, the boat curved past the deadhead. She put the boat into neutral until it lost momentum, then shifted into forward.

Slowly they headed out of the bay.

She increased speed and stepped up on the gunwale, straining to see ahead. The river opened out before her, midnight blue like the sky. Just then, she remembered the running lights and flicked the switch: they all worked except the stern one. So it *had* been damaged. But the dashboard had its own lamp, and by its illumination, she could see the flash of Lafcadio's eyes as he stood over Gran. Emmeline throttled up a bit more. She noticed she was gripping the throttle tightly and relaxed her hand. Easy, easy. Be the level-headed one.

Suddenly she thought of the book. Where was it? Somewhere in the darkness it crouched, biding its time. It didn't like to be ignored; it wanted to be *read*.

There—lights! Lots of coloured lights. She turned the wheel cautiously and, through the near darkness, glimpsed a small dock. Lafcadio jumped up onto the transom and meowed encouragingly. Emmeline took another breath: now came the hard part. Gran always said that anybody could dock *Permanent Wants* if they took their time. She throttled down. The lights drew closer; she could see tires along one side of the dock. Reducing speed even more, she eased the boat in, put the gear into neutral, and shut off the engine while it was still gliding forward. Then she rushed to catch the edge of the dock. She didn't quite make it, but the bump was not serious.

Yes!

She switched off the engine and heard something in the silence that cheered her immensely—the crickets. Their chirping was faint but steady. Hastily wrapping a tie rope around a cleat, she jumped on the dock and was halfway up the path to the house when she ran into Jo.

"Emmeline!" said Jo, flashlight in hand. "What is it? What's happened?"

The girl grabbed Jo's hand and pulled her towards the boat. Lafcadio was meowing again. Emmeline quickened her pace. Had something happened to Gran? And then her heart leapt—in the beam of Jo's flashlight, she could see Gran awake. Her grandmother sat on the cockpit settee, blinking in the light and rubbing her head.

"Teo!" said Jo.

Gran looked up, wincing. "Em. Jo."

"Are you all right?"

"I think so. What happened?"

"I don't know. Em must have brought you here. You don't remember?"

"No," said Gran. "I think I banged my head—I've got a pretty good bump there." She made room on the settee for Em, who had jumped down beside her.

"Listen," said Jo, "we're all going to have a nice cup of tea, and then you're going to see a doctor, Teo."

"I'm okay, Jo, really." Gran reached down to stroke Lafcadio, who was purring so loudly he almost drowned out the crickets. "I just need to rest a moment."

"You do that. I'm going to put the kettle on and call Doc Swanson. He won't mind stopping by for a moment."

"Go," said Gran with a sigh. "Anything to make you happy."

Jo disappeared up the path, and Gran was silent a moment, listening to Lafcadio and the crickets. "Did you really bring me here, Em?" she said.

Em nodded, twining her fingers in Gran's. Gran smiled.

"I was right out of it," she said. "The last thing I remember— maybe I dreamt it, I don't know—I was reading that book, and I came across something about language, and problems with language, and all your symptoms were there. Exactly your symptoms. And it explained how to *treat* them."

Emmeline became very still. Lafcadio, sensing something, stopped purring and looked up.

"I'm sure I could find it again," said Gran. "Once we've had our tea, we'll have another look. Where did we put the book again?"

Emmeline jumped up and banged open the door of the galley. She understood now how the book worked. The Great Jewelled Net swept through the entire universe and came up with all those things you had *lost*—and nobody can resist the things they have lost. She knew beyond a doubt that the book was insidious and dangerous, as unhealthy as the house where the old lady lived—the lady who could not throw anything away, who could not even bring herself to empty her own *bathwater* . . . Emmeline's hand groped on the top shelf. She would destroy the book, tear it apart, throw it overboard. But her searching hands found nothing.

"Oh, it's okay, Em," called Gran. "It's here in the catch-all."

Emmeline stood in the doorway, breathing hard. Gran was leaning close to the dashboard light, absorbed in the book. Lafcadio was at Gran's feet, meowing as urgently as before, and the crickets were cheeping away valiantly. Gran seemed to be sitting in a charmed circle, shut off from everybody else by the book. And Emmeline knew what she would find in there—something about Grandpa Silas and their life together, something that would pierce her heart. She closed her eyes.

no gran no

Everything seemed suspended. The crickets kept up their two-part plainchant, and Lafcadio crouched like a coiled spring. She could say it. She swallowed. Say it: *Please, Gran* . . .

The crickets suddenly fell silent, and Emmeline opened her eyes. Gran was staring at her.

"Was . . . was that *you*, Em?" she said.

Em blinked. She wasn't even sure she had spoken out loud, but *something* had happened. The boat was still perfectly quiet; she could hear the humming of the galley refrigerator behind her.

"I thought . . . I thought I heard you speak." Gran stood up, putting the book down, and took a step towards Emmeline. "You spoke, didn't you?"

They stood there for a moment in the semi-darkness, and Emmeline knew that the charmed circle had been broken. At that moment Lafcadio bounded onto the settee, seized the book in his jaws, and leapt onto the dock. Gran turned just in time to see him disappear into the darkness.

"You *did* speak," she said, turning back to Emmeline. "I heard it."

Emmeline ran to her grandmother, gave her a brief but powerful hug, and stepped onto the dock. She didn't want to lose Lafcadio. In a second she had pounded down the dock to the edge of the lawn, where the cat, faintly illuminated by candlelight, was locked in savage combat with the book.

"What's he *fighting*?" called Gran after her.

Lafcadio was shaking the book as if it were a vicious rat, scattering coins and seashells and other trinkets all over the lawn. He put his paws on it, got a better grip, and continued his attack. As Emmeline came up, he gave the book a particularly wild shake, ripping something small out of the interior. Ignoring the book, he held the small thing in his jaws, panting, and allowed her to take it. She felt something oblong and soft.

"What on earth?" said Jo, coming out with a tray of cups.

Emmeline held the thing up to the candlelight. It was a miniature leather-bound book, smaller than a pocket notebook and as perfectly formed as the miniature Mona Lisa or Eiffel Tower. She could open it with her thumb and forefinger; the pages were as fine as flower petals. But she didn't have time to look at it closely. Lafcadio had leapt onto the porch and now stood on his hind legs against the railing, straining towards one of the candle-lanterns and meowing urgently. And suddenly Emmeline knew what he wanted. She came up behind him and, stepping onto a chair, thrust the little book into the flame.

There was a flash of green light, and the little book was snatched from her hands. Behind her she heard a crash of crockery—Jo had dropped the tray.

She looked at her hand in disbelief: the book was gone. Jumping off the chair, she ignored the astounded Jo and took a few steps towards the spot where the big book had been lying. It had disappeared as well; the rosy candlelight illuminated an empty lawn.

Em was bursting to call Madison. The two grown-ups were in the living room—Doc Swanson had come and gone, pronouncing Gran fit as a fiddle—and in Jo's kitchen, Emmeline dialled Madison's number with a shaking hand. Her head was still in a whirl. The little book had disappeared, taking the *big* book with it. What had happened? Then, just as she dialled the last digit of Madison's number, she remembered something Jo had said. If the Book of Everything contained the entire universe, it would have to contain *itself*. Maybe the thing Emmeline had burned had been exactly that: the book in miniature. Lafcadio had found it, somehow; he had gone for the living heart of the beast—its only vulnerable part.

"Em, guess what?" said Madison when she got on the line. "I made a medieval diorama at science camp, and it had peasants and cows and horses and chickens and a dragon swooping down on the peasants, and Jody—that's our camp counsellor—"

A wave seemed to be unfurling in Emmeline's mind, a wave that had been gathering force for a long time . . .

"And Jody said, 'It's supposed to be a *science* project.' And I said, 'But it's got a dragon, doesn't it?' And she kind of went *hunh!* And I said, 'Well, I'll put in some *igneous rocks*. Will that make it scientific enough for you?' And she said—"

The wave broke in Emmeline's mind; the floodgates burst.

"*Spaseebah!*" she said loudly.

There was shocked silence at the other end of the line.

"*What?*" said Madison.

"*Spaseebah,*" said Emmeline, more temperately this time, and hung up. Then she smiled. She knew a word that Madison didn't know.

John is never still. Even when he's sitting, he fidgets or rocks or makes clicking sounds to himself. Often he gets up and walks around the room, checking out shapes and shadows I cannot see, banging on things, smacking his lips, clicking. In a car he has to wear a harness because he gets so fidgety he will try to open the door and jump out. He is a likeable kid, with his mild blue eyes and a lifetime interest in noises, but he *can* get on your nerves. He hasn't said a single word in his twelve years.

Meredith is ten, a tiny girl with large glasses and a hearing aid; her cerebral palsy makes her sit crookedly in her wheelchair. She cannot speak either, but her language skills are actually quite good. Taped to the tray of her wheelchair is a letter-board; if someone stands beside her to guide her hand, she can point to letters and spell out words. Of all the children here, she is the one who asks the most questions. She has a small, sweet huddle of a face that reminds me of some spring flower. The carrying bag on her wheelchair is decorated with Hannah Montana decals.

At thirteen, Connor is the oldest of the group. He is tall and gangly, with spiky blond hair, quick eyes, and a face that is starting to shade into a teenager's. Deaf since birth, he loves drumming, which he does as loudly and wildly as he can. He also likes press-on tattoos, and once he came to the circle wearing a clip-on nose-ring. (When John showed an interest in it, he casually took it off, stilled John's rocking with a quiet hand, and clipped it on to the other's ear. John took this as a gift and spent the rest of the session clipping it on to different parts of himself.) Connor's challenge is his epilepsy. Generally he is very fluent in Sign—much more fluent than I am— but his condition can affect his ability to use hand shapes. When he is going through a period of frequent seizures, he often sits a bit apart from us, sometimes tapping out rhythms on his knees.

Ali's problems are a bit like Emmeline's, though more severe. He can't speak, read, or write. Unlike Emmeline, however, he has never been able to learn any signs. When he first came to the circle, he had stopped listening to people. He sat in the corner, his eyes a dark frost. He never cried, never threw a tantrum, never actually *looked* at anybody. But now he listens to Emmeline—or rather, listens to me and Gran as we try to bring out Emmeline's stories.

Sometimes we get other children as casual visitors, but this is the main group: John, Meredith, Connor, Ali, and Emmeline. Kate, the Sign language teacher at the hospital—the same Kate who taught *me* Sign while I was doing my training—often sits in. It's great when she's here, since she's the only one who can converse with Connor at his own speed. Parents come, too, of course; John's mother is here every session. Generally Gran comes, too, but when it's her granddaughter's turn, she tries not to say too much. The circle is for the kids.

Today will be Emmeline's last day in the circle for a while. She's going to Toronto to do a special program, one that uses music to help children overcome problems with language and learning.

John's mother has brought in a cake, and Emmeline's father has brought in Coke and lemonade, and Meredith's mother and brother have brought a card that everybody has signed in their own way (lots of squiggles). John takes paper cup after paper cup, puts them upside down on the table, and crushes each one with a blow. He is delighted when they make a clean sound of collapse. Connor tells a joke in Sign, one too rude to be translated. Today is not a storytelling day, just a festive day.

"So Emmeline is leaving today," I say, signing as I speak. "We'll miss the stories about *Permanent Wants*."

"But I know there are lots of other stories here," says Gran, looking around the circle. "Stories just as good."

Her words remind me how much has changed since I brought Emmeline to the circle. I'd been her speech and language therapist for two months when I decided that other kids with language problems should really hear the stories I was hearing. This wasn't a story circle at all when Emmeline joined it. We used to do very simple activities, usually games with pictures and words. But Emmeline was burning to tell the others what had happened to her in the summer. She started by bringing in objects—the atlas that contains Zeya Shan, the little pirate ship in a bottle from Kingman Drake, a fossil from Squamish Island, and other mementoes. Then, with lots of help from Gran, she started talking about the objects using Sign. Often she just showed the other kids her "ship's log," the big scrapbook that contained the images of the summer, and they had to fill in the details as best they could. And she spoke only one word the whole time—*spaseebah*. (When I asked Gran how on earth Emmeline's first spoken word in a year could be *Russian*, she just said mildly, "It was that kind of vacation.")

And two things happened as a result of all this. First, the kids wanted to tell *their* stories, too. It didn't seem to matter to them that they couldn't speak like other kids. From Emmeline, they picked up a way of storytelling that uses objects, sketches, signs, gestures, facial expressions, bits of music, and just the feel of things (rough or smooth, prickly or soft). The stories told this way appeared in bits and pieces, and the listeners had to put everything together. In a way, *everybody* created the story, just as every goose creates the V-shape that drifts honking overhead.

The second thing that happened concerned Emmeline herself. You could call it a breakthrough.

She had told me, as best she could, where she had got the word *spaseebah*, and though I wasn't really clear on the details then, I understood well enough that she had got it from a dream—and that she had been playing her violin in the dream. That's when I began to wonder if her violin could somehow be used to *free* her language. She had such fluency with music; if only that fluency could be harnessed to make the words flow just a bit better. So I asked her to bring in her violin and play the tunes that went along with the summer. I also got her to think of words that went with the tunes, and to try saying them while she was playing. At first, she just hummed loudly or said a few karate shouts. But one day, while she was playing "The Roaring Boy," she chanted "boy roaring *boy*" in time with the music. Just three words, but what a big day for us. Since then, she's done it with other tunes, too. While playing "The Road to Lisdoonvarna," she even said, "Road . . . is my road . . . this is my *road*."

And it was Emyla who put her on that road.

"Thanks, Emmeline," I say. "Thanks for your stories. We'll be thinking about you."

The others are unusually quiet. Even John is barely stirring, just clicking softly to himself. Emmeline does not look at me, but makes a few quick signs. I have to concentrate.

It's not . . . That's all I catch.

"Sorry, what was that?"

She signs again—the fingers of her right hand moving along her left and down along the fingertips. Then she draws her thumb along the underside of her chin. *It's not finished.*

"No, you're right," I say, taking a stab at her meaning. "It's not finished. You'll be back here soon with more stories."

She sighs. No, that wasn't it. I glance at her mum and dad, who look happy but tired. Like Gran, they've gone through a lot over the past few months.

The cake disappears; Connor tells a few more jokes; the parents gather up coats and sweaters. Emmeline gives the other kids a hug—everybody except John, who is studying a fly in the corner of the room and doesn't want to be bothered. But eventually even John goes, and only Emmeline and her family are left.

Emmeline tries again: *It's not finished.* I am hoping that somebody will come to my rescue, and fortunately somebody does.

"I think," says Emmeline's father, "what she means is . . . We were talking last night, and Emmeline said she would love to have the stories written down. So that other people can read them."

"That's a great idea," I say. "You should do it now, while it's all fresh in your minds."

Emmeline's mother and father exchange glances. Gran brushes some cake crumbs from her lap.

"The thing is," she says slowly, "you know all the stories now. Some of them you've even heard *twice.* Plus you know the places we talked about—you've been out to visit them. I gather you've even spoken to some of the people we met."

I didn't think anybody knew that. In the last two months, I've certainly learned to respect Gran.

"I was quite sure you weren't making the stories up," I say quickly. "But I needed to understand what actually happened. I just wanted all the *facts.*"

I never did get all the facts—not even close. But I did manage to learn a bit more about the people in the stories. Henry and Prue Van Troon, who hunted for the language of Eden, are hoping to adopt the pale-haired deaf girl, Belle (she seems fine with the idea, since Prue is interested in art, too). Tom, the boy who worked at the Reptile Haven, is back in Toronto; Emmeline will be able to visit him there. And Dexter Nervish is now leading a campaign to have his little Rideau Valley village twinned with Ulan Bator, Mongolia. What those Mongolians really need, he says, is a good healthy dose of civilization. Good luck to him, I say.

"So you see," says Gran, "we think *you're* the person for the job."

My heart sinks. As if I needed something else to do.

"Anyway," adds Em's mother, "the stories might help other people, don't you think?"

Okay, yes, she's absolutely right about that. I've seen what has happened here. In a hospital, a place these kids once dreaded, stories have begun to flow. Meredith uses the letter-board, Connor uses Sign, John uses his mother, and Ali *reacts*. They bring in objects and pictures, as Emmeline did; they make faces and gestures; they drum and hoot and wriggle. Nothing is explained much, but maybe that makes for the best kind of story. And as the stories flow, I see the children slowly moving away from me. I see them sailing ever closer to a country that has long been denied to them, the same summer country—green and endless and eternal—that Emmeline explored on *Permanent Wants*.

You're right, Em. It's *far* from being finished.

I sign very quickly to her, and she gives a huge smile.

Acknowledgments

This book brings together all the things I'm interested in—music, language, darkness, animal powers, pirates, forgotten countries, forgotten classics of literature, and tiny bug-eyed lizards with long, picturesque names. A lot of people helped with the whole mish-mash. Theresa Grant, Marie-Christine Haubert, and my cousin Sam Williams read parts or all of the manuscript. Dana Campbell lent me some books on American Sign Language and invited me to join her class of special-needs kids. Dave Trattles gave my brother Scott and me a wonderful handcrafted birthday book that inspired the Book of the Jewelled Net. My niece Saraya gave me some facts about karate; my niece Brigh gave me a description of her medieval diorama; and all my other nieces gave me bits of wisdom and experience that I've pondered and hoarded. Thanks, all.

Jamieson Findlay is a freelance writer, teacher and science journalist. His first novel, *The Blue Roan Child*, received international critical acclaim. He lives in Ottawa.